Praise for Bria.. . ...

'Millions tune into a virtual reality program
while society collapses around them in this thoughtful
cyberpunk novel from Pinkerton...builds to a clever,
desperate climax. Fans of stories centered on the conflict
between the virtual and the real will find plenty to enjoy.'
Publishers Weekly on *The Nirvana Effect*

'Surprising plot twists, exciting action...Pinkerton wields
fast pacing and an entertaining, electrifying plot.'
Publishers Weekly on *The Gemini Experiment*

'Part spy thriller, part SF adventure, Pinkerton's latest is a
fast-paced and action packed novel with well-developed
characters that will have strong YA and adult appeal.'
Library Journal on *The Gemini Experiment*

'*The Gemini Experiment* is a thrill ride filled with twists
and turns that keep the reader guessing and entertained
all the way to the stunning conclusion. Brian Pinkerton
has created a wonderfully constructed story, frightening
in its believability...an exceptional read.'
Cemetery Dance on *The Gemini Experiment*

BRIAN PINKERTON

THE INTRUDERS

This is a **FLAME TREE PRESS** book

FLAME TREE PRESS
6 Melbray Mews, London, SW6 3NS, UK
flametreepress.com

US sales, distribution and warehouse:
Simon & Schuster
simonandschuster.biz

UK distribution and warehouse:
Hachette UK Distribution
hukdcustomerservice@hachette.co.uk

Publisher's Note: This is a work of fiction. Names, characters, places, and
incidents are a product of the author's imagination. Locales and public names
are sometimes used for atmospheric purposes. Any resemblance to actual
people, living or dead, or to businesses, companies, events, institutions, or
locales is completely coincidental.

Thanks to the Flame Tree Press team.

The cover is created by Flame Tree Studio with
thanks to Nik Keevil and Shutterstock.com.
The font families used are Avenir and Bembo.

Flame Tree Press is an imprint of Flame Tree Publishing Ltd
flametreepublishing.com

A copy of the CIP data for this book is available from the British Library
and the Library of Congress.

1 3 5 7 9 8 6 4 2

PB ISBN: 978-1-78758-778-6
ebook ISBN: 978-1-78758-780-9

Printed and bound in Great Britain by Clays Ltd, Elcograf S.p.A.

BRIAN PINKERTON

THE INTRUDERS

FLAME TREE PRESS
London & New York

Before there was human life on Earth as we now know it, there was a predecessor human race that squandered the potential of the species. This breed of *Homo sapiens* succumbed to primordial instincts of greed and destruction, leading to its eventual demise.

These crude ancestors remain embedded in our DNA. While there will be skeptics and nonbelievers who dispute the revelation of a previous, mirror society, it is my duty to document this lineage. A failed humanity remains in our roots, in danger of reactivation. We were bestowed with a second chance, a miracle from above, and from that carved a better path for civilization, rescuing the planet before time ran out. But for how long?

This is a lesson in history and humility, one I am uniquely qualified to give. I am authorized to chronicle this legacy because of my direct experiences and courageous passion to bring it to the surface with unflinching candor.

This book should be required reading for every citizen around the world. From the past, we will recognize warning signs for the future. This alone can save us from a second round of extinction.

Zeke Abernathy Gorcey, *Revealed! The Untold Story of the Human Race* [A work in progress]

PROLOGUE

When the hot sun slid from overhead and splintered into rays between the trees, Connor knew it was time to leave the river and head back to camp for dinner. His father was clear with the instructions: return to the RV before dark and be quick about it. "Don't make me come get you."

But Connor and his little brother, Evan, still had two more muddy worms residing in the shallow plastic container, and it would be a shame to let them go to waste. The one dozen nightcrawlers cost four dollars, purchased from a rickety bait shop next to a gas station during a trip to refuel the hungry tank of the family's mobile vacation home.

Connor had an itchy feeling that one more catch awaited, maybe the biggest one yet, if he could just indulge in a few more tosses into the active Indiana stream.

"We're going to go soon," Connor told Evan in a voice of marginal authority. At thirteen, he was four years older than his sibling, although not always successful at telling him what to do. Evan was good at tuning people out – usually lost in his daydreams or vacant thoughts – and when you told Evan something you needed to state it multiple times to penetrate his thick head of stringy blond hair.

"Five more minutes," Connor said.

Evan had put down his pole and was tossing small rocks into the river.

"Stop it, you'll scare the fish."

Evan threw one more rock to reinforce his brotherly independence and then wandered over to the fish bucket.

Inside, the afternoon's three catches commingled: two smallmouth bass and a rainbow trout with a pink-red stripe and black spots. He poked his finger in the water.

"Don't touch those, we're going to take them back to Dad."

Earlier, their father had told them to 'bring back dinner', although not entirely seriously, since he was planning to grill hamburgers, served with store-bought potato salad. He had scouted the fishing location for his boys, deemed it satisfactory (not deep enough to drown in) and allowed them to fish on their own for a couple of hours with strict instructions to return before it got dark. The walk back to camp would take about fifteen minutes, he told them.

Connor remembered those words with a tug of anxiety but continued to fish anyway as shadows broadened like dark puddles around him.

The worm on his hook disappeared, but it encouraged him to keep going – something out there was biting.

He hooked one final worm, puncturing it multiple ways in the manner he'd learned from his Boy Scouts merit badge, until the bait became a chubby knot with a tail.

He threw his line into the river and waited for any sudden dip of the red and white bobber.

He chased away thoughts of the ticking clock to dinnertime. He would just walk faster back to camp.

For weeks – that felt like years – Connor had looked forward to this trip. Fishing was number one on his list. He also wanted to climb mountains and spot a grizzly bear.

The Reynolds family's summer vacation had been planned a long time ago, in the cold and dreary winter months, and been the source of great anticipation ever since. The boys' father had displayed the route on his computer and discussed every stop along the way, from their Parkersburg, West Virginia home to Yellowstone National Park in Wyoming. This first stayover in Engles, Indiana, felt like one of Connor's Boy Scout camping trips, except calmer without the chaos of a couple of scoutmasters trying to wrangle seventeen hyperactive boys in the wild. There was also the added comfort of not sleeping on the ground in a tent. The RV, rented from a colorful lot with a big selection, was like a clubhouse on wheels with small, curtained windows and a multitude of little cabinets. The compact vehicle hosted a cramped kitchen with a stovetop, fridge and microwave, a tiny bathroom with toilet and shower stall, a diner-like eating booth, a mini master bedroom for the adults and a foldout couch for the boys. Connor didn't like sleeping in the same bed as his little brother, and it was the source of much kicking and poking. When they weren't bickering, they were giggling, sometimes late into the night until a parent intervened.

Fishing only barely interested Evan, and his restless impatience had been a persistent nuisance across the past couple of hours.

"I'm bored," Evan said now, for possibly the tenth time overall, wandering circles around Connor, kicking at the dry, hard-packed dirt.

"Shut up."

Connor hated to think of himself as an older, leaner version of his pudgy brother with the whiney voice, but the similarities were inescapable. They looked alike, as they should, right down to the stringy blond hair, long eyelashes and pug nose.

Five and then ten minutes passed. The darkness was growing serious.

Connor grumbled a swear and reeled in his line. The hook was bare. How long had it been that way? Well, it didn't matter. He was done. Out of bait.

"Get your stuff, let's go."

"I'm hungry," Evan said. He had devoured his snack – a small packet of vanilla wafers – almost immediately upon arrival. The empty wrapper was hastily half-stuffed into the back pocket of his shorts, emerging like the beginning of a tail.

"Dad's making hamburgers. Maybe he'll grill our fish."

"I don't want to eat them," Evan said, with a slight tone of alarm.

"Well, let's at least show them to Dad and Mom." He was proud of his catches and wanted to produce evidence of his success.

"Mom's not going to eat those either," Evan said.

"Shut up," Connor said. He said that a lot to his younger brother, sometimes without conscious thought, like a reflex, an efficient way to slap punctuation on a conversation he wanted to end.

"No, you shut up," Evan grumbled under his breath.

They gathered their things, including the empty worm bucket. (Connor was a serious proponent of 'Leave No Trace Behind', a motto of the Boy

Scouts.) They advanced on a twisty, well-worn path of trampled grass and dirt that led back to the campground.

"If we walk fast, we won't be late," Connor said.

The surroundings grew dimmer with uneasy acceleration, threatening to outpace their footsteps. The environment was looking less familiar.

After twenty minutes of walking, Connor realized they were on the wrong path.

He stopped abruptly for a moment, feeling a chill in his bones.

"Are we lost?" Evan said.

"Shut up."

"It's getting dark." His tone became a whine, the prelude to a cry.

The canopy of trees above seemed to crouch lower.

"We're not lost. We took a wrong turn back there. Let's turn around. Follow the path."

"You got us lost," Evan said. "I'm hungry."

They backtracked for ten minutes and reached a large bald patch that split in multiple directions like tentacles.

"This is where we went the wrong way. Go that way." But Connor's voice wavered with uncertainty.

"Will Dad come find us?" Evan said.

"He won't need to."

Thirty minutes later, dirty and frazzled, suffering a few more wrong turns and backtracking, the boys reached the familiar campground.

Dense trees and knotted brush gave way to a clearing that revealed civilization: an assortment of hulking recreational vehicles spread across a large lot, each one settled in place with open awnings and lawn chairs. The campground's simple play area came into view with its jungle gym and red slide. A small cabin anchored the front entrance of the lot where a mustached man in a ranger's uniform had signed them in and assigned them a space late the night before.

Everything was familiar except for the absence of people. The area held an eerie stillness. It was the look of abandonment.

"Where is everyone?" Evan said.

His question was met with silence.

The campground was losing color as the sun descended deeper into the forest.

Connor had fully expected to see his parents outside their RV, grilling hamburgers, setting up the picnic table and probably wearing mad faces because the boys were late. But the grill stood silently, unmanned. The nearby picnic table remained bare.

His parents' absence immediately alarmed Connor. Maybe they had gone looking for him and Evan? Then his father would *really* be mad.

"Let's check inside."

They leaned their poles against a tree and put aside the fish bucket and backpack of supplies.

"Dad, Mom," Connor said, anxiety lifting his voice an octave. He climbed a metal step and pulled open the thin screen door to the RV. "We're back," he said, entering, with Evan close behind.

As Connor stepped forward into the cabin, his foot kicked into something big, causing him to stumble.

Connor glanced down and saw his father crumpled in a heap on the floor.

He cried out with a gasp.

Evan peered around his brother, and his eyes widened.

"*Dad!*"

Connor crouched down. He hesitated and then nudged his father's shoulder. He didn't look injured, no blood or marks, just a terrible limp presence, as if the life had been sucked out of him.

As Connor tried to rouse his father, Evan stared ahead, frozen. He had just discovered their mother.

Her pink bare legs protruded from the small bedroom, laid flat, one sandal kicked off. She was stretched out in the narrow space, half inside the bedroom, arms bent at random angles. She looked like she had taken a bad fall.

"Dad, wake up! Wake up!"

Connor couldn't pull his father out of his deep unconsciousness, and a fear hit him that ran his blood cold.

Is he dead?

He quickly moved past his father to reach his mother. He tried to jostle her awake, but she was equally unresponsive.

"We have to get help!" Connor shouted.

Evan's gaze locked in horror at the strange sight of his father's slack expression, eyes thin and just barely exposing themselves. He started to cry.

"Go, go!" said Connor, giving his brother a push. "We have to get help."

A jumble of Boy Scouts first aid training raced through Connor's mind, but all of it relied on knowing the nature of the injury – stopping bleeding, reviving a drowning victim, applying a splint to broken bones. Despite nearly being a young man, he felt reduced to a helpless child, in desperate need of an adult to make everything right again.

Connor dashed across the gravel to a neighboring RV, old-fashioned and smaller. When they had first arrived, his parents introduced themselves to the occupants, a gray-haired couple, someone's kindly grandma and grandpa. They said they were from Kansas. The grandpa was a retired Air Force officer. The grandma offered cookies from a tin to Connor and Evan.

Connor pounded on their door, loud and urgent.

Behind him, Evan was bawling.

No one responded. The door rested against the latch without being fully shut, so Connor pulled it open for a look inside, introducing his presence with a shaky, "Hello?"

As soon as he opened the door, he saw the old couple on the floor of the cabin, entangled with one another, a sprawl of bony arms and legs, also unconscious.

Connor screamed and jumped backward. He knocked his brother to the ground.

Now they were both hysterical.

Tears blurring his vision, Connor ran fifty feet to the next camper, a rounded trailer hitched to the end of a car. He never made it to the door. He stopped abruptly in his tracks when he discovered bodies dropped in the dirt, three of them, two adults and a little girl in a pink dress.

Not moving.

Connor ran screaming to the welcome cabin at the campground entrance. This was the only place of authority, where the mustached man took their money and gave them papers, instructing them where to park and telling them to enjoy their stay.

Connor banged on the wooden door and got no response. He was prepared to go inside when his brother screamed:

"Connor, *look!*"

Evan pointed down the road to a gray sedan with its front hood crumpled against a big oak tree. In the weakening light, Connor could see the outline of somebody in the front seat.

He ran to the car, hoping and praying that someone inside could help him. But it was another body. He discovered the man in the ranger's uniform, eyes open and mouth twisted in a grimace, frozen unnaturally. His hands remained on the steering wheel. He looked like he was in suspended animation, stuck in a moment of shock.

"Is he dead?" Evan said. Connor reached through the open window and gave the man a poke. He lurched forward and Connor shrieked.

The man's face fell into the steering wheel with a dull thud.

"Call 911, call 911!" said Evan in between bursts of sobs.

Oh my God, yes, of course, thought Connor. He needed an ambulance – lots of ambulances – from where? How close was the nearest hospital? Police department?

When they first arrived at the campgrounds, his father had said cheerfully, "We're really way out in the boonies now."

At the time, it was a fun concept, an adventure. Now it was absolutely horrifying.

Connor pulled his cell phone out of his pocket. As he had experienced earlier in the day, there was a signal, but it was very weak, a dim pulse of life.

His hands trembled so badly he struggled with tapping out the three digits.

Then the buzzing started.

"What's that?" Evan said.

Connor froze. It sounded like a swarm of bees.

Evan searched the skies.

The sunset was nearly complete. The overhead canopy of trees meshed with the newly darkened sky into an abstract ceiling.

The buzzing grew louder, swiftly reaching an intensity that no longer resembled a cloud of ordinary bugs.

Evan, crying, covered his ears and shut his eyes tight.

Connor swooned in a circle, searching for the source of the horrible noise.

In an instant, the buzzing became a shrieking blast that exploded from the blackness and consumed his senses. It filled his ears, speckled his vision and attacked his smell and taste with something odorous and overpowering.

Evan abruptly stopped crying. Connor could no longer see him because he was blind. His eyes burned with fire.

The older brother opened his mouth to scream but could barely emit a tortured squeak before his bones became jelly and he dropped to the dirt, sucked into a swirl of nothingness.

CHAPTER ONE

Greg Garrett sent another text message, this one reduced to a simple, direct question:

Are you mad at me?

His wife, Janie, had ignored his previous texts – and left his three phone calls unanswered to amplify the silent treatment.

Greg knew he hadn't left town on the greatest of terms, leaving the house to catch his flight without time to resolve their latest bundle of bickering.

"Maybe we won't be here when you come back," she had said sharply, six-month-old Matthew in her arms and eight-year-old Becky looking up from her iPad, seated across the room on the middle cushion of the couch.

"We'll discuss it later!" he shouted to shut her down, struggling to pull a suitcase and bulging messenger bag through the front door while checking his phone for the Uber's arrival.

"If there is a later!"

And now he was four days deep into his latest business trip and any reconciliation clearly was not going to take place remotely. The few texts they had exchanged before this silent treatment were mostly unpleasant.

Greg was mad, depressed and resigned to the fact that the marriage had hit a rotten patch. The primary catalyst was clear – his new job.

Despite her objections, he had accepted a big promotion at work. It fed his ego, offered a considerable pay boost and required near-constant travel. With a new baby in the household, it was obvious which of those three components had set her off. She didn't want him to accept the job at this stage in their life. She wanted him home more often, helping out, rather than spending every week on the road, hopping from hotel to hotel, a chronic absence.

When he was the district manager of Indianapolis for Imperial Inn, he could visit the company's six Indy-area properties in day trips. He was very good at his job, and that led to his current predicament. Corporate headquarters liked him – and more importantly, they didn't like his immediate boss, a frumpy minimal-effort man named Harvey who failed at 'problem-solving', 'data-driven decision-making' and 'innovative thinking'. Harvey had been the head of the Midwest territory for more than two decades with archaic approaches and an arrogant attitude that didn't gel with the latest, youth-driven executive leadership team. They canned him and recruited Greg, based on his performance record and, he suspected, his tireless agreeability.

The broadened parameters of his responsibilities stretched from Nebraska to Ohio and reached north into Minneapolis and south into Kansas City. The district managers now reported to him, including the open position for his Indianapolis job. Their slowness to fill it only added to his workload.

Janie was apprehensive about the amount of travel required by the position. She was adamant about *not* moving from their Engles home to be closer to the hotel chain's Midwest office in Chicago. She had grown up in rural Indiana, her mother lived in a nearby town, and she had no interest in relocating to a big city, citing crime statistics and inflated costs.

Greg promised they would not move, and Janie believed this would be a deal breaker with his employer. She was stunned when Greg delivered the news that the company was open to him working remotely with biweekly trips to the Chicago office. In a weary moment, she let him make the final decision and quickly regretted it. Greg accepted the job and before long, he was traveling, traveling, traveling.

Every night was a different hotel but the same routine. He met for a half day with the hotel manager and local district manager to review financial performance, operational controls, regional marketing, social media presence and guest satisfaction. He led a development session with the hotel's staff to provide coaching and ensure compliance. Each hotel was measured on Key Performance Standards and trained to adhere to a Strategic Vision Framework. He refreshed his presentation template for every visit, bringing particular focus to slides on local challenges and opportunities.

Each market had its own issues, whether driven by external trends in the competitive environment or internal problems like team turnover or sloppy procurement practices.

The final phase of each visit was dedicated to his own personal observations, logged in a series of checklists. He stayed the night, like a guest. He reviewed the fitness center, the pool, the breakfast buffet, the housekeeping quarters, the vending machines, even the strength of the Wi-Fi signal. He tuned in to the sights, smells and sounds of the hotel and the impact of every moment of the hospitality experience.

He could easily integrate with the guests without earning a second glance. Greg was cursed or blessed with ordinary qualities – average height, weight and looks with a pleasant, forgettable face – that meshed with his calm, steady demeanor. Wherever he went, he blended in.

Upon arrival, he would randomly select an unoccupied room rather than take a specific assignment. He knew that if the staff locked in the reservation, they would overprepare the space and it wouldn't represent a real guest environment. The hotels were rarely at capacity – a separate, larger issue – so he didn't require an advance booking.

Once inside his guest room, he ran a formal inspection – everything from the towels to the television remote. He looked under the bed with a high-powered flashlight. He checked the shower's water pressure and temperature. He reviewed the ease of opening and closing the shades. He tested the air and heating.

He regularly capped off the ritual with an order from the room service menu, always something different, and took notes on the food's promptness and freshness.

By eight o'clock, he was typically spent, done with scrutinizing, lapsing into a tired, fuzzy boredom. He would turn on a local sports game, not to root for anybody but to provide a familiar anchor – baseball, basketball, football – in his transient life. The chatter of the sports broadcasters filled the room's emptiness with ambience.

Eventually, the game of the night ended, the TV went dark, and he killed the lights and settled in for sleep.

Sleep never came quickly.

He would listen to the hum of the air unit, the random thumps and clicks, footsteps on the hallway carpet, muffled voices in the walls.

Tonight it was even harder to drift off, given the unresolved fight with his wife that looped in reruns in his head.

Fortunately this was the last stop on his latest hotel tour and tomorrow at this time he would be home again to patch things up.

He understood her resistance to separation. He knew they were best when they were whole. And these days he felt anything but whole. His entire life felt uncomfortably detached – removed from his family and apart from his company's offices. He was a floating soul.

He stared up at the colorless ceiling and for a surreal moment he couldn't recall where he was. The hotels easily blurred into one another, especially with their identical layouts and room decor. Even the bland framed artwork, bought in bulk, was familiar in every city.

He thought back to the ball game that had droned on the television tonight – Minnesota Twins – and his current location returned to him: Roseville, Minnesota.

Greg heard disembodied voices – a female adult, then a child – in the wall behind his head. They murmured in the dark like ghosts. He began to think about the history of this room. The Roseville hotel was built eleven years ago. How many people had stayed in this very space over the years? He conducted some loose math, allowing for a seventy percent occupancy rate, and easily topped a couple thousand.

He imagined the ghosts of the previous occupants hovering in little wisps around the room. He could almost sense the lingering residue of their presence, watching him in the dark. He was one of them. He would leave his own existential crumbs here and then move on.

I'm floating, we're all floating through life, he thought in a muddle of semi-consciousness before entering true sleep.

★   ★   ★

Greg returned to an empty house in the middle of a sunny afternoon. He took a cab home from Indianapolis International Airport, strolled up the short walk to the front porch and let himself in, entering an unusual silence. Janie had apparently taken the kids somewhere and, of course, not told him. He unpacked, sent her an inquisitive text that she promptly ignored, showered and changed clothes.

It was technically still a workday so he settled into his home office, flipped open his laptop and caught up on work email. He expected the front door to open at any minute with the return of Janie, Becky and Matthew. Soon it would be dinnertime.

He prepared his defense for the argument to come. The hotel industry was going through a rough patch and Imperial Inn was struggling to return to former glories. He needed to put in extra travel now, but things would calm down and he would be home a lot more in the future. After this current round of in-person visits to introduce himself, he would be able to delegate more to the district managers. He could schedule subsequent meetings as online encounters through Zoom or some other platform. It was just important that each Midwest hotel in the chain meet him in person this first time.

He was well rehearsed for a dialogue that didn't arrive. Dinnertime came and went. Shadows began to extend across the front yard.

He tried calling her. No answer.

Now he was truly alarmed. Where were they? This wasn't a simple trip to the park or to see a neighbor or buy groceries. This didn't feel right.

Had she left him, taking the kids with her?

During one particular argument, she accused him of not wanting to spend time with his family.

That comment hit hard because, in truth, he *did* sometimes look forward to getting away and being alone for a while, a luxury that Janie didn't have. She dealt with the colicky baby, following full days with sleepless nights, while he slumbered in quiet comfort and solitude in a hotel room served by a staff working overtime to impress.

Janie had quit her job in commercial real estate after Matthew was born, a surprise pregnancy. Her allegiance was with family.

When the household got hectic, Greg was secretly grateful for long stretches of travel. He would never say it out loud, but maybe Janie was right. He welcomed his family's absence. He was a phantom father.

As his mindset shifted from defensive to guilt-ridden, Greg slapped the laptop shut. He pulled himself out of his home office.

Enough work. He was starving.

He tried calling her again, and again no answer. He sent Janie another text: *I'm getting worried. Please respond. Where are you?*

Then he microwaved a cardboard container of mac and cheese, the fastest and simplest meal he could find.

He stood by the front window as he ate out of the box, hoping to see his family's return. But the street remained empty.

The house felt incomplete without her – she typically brought it to life with her dominant personality. Janie had dark brown eyes, flowing brown hair and a commanding voice and presence that defied her slight, short build. She typically moved through the rooms with an active purpose, a bundle of energy. Now it felt like someone had pulled the plug.

The silence was uncomfortable.

Finishing the box of mac and cheese, he moved away from the window to head back to the kitchen. Then he spotted something that took his breath away.

Janie's purse sat on a chair in the adjoining dining room, its strap tossed casually to one side.

She left without her purse?

He quickly stepped over to look more closely and saw her car keys clearly visible inside.

Greg threw his fork and mac and cheese box in the kitchen sink. He ran into the family room to open the door to the connected garage.

The blue Ford Escape they shared sat idle.

Immediately panic settled in. He couldn't believe he didn't look in the garage earlier. In his mind, the car was logically gone with them. It never dawned on him to check.

He returned to the purse and probed its contents. Her cell phone was missing, but that didn't surprise him. She often stuffed the phone in her jeans back pocket so it was always accessible as she moved about the house and in the yard with the kids.

He pulled out his own cell phone and called Janie's mother, who lived nearly three hours away in Mishawaka. She was a sour woman and always talked down to Greg.

She had no information on her daughter's whereabouts.

"What, you can't keep track of your own family?" she said in her usual snide tone. She began to batter him with a backlog of her usual complaints about not seeing the grandkids often enough.

Greg closed his eyes tight. This was infusing more drama, not reducing his pounding stress. He couldn't stop himself from pushing her away with a lie. "Oh, never mind, she just pulled up in the driveway. All is good. Talk later."

Janie's mother muttered a barely audible goodbye and returned her focus to a loud television blaring in the background.

Greg wished he had someone else to reach out to about his rising crisis. He had no siblings, his father was deceased, and his mother was in a memory care facility in Nebraska, fraught with her own absences and disorientation.

He called Janie's friend, Stacy Fernstrom, who lived a few blocks away. Maybe they had gone over for a visit? He kept his voice calm, casual.

"Sorry, she's not here," Stacy said. "Did you check the school playground?"

Greg checked the playground next. He jumped in the SUV and drove slowly, watching the sidewalks. The playground was empty, with a motionless swing set, idle slide and unoccupied jungle gym. He drove up and down several streets, seeing occasional people, but no sign of his wife and children.

Greg returned home and called the sheriff's office. He spoke with Deputy Tom Billings. He speculated out loud about a kidnapping, as absurd as it felt.

"Is there any sign of forced entry?" Billings asked.

"No, no," Greg said, perspiring under his clothes.

"Anything out of the ordinary, like there was trouble?"

"Nothing's disturbed. They're just not here."

"Well, it's only been a few hours, right?"

"I don't know. It could be a lot longer. I haven't talked to her in days."

"When you left, did she say anything about plans to go anywhere, a trip?"

"No. No way. We have a six-month-old."

"Did you check with friends, her family, look around the neighborhood?"

"Yes, all of that."

"Did you have a fight or anything that might have caused her to go off somewhere?" Billings asked. "It's happened before, where we file a missing persons report, and it's really just someone storming off for a while and needing to cool down."

"We did…. We did have an argument before I left," Greg said, somewhat reluctantly.

"Well, that could be your problem right there."

"She didn't take the car."

"Maybe she called an Uber."

"But why would she do that with the car sitting here?"

"Who has the title on the car?"

"Well, I do, but—"

"There's your answer. Legally, it's not her car. Listen, I'm not saying this is the start of a divorce or separation, but you've got to consider anything."

"Wouldn't she at least tell me that she's left me?"

"Well, you know what they say. Actions speak louder than words."

"She wouldn't just disengage with me like this. Not so completely."

"Did you try calling the hotels in the area, the motels?"

"No – not yet." Greg was instantly struck by the irony that she could be holed up at the local Imperial Inn.

"You do that next. I'll check with the hospital. If you don't hear from your wife by morning, we'll open a formal investigation. But I'll be honest, nine times out of ten there isn't any real trouble. Somebody just leaves in a huff and for whatever reason cuts off communication. You said there was a fight."

"An argument."

"An argument, whatever. She got mad, she took the kids and went somewhere."

"But she didn't even take her purse."

"People get blinded by rage, they just storm off sometimes."

"That's not what happened here."

"Like I said, it's been just a few hours. Make more calls to her friends, check places she might go. Someone could have picked her up, people don't just get sucked out of their houses." There was a hesitation, and then he asked, "Any chance...there was another man in her life? Someone she could've run off with?"

"Oh God," said Greg at the mere notion. "No, no. I really don't think so. There's nobody, I can't imagine...."

"I just mention it because I've seen it happen."

Greg tried to envision Janie having a secret boyfriend, and it seemed ludicrous. She was too busy being annoyed with *him*. "I'd say it's highly unlikely." But so was this entire disappearance.

"Don't you worry," Billings said. "This time tomorrow, I bet you'll have your answers."

"If they're not home – if I don't hear anything by morning – then I want a full investigation. I'm serious, Tom."

"I don't doubt that you are. We're looking out for you."

After the call ended, Greg felt sick in the pit of his stomach.

★   ★   ★

Greg lay awake in bed, alone and in silence, feeling like a stranger in his own home. He had left most of the house lights on, except for the ones in the bedroom, placing him in semi-darkness. The unnatural stillness took on a disorienting quality, like he had simply transferred to another hotel room.

He wanted to sleep and then wake up in a brand-new day with immediate answers, or at least new possibilities.

The local hospital and sheriff's office had no evidence that his family had encountered any harm. Area hotels and motels had not admitted anyone with his last name. Janie's friends and family could offer no helpful clues.

In a state of sleepy delirium, he wondered if this was all some kind of cosmic punishment for neglecting his family. Had they been taken away from him because he had failed at being a good husband and father?

Sometime between one and two a.m., Greg drifted off, woke up a few times, and then finally entered something resembling real sleep. Exhaustion won out.

The next time he awoke, it was deep and dark into the night. An unsettling sound stirred him back to consciousness. At first, it lived in his dreams. It slowly transitioned to reality.

Greg opened his eyes.

He didn't move. He listened.

The sound was unmistakable.

He could hear his baby son, Matthew, crying somewhere in the house.

CHAPTER TWO

Greg raced through the house, flipping on every light switch, expecting to find his wife and children making a late-night return. It was clear: Janie had slipped into the house quietly and discreetly with the kids in tow to avoid a confrontation and her intentions had been shattered by baby Matthew's outburst. For less than a minute, he was flooded with relief. But it quickly evaporated when his family was nowhere to be seen. The crying abruptly stopped, replaced by dead silence. The house remained empty, the front door secured. There was no sign of anyone anywhere.

Did I just dream that?

Greg's skin stuck to his pajamas with sweat. He felt angry that his overactive imagination had tricked him with such cruelty.

False alarm. No crying baby. No family. He remained alone.

He drank a glass of water at the kitchen sink. He tried to calm the flutters in his chest. He gripped the counter and took several deep breaths.

One light at a time, he returned the house to darkness. He slid back into bed. He stared at the ceiling for a long while and finally drifted off.

He awoke minutes later to the strains of a sad, soft wail.

The sound was unmistakably an infant. It drifted in and out, like a strange breeze. This time, Greg did not jump out of bed. He froze, listening with eyes wide open. There were no additional noises to provide context. No voices. No footsteps or doors. Just the crying, less shrill this time, a persistent rise and fall of restless discomfort.

He tried to locate the sound.

It was close, maybe one room away.

Greg slowly peeled back the sheets. He placed his bare feet on the hardwood floor. The baby's whine continued, distressed warbling with stutters of crying.

It's got to be Matthew. It sounds like him. Who else would it be?

Greg stepped softly out of the master bedroom and took a turn in the hallway. He entered the adjoining baby's room. It was very dark. Instead of turning on the light, he advanced slowly to the crib, not wanting to do anything to disturb the environment.

The crib was empty. He felt inside. The bedding was cool to the touch.

The crying continued uninterrupted.

Now it sounded like it was coming from the master bedroom he had just left. How was that possible?

Greg returned to the hallway, not saying a word.

The entire house was dark and lifeless – except for the baby crying.

He tried to pinpoint the precise location of the sound.

In the master bedroom, it sounded like it was coming from the baby's room.

In the baby's room, it sounded like it was coming from the master bedroom.

How was that possible?

The crying persisted, tiny and frightened. As he stood in the hallway, his eyes slowly scanned the surroundings from left to right, then right to left.

Then his gaze lifted upward.

Oh my God.

The attic?

Greg gasped. He raced into the kitchen, yanked open the utility drawer, snatched a flashlight and turned on the beam. He grabbed a small step stool next to the sink and brought it into the hallway. He stepped on the stool and raised his arms as high as he could to grip a silver handle. He pulled down the ladder leading into the attic.

The infant sobs intensified.

"Matthew!" he shouted. He climbed the steps with a firm grasp on the flashlight.

The crying reached near-hysteria, shrill and piercing.

Greg's upper body entered the attic. He immediately began bouncing the flashlight beam across the open space, illuminating sides of cardboard boxes, plastic buckets and old storage trunks. He swung the flashlight wildly, probing every corner and crevice.

The crying stopped.

The house returned to dead silence.

Sweaty and panicky, Greg continued to aim the flashlight in quick jumps around the attic, examining the floor and then looking up into the crisscross of wooden beams in the low ceiling.

Nothing looked out of the ordinary. He pierced every shadow with light and found only the expected contents of the attic, layered with undisturbed dust.

"Hello?" he said. "Is somebody there?"

The only noises Greg could hear were the ones he was making himself.

He retreated down the creaky attic ladder. He pushed it back into place in the hallway ceiling. The attic entrance sealed with a thump.

He put away the step stool but retained a tight grip on the flashlight. He brought it with him into the master bedroom.

He stood by the bed for a long stretch, listening for the return of Matthew's cries.

He heard nothing.

My mind is playing tricks on me. I'm exhausted. I need real sleep.

Greg turned off the flashlight. He released it from his sweaty grip, placing it on the nightstand.

He returned under the sheets.

In a few hours, it'll be daylight.

Maybe the morning sun would bring normalcy.

He calmed himself the best he could. He decided against a sleeping pill because he didn't want to be groggy to face the next day.

He tried to force nothingness on his thoughts. After a few starts and stops, he finally slept for a stretch of time, close to an hour.

Matthew's crying made an appearance in his dreams.

Then Greg awoke and the crying continued. He wasn't dreaming.

Now it was louder, fiercer, as if enraged or stricken with pain.

"*Matthew!*" screamed Greg. He tumbled out of bed and hit the floor hard. Dazed, he scrambled on his hands and knees toward the sound of the crying. It filled his ears and pounded his heart.

It's coming from the wall.

Greg reached the bedroom wall and placed his hands on it.

Was the wall vibrating or was it him?

"Matthew?"

The crying persisted in frantic bursts, stabbing him like a knife.

Greg began clawing at the wall, shouting his son's name. He wanted to embrace him to stop the pain. He scratched frantically in desperation. Tears flowed from his eyes.

Greg moved out of the room. He rushed down the hall to the door to the basement. He descended the concrete stairs and raced to the workbench, where he quickly sifted through his tools.

He found a large hammer.

Greg returned to the master bedroom. The cries were stuck in the wall, he was convinced of it.

Matthew was trapped, somehow, between the two bedrooms.

Whack!

Greg struck the wall hard and broke open a small hole, splitting plaster.

Whack! Whack! Whack!

He continued to strike the same spot, widening the hole, to release the screaming baby.

"Matthew, I'm coming!"

He broke into the wall and reached inside, pushing away wires and chunks of plaster.

"I'm here, I'm here!"

The crying encompassed him in surround sound now, impossible to place in one direction, louder than natural, screeching like nails on a chalkboard, a truly horrific sound of raw anguish.

Greg pounded at the edges of the hole to make it bigger. He had to free whatever was inside. Was it traveling the four walls of the bedroom?

Greg disintegrated into confused crying. His sounds meshed with the crying baby's amplification, one blast of sound, and he thought his head would explode.

Greg passed out and hit the floor.

★   ★   ★

Rays of sunshine reached into the room. Birds chirped sweetly outside. Occasionally the sound of a moving car rustled by. Greg awoke and slowly sat up, momentarily puzzled to find himself on the floor.

Then he remembered the night before. It hung in his head like a bizarre dream. But the gaping hole in the wall in front of him confirmed it was real.

The hammer lay on the ground nearby. His palms were scratched and bloody from tearing at portions of the wall with his bare hands.

"Oh my God," he said quietly.

He remembered his frantic pursuit of Matthew's phantom cries.

Now, in the plain daylight, it seemed silly and outrageous.

When Janie came home, how would he explain this big hole in the wall? When. If.

He got up and wandered the house. There was still no sign of his wife and children. Despite the human sounds of the night before, no one had physically returned. The house was empty.

He checked his phone for the millionth time, and it disappointed him yet again with no correspondence from Janie. He tried calling her, and it rang once before going into voice mail.

He sent another text.

This time, he received a prompt notification: Not Delivered.

Had she shut off her phone? Or was it something more sinister?

His heart began pounding all over again, encased in a shell of fatigue.

Greg knew what he had to do next. He called the sheriff's office.

This time, he reached Sheriff Casey himself.

"I'm ready to fill out a missing persons report."

Casey promised to come right over.

Then Greg's cell phone buzzed with a text. He eagerly checked it, then groaned.

It was his boss, Carl Peters.

"Read your emails," it said.

THE INTRUDERS • 25

Greg stepped into his home office, logged into his company's network and reviewed a chain of messages about a broken water main at the Cedar Rapids, Iowa location and some resulting chaos. The district manager was gone on a boating trip and had left things to a panicked, clueless staffer.

"I can't deal with this right now," Greg said out loud.

He quickly called his boss.

"I'm having…a bit of a family situation," he said to Peters, not wanting to go into details, especially since he didn't have many details to offer.

Peters responded with a dry speech about work-life balance and how the balance required sacrifices on both sides, with this current company crisis requiring his undivided attention to his professional obligations. Peters also threw in some digs at the 'remote working thing' and how it required a special kind of focus and dedication to justify his absence from the 'rest of the team' at the Chicago office.

"I'll talk to Cedar Rapids," Greg finally promised. "I'll get it taken care of. I'll make some phone calls right now."

"We have some very angry customers, make sure they get some vouchers and personal attention. And find out why Benny Matikowicz is on a goddamned boat."

"Will do."

The call ended, and the doorbell rang.

Greg quickly responded. He let in Sheriff Casey and Deputy Billings.

He told the story of coming home to an empty house and being unable to reach his family. Billings nodded a lot; he had heard the same information the night before.

Casey began strolling the house, glancing in rooms. "No signs of forced entry, nothing disturbed, nothing unusual?" he asked.

"No," Greg said.

Then Casey glanced into the master bedroom and said, "What's that?"

He pointed to the big hole.

Greg froze. If he explained he had heard the sound of a crying baby inside the wall, Casey would question his mental state. He didn't need that right now. There was no way to make it sound normal.

"Fixing some wiring," Greg mumbled.

Casey nodded and continued his walk around the house, stopping where he had started, the living room. Billings was already tapping something out on his iPad.

"And you reached out to family and friends, anyplace she might go?"

"Yes."

"Do you happen to know what she was wearing?"

"No, like I said, I've been on a business trip since…Sunday."

"And she didn't take any suitcases, travel bags?"

"No. Like I said, not even her purse."

Casey nodded. "Email us some pictures of her and the kids. You might want to post them yourself on social media…."

Social media? thought Greg. It felt humiliating, especially if she had simply walked out on him. But he nodded anyway.

"Usually we wait twenty-four to seventy-two hours before we activate a full-out investigation," Casey said. "Ninety percent of the time, it resolves itself in a day or two. But this does feel unusual. It's hard to disappear around here with a baby and eight-year-old."

Then he asked, "You're still legally married, right?"

Greg said, "Yes. Of course."

"The reason I ask, if you're legally married, there's no court order of custody. It's legal for one parent to take the children. I can't file this as a kidnapping."

"She wouldn't…kidnap our kids," he said. "She's a good mother. This isn't…she's not a criminal. I'm just worried they went somewhere, I don't know, on a walk or something, and they got hurt or trapped."

"We'll canvass the area," Casey said. "I promise you, we're on it. You hear anything, any new information, I want you to share it with us as soon as you can."

"Absolutely," Greg said.

Greg felt better with the commitment of law officials helping him.

But his mood progressively darkened during the day as the terrible silence continued, hanging heavy over the house. He still couldn't reach Janie and the kids and had no clues to their whereabouts. It knotted his stomach.

Throughout the day, Carl Peters continued to poke him with work issues, ranging from troubles at assorted properties to revisions to the budget forecast. Greg tried to handle his job as if nothing was happening, but he was in a daze, unable to concentrate. He shut down his laptop early.

He debated calling Janie's mother again, but knew she would blame him for the disappearance or suspect he was holding out on the real story of why Janie might leave so abruptly.

At dusk, with the daylight dying once more, he became overwhelmed with despair. He couldn't go through another night like the one before. He called the sheriff's office. Casey promised that his men had been on the lookout, covering the community, and would continue their search.

Greg sat in the living room, clutching his phone, staring at the front door, imagining the moment his family would return. He could even hear Becky exclaiming, "Daddy!"

By ten o'clock, he felt jagged with frayed nerves. He knew he needed rest to keep his mind sharp. He couldn't endure another night of fragmented sleep, constantly interrupted by panic.

Greg took a sleeping pill with a shot of vodka.

He lay sideways in bed, staring at the awkward, gaping hole in the wall. He made plans to repair it the next day, getting supplies at the local hardware store, one of those drywall patch kits. The damage was a source of embarrassment, the product of half-awake delirium. The sounds of the crying baby had not returned since he woke up on the floor. Clearly his amped-up anxieties were playing tricks with his mind. He turned off the nightstand lamp.

Greg fell asleep.

Hours later, he awakened in full darkness. A low whining sound moved through the house. He felt his heart start hammering. Was it the wind? He listened carefully, fists clutching the sheets.

It was human.

A slight, wordless moan drifted in the air above and around him. The tone was mournful, and it sounded like Janie.

This is not happening.

Greg told himself he was dreaming. He shut his eyes tight. He continued listening to the rise and fall of painful moans. *My God, it sounds like a dying animal.*

Then Greg realized he may have landed on an explanation. The cries the night before, the moaning tonight…something was sick or dying in his yard. Surely that was it. A hurt dog, an injured cat, a wounded rabbit…. What the hell else would make such a pathetic noise?

Then the mournful noises stopped.

For a full minute, the house was silent.

Greg thought morbidly, *Well, whatever it is, it must have died.*

He shut his eyes again. He tried to relax, but he wasn't ready to sleep.

Greg felt his breathing calm down, his chest rising and falling in a steady rhythm. He released his grip on the bedsheets.

He wanted to purge his thoughts, empty his head. Then he felt a presence – an eerie sensation that he wasn't alone.

He opened his eyes.

A stab of fear lit up his body. Something hovered above him.

He watched as wisps of light, like lingering smoke, drifted in the air. He studied the patterns and could see the outline of a face.

He opened his mouth to cry out but was too frightened to make a sound.

Illuminated sketches came into focus, producing identifiable features: Janie's eyes looking down at him, the slope of her nose, the crease of her mouth. He could see Becky, trying to speak but silent. Floating between Janie and Becky, the shape of an infant came into view. Greg could see Matthew's tiny bald head and pinched expression of discomfort.

This can't be real? Can it?

He was afraid to move. The images lingered in and out of visibility in the charcoal shadows of the ceiling. The faces looked sad, struggling to communicate, pulsing between light and darkness.

Greg very slowly moved his right arm across the bedsheets. He reached for his cell phone on the nightstand. He took ahold of it without removing his eyes from the ghostlike visions swimming above him.

Greg brought the phone to his face. He swiped his thumb to activate the camera.

He could see blurry white trails framed on the screen, defying the darkness.

Hands trembling, he moved his thumb to tap the red button for a snapshot.

He took the picture, creating a sudden flash that lit up the entire room.

An explosion of high-pitched shrieks bombarded his ears and invaded his skull before abruptly slamming to a hard stop. Greg found himself screaming with them, then alone. The phone fell to his chest.

Panting, he faced a silent, darkened room once again.

For a moment, the camera flash left residual spots in his vision, like a film negative.

He could still see their faces.

Then they faded away.

The still of night returned.

CHAPTER THREE

Greg waited up the rest of the night for the images of his family to reappear. He studied the room, heart pounding, gripping his phone. The nightstand lamp was on to keep him alert and grounded in his surroundings.

The photo he had taken showed nothing. It was just a white flash, lighting up the bedroom ceiling, without anything resembling the pained faces he witnessed etched in the shadows.

Am I going crazy? Isn't this what happens to crazy people? They hallucinate.

The morning made a slow entry, easing the house back into unassuming familiarity as daylight filled the rooms. He finally peeled away the sweaty bedsheets and went into the kitchen to make a cup of coffee. As he sipped it, he tried reaching Janie again on the phone with the same disappointing results.

He just wanted to know: Did she abandon him intentionally or did something bad happen?

He was rooting for the former, the lesser of two evils, even though it made him sick inside.

He called the sheriff's office to let them know another night had passed without his family's return.

Deputy Billings picked up. Greg had known Billings for many years, having worked with him on minor crime incidents at the local Imperial Inn. Greg felt more comfortable with Billings than Sheriff Casey, who could be gruff and standoffish.

Greg decided to tell Billings about his experience with the ghostlike visions. It spilled out desperately with a pent-up release, like a confession.

Billings listened carefully and said, "You've been under a lot of stress."

"Do you think there's anything to it?"

"Well, personally, I've never had that kind of experience. I know there are some people who believe in it."

"I sound crazy, don't I?"

"No, no," Billings said. "I mean, under the circumstances...."

"If I saw ghosts, does that mean they're dead?"

"I, I don't know." Billings clearly didn't know how to respond to this conversation. "Maybe you can talk to an expert in the paranormal."

"Do you know someone?"

"Well, not exactly, but I have other names," he said. "Like counselors."

"Psychiatrists?"

"They help people going through a rough patch with their families."

"I don't know," Greg said. "Maybe that would help. But this is more... visceral than just being upset. I saw something, Tom. I *heard* it."

"Tell you what. Why don't you come in? We'll sit down and have a chat. I can give you some names. There's a woman, Dr. Rombeck, she did wonders for my sister."

"You want me to come to the station?"

"I think it would be a good idea," Billings said. "We have procedures, and we need to cover some bases."

"What does that mean?"

"I don't want to create alarm here," Billings said. "This is just the next step. There's a line of questioning."

"Wait a minute," said Greg, feeling a new surge of anxiety. "Are you saying I'm a suspect?"

"No, and we want to rule that out."

"What the hell," Greg said. "You think I butchered my family and buried them in the backyard?"

"No, of course not."

"I thought you were going to help me find them."

"Of course we are."

"Then let's talk about that, rather than wasting time investigating me."

"We have to do both," Billings said. "It's procedure, that's all. Believe me."

"Fine. Jesus. Let's get this over with. I'll be over in an hour."

Greg ended the call and put down the phone. He finished his coffee in one gulp and threw the mug hard into the sink, where it broke into pieces.

As he was getting dressed, his cell phone rang.

He rushed back into the kitchen, shirt unbuttoned.

It wasn't Janie or anybody that would be helpful.

It was his boss, Carl Peters.

Greg let it go to voice mail.

After a message alert beeped with a red badge, he listened to the recording.

"What the hell, Greg," said Peters. "You didn't follow through with anything yesterday. Do I have to do your job? What's going on? Do I need to—"

Greg shut it off. He didn't need to hear the rest.

He finished getting dressed and drove to the sheriff's office.

He sat down with Casey and Billings and endured a long stretch of questioning about his whereabouts of the past week. He told them about his business travel, providing names and locations, easy evidence.

When they were done with him, they brought him over to a young woman, Rachel Mills, who managed the administrative side of the sheriff's office, including the website, social media and press relations.

"Rachel's going to show you how to get the word out through Facebook, Twitter, stuff like that," Sheriff Casey said. "We'll get the whole community behind you. Somebody's bound to have seen or heard something."

Greg said, "I don't know if I want to do that."

"Why?" responded Casey in a tone that sounded accusatory.

"It's just...." He searched for a word and found the wrong one, but it reflected his current feelings. "Embarrassing. Putting it out there for everybody. It feels stupid, like I've misplaced my family. It's something you would do if your dog ran away."

"Suit yourself," Casey said, looking him over. "Just thought you'd like some help."

"Maybe later. Let me think about this. I'm still hoping...they're just going to come home, walk through the front door, and explain everything."

"That would be stellar," Casey said. His voice was patronizing. Greg was done, ready to leave.

He returned home with a renewed hope that Janie, Becky and Matthew would be waiting for him.

The house was empty.

He made himself a sandwich. It didn't taste like anything, but he was hungry. He cleaned up the broken pieces of coffee mug in the sink, feeling guilty about the outburst.

His phone rang, and he seized it.

ERYN SWANSON.

Who the hell is Eryn Swanson? he thought.

He answered, and a friendly voice introduced herself as a reporter for the *Engles Express*, the local paper.

He groaned inwardly.

She started asking him about the missing persons report, and he cut her off, asking, "How do you know about this?"

"It's public record," she said. "It's filed by the county."

"Great," he said, tired and unable to hide his grumpy tone. "So you want to write about my tragedy?"

"No," she said. "I want to help."

"Help?"

"If I put this on the front page, our entire readership will be on the lookout. Someone might have seen something, any kind of clue. Listen, it will be tasteful. You know us, we're not some tabloid. We're the voice of the community. Do you have a nice photo of the family we can use?"

"I don't know," Greg said. "I have to think about this." He wondered if he sounded like a jerk turning her down. He was just very unsettled by the notion of making his problems headline news. What if Janie left with the kids because she couldn't stand him anymore? What if this reporter interviewed him, and he let his guard down and started talking about ghosts and weird voices in the middle of the night? What would that accomplish?

And maybe if he resisted the offer to make this front-page news, the whole thing would prove to be unnewsworthy. There was always the chance that Janie and the kids would return any minute. It had only been... how long?

Forty-eight hours?

Eryn read a lack of commitment in his silence and put the ball in his court.

"Take some time to think about it," she said. "In the meantime, I'll send you another story I did about a missing person, just recently. A woman's brother, other side of town."

Greg perked up for a moment. "There was another?"

"I know, kind of unusual to have two cases so close together, right? Just goes to show you, these things happen. You're not alone, Mr. Garrett. You didn't hear about the man on the west side?"

"I must've missed it," he said. "I travel a lot."

After the call ended, she texted him the link. He read the story.

Indeed, it was a straightforward presentation of the facts, compassionate and asking for the public's help.

Eryn had interviewed Susan Bergan, a tax consultant, about her missing brother, Steve. Steve was in his mid-twenties and lived alone in a small house he rented on a road bordering the forest preserve. He worked as a heating, air-conditioning and refrigeration mechanic. His sister said she talked with him on a regular basis, and then without warning he became unreachable.

She finally got the landlord to let her inside his house, and he was gone. She examined every room and nothing was disturbed. Steve's employer said he had stopped reporting to work, without a word.

Accompanying the story, there was a photo of Steve smiling and holding a frosty beverage in a clear plastic cup with activity in the background that looked like a barbecue. He had long hair and a full-grown beard. He wore a Foo Fighters T-shirt.

Greg tried to imagine a version of the story with his information plugged in. He had no doubt Eryn Swanson would write an article that was sensitive and respectful.

He emailed her and said that if he couldn't locate his family in two more days, he would agree to a story.

She quickly responded that she would notify her editor, and they would hold space on the front page of next week's edition.

As they talked, Greg's boss buzzed to get through. Greg didn't answer. He knew he needed to give Peters some type of explanation for his sudden detachment. Extended silence would not be wise. After he finished talking with Eryn, he finally called his boss.

Greg explained his situation in vague terms. He said he was having 'issues at home'. He wasn't expecting sympathy but the response was worse than he imagined.

"Well, when do you think this 'issue' will be over?" asked Carl Peters, annoyed.

"That's the thing, I don't know."

"If you're having marital problems, I get it, I've been there, but you can't walk away from your job. Things are crazy busy. You knew there'd be heavy lifting when you accepted this promotion."

"I just need another day or two to clear my head and get this resolved," Greg said.

"All right," said Peters, immediately picking up on Greg's words. "Another day or two."

Greg just as immediately regretted giving a specific time frame. He had no way of knowing whether or not things would be better or worse in a couple of days.

The phone call pissed him off and ended with both sides angry.

He forced Peters out of his head. He reread the article about Susan Bergan's missing brother. The similarities were unmistakable. Gone without a trace. No signs of forced entry or robbery. No response to calls and text messages.

Then Greg had a crazy thought: *I wonder if this woman has experienced any ghosts?*

Perhaps if he contacted her and exchanged stories, they would discover common threads that could offer real clues?

He found her phone number online, called it and left a message when she didn't pick up.

Then he went to the hardware store to buy materials to repair the ugly hole in the bedroom wall. It gave him something to do, and he was antsy. He couldn't bear spending the afternoon sitting around, watching the front door, feeling time crawl.

Back home, he started to apply the drywall patch, and then his cell phone rang.

As always, it triggered a huge surge of hope and terror. Good news, bad news, no news?

It was Susan Bergan.

"Hey," she said, a pleasant but tired voice. "I got your message. Yes, let's talk. I.... It's so weird.... I'm free in a couple hours. Do you want to meet for coffee?"

"*Yes*," said Greg, and it was the most affirmative thing he had said all day.

CHAPTER FOUR

Greg met with Susan Bergan at Ridgeview Diner, and they occupied a red booth tucked in the back by the kitchen doors, out of view. The town was small enough that they would probably be recognized, and both wanted privacy and the ability to talk freely about their personal crises. They had a shared obsession.

"It was just like, poof, he was gone," Susan said. She looked to be in her early thirties, with straight red hair, square shoulders and a plain face with light freckles. Her pale blue eyes stared solemnly, and she wore no makeup.

Greg nodded. "Same here, it's like they suddenly ceased to exist."

"What did the sheriff say to you?"

"They issued a missing persons bulletin and all that. But I can tell they're skeptical about the whole thing. Like I'm holding back on something. I mean, it's possible my wife left me, we've had some rocky times. But to take the kids – an eight-year-old and a six-month-old baby – and not even say anything, that's just not her. Her mother claims to know nothing. I have no reason to suspect she's lying. We don't have enemies, we don't have much money if this is a kidnapping. I've looked everywhere they could have walked to, you know, the park, the forest preserve. I'm starting to question my own sanity."

"Don't," Susan said, cradling her cup of coffee, looking Greg in the eye. "I started to do the same thing. But we're not crazy. Something happened. The sheriff, the deputies...they've been all right, but I can tell they've reached their own conclusions about my brother."

"And that is...?"

She hesitated, then leaned in, confiding. "Steve...had a few run-ins with the law. Nothing major, he just liked to drink. A lot. He was in and out of rehab. He got picked up a few times for stupid things, passed out at a laundromat, getting in a bar fight, DUI…. So they think he's on a bender."

Greg's cell phone buzzed on the table, where he had laid it flat by the salt and pepper. He stared at it.

It was his boss.

He chose to ignore it.

"Do you have to get that?"

"No," Greg said. He asked Susan, "Is his car missing?"

"No," she said, surprised by the question. "It's a pickup truck, but no…. It's still sitting in the driveway. So it's not like he's in a car wreck, in a ditch somewhere or went on a road trip."

"Same," Greg said. "Our car's still in the garage. That's the weirdest part. Why wouldn't she take the car, with the baby car seat? Did someone pick them up? Who?"

"Did you tell the sheriff about the car?"

"Yes. I told them everything."

"Maybe we need to hire a private investigator."

"Do you know someone?"

"No."

She sighed and impulsively checked her phone, sliding it out of a simple, leather saddlebag. Her expression did not change – no messages. She let the phone drop back in the bag and returned her hands to the coffee cup, not drinking from it, just clutching the sides.

"Do you want to know something else that's kind of weird?" she said. She half-smiled, reflecting on a memory. "The last time we spoke, Steve said the strangest thing. We were on the phone. I was just checking in with him because of, you know, to make sure he was doing all right. All of a sudden, he says, 'Whoa. That is crazy. Are you seeing this?' I said, 'What?' He said, 'It's raining, like, silver streaks. It looks like tinsel from a Christmas tree.'"

Greg stiffened, struck by her words.

She continued. "I said to him, 'It's not raining here.' And he kept going on about the color. I thought maybe he was high. I told him it was probably just the reflection of the light or something, and he said, 'No, that's not it. The rain is *silver*.'"

"Wait, hold on," Greg said. He grabbed his cell phone from the table. He pulled up a texting exchange with Janie from earlier in the week. He handed it to Susan. "Read this. It's my wife."

The conversation started with a text from Greg: *Finally arrived in MN. Flight was delayed. Tired. Going straight to the hotel. How are the kids?*

Fine. Just had some weird weather.

Weird?

Rained for like fifteen minutes and only our house. Didn't even reach across the street.

That is weird.

Didn't look normal. Not clear, it was shiny.

Cab is here. Gotta go.

Bye.

Another text conversation followed from a day later, new topics, essentially arguments about his extended travel schedule.

Greg took the phone back. "You don't have to read the rest. That's just us bickering."

"When did she send that?" asked Susan.

Greg had to think for a moment. His sense of time was wrecked by the turmoil of the past few days.

"Sunday," he finally said. "When was yours?"

"Weeks ago. Like three weeks."

"It's a really weird coincidence," he said. "The part about the rain."

"Next time it rains, we'll have to check it out," Susan said. "I haven't noticed the coloring. Maybe it's getting polluted. God only knows what kind of toxins are in the air, even out here."

"So that's all we've got, funny raindrops," Greg said. He wished they had found a stronger connection, with more obvious clues. He decided to advance to the next topic, something he had been holding back until they got further into the conversation.

"Speaking of weird things," he said. "Have you had any…strange visions or heard weird sounds…like a…." The next word came out awkwardly but he had no other convenient way to put it. "Ghost."

"Ghost?" From her blank expression, it became obvious she did not relate.

"I'm the first to admit, it could be my mind playing tricks on me," Greg said. "It's happened the past two nights. The first night, I woke up, and I thought I heard the baby crying. I searched the house, there was nothing. The next night, I saw these images…like I could see their outlines, sort of drifting in the air."

She looked at him with sympathy and offered a simple shrug. "No, nothing like that. You're asking me…have I seen Steve's ghost?"

He didn't want to undermine the credibility of everything else he had told her. He dismissed the subject with a wave of his hand. "I'm sorry. Forget it. I know it sounds bananas."

"No, this whole thing is bananas. I could believe just about anything right now. None of it makes sense."

"It was probably one of those half-awake dreams."

"I'll be on the lookout for anything like that."

Greg released a small, sad laugh. "Listen to me. Ghosts. I'm losing it. Lack of sleep."

"We're going to stay in contact," she said reassuringly. "I don't know what's going on, but we're going to help each other out. I promise."

★   ★   ★

Greg returned home amped up with extra anxiety from three cups of black coffee. He parked in the driveway and paced around the exterior of the house, searching for clues. He studied the windows for anything unusual, like signs of a break-in. He stared into his neighbor's yard. He saw nothing out of the ordinary.

Greg's house sat in a rural area of large, grassy properties. A simple playset sat perched in his back lawn, offering the painful image of an empty, unmoving swing. There was a small playhouse, empty. He wanted to shout out his children's names. He felt helpless.

Then he filled with anger. If Janie was responsible for taking the children away, without a word, he would never forgive her. He could never trust her again. It was sick, grounds for divorce. So what if she was upset with his heavy travel schedule, he was earning better money so they could start saving for the kids' colleges.

As he circled the house and returned to the front yard, Greg stepped into something soft. He immediately pulled back and swore, expecting to see dog shit.

But it was something else.

"What the hell?" he said out loud.

Greg stared down at a strange patch of sticky mud, approximately a square foot in diameter. It was surrounded by grass. He saw a scattering of small yellow dots in the mud, unlike anything he could recognize. Seeds? He inspected them more closely, bending down and touching one. It had a rubbery texture, deflated like some kind of tiny hatched egg. The impression of his shoe had flattened a number of the eggs, leaving a slight white residue.

What the hell is growing on my lawn?

He wandered across his front yard, head down, looking for more signs of this strange cluster.

He found four more.

He found one at the side of the house, then three in the backyard.

They all looked the same: moist and gooey, spotted with tiny, emptied shells with a shade of rotten yellow.

He pulled out his cell phone and took a picture. He would go online and do some research. *What could it be?*

Greg walked over to his property line. Did the neighbors have this same crap on their lawn? He advanced into the O'Malleys' front yard, head down, inspecting the grass. He spent several minutes strolling across their property. He found no signs of the soft mud and yellow shells.

Greg returned to his own yard. He crossed it to look at the terrain of his neighbor on the other side.

Nothing. Green grass, occasional weeds, some normal bald spots of dry soil, nothing out of the ordinary.

Greg thought about the 'tinsel rain' experience he had shared with Susan Bergan.

This has to be related, right? Something abnormal is happening to my yard.

He thought about texting her a photo and trying to explain it, a potential outbreak of tiny worms or larvae, but there was no sign of whatever emerged from these yellow casings.

He worried he would sound absurd again, like when he told her about seeing ghosts.

But he really wanted to know if her brother's lawn experienced this same phenomenon.

So he looked up Steve's address on his phone, hopped in his car and drove over there.

Steve lived in a small ranch house in a low-income area of town situated near a forest preserve. Greg parked in front of the home and studied it: dark windows, peeling paint and scraggly bushes. His eyes immediately went to the lawn. It had not been cut in ages, on the verge of wild. But the gaps were immediately visible from areas of dead grass and mud, sprinkled with yellow specks. From afar, the yellow presence looked like tiny weeds, perhaps the start of dandelions. Greg strolled closer and recognized the same odd, deflated shells he had discovered on his own lawn. He continued walking across the yard and found several more clusters. It took his breath away.

Greg heard a car pull up in front of the house. He raised his head to look. It was the sheriff's car.

Sheriff Casey stared at Greg through large sunglasses. "Whatchya doin' there?" he called out from his open window.

Greg stared back. "Looking for clues."

"Me, too," Casey said. Then he smiled, although not entirely friendly, and stated, "Maybe I've just found one."

Greg knew he looked suspicious but didn't care. He thought about telling Casey about the yellow clusters but decided to wait until he talked to Susan. He needed to process this discovery and make sense of it. He doubted Casey would help with that; he was dull and pragmatic.

"We examined the house thoroughly," Casey said. "There's no reason for you to be here. How about you just worry about your own affairs."

"Do you think there's a connection?" asked Greg, approaching the patrol car.

"No," Casey said. "Unless your wife was a heavy drinker. You think they went out on a bender together? Or she's having an affair?"

That last thought had never entered Greg's mind, but he quickly dismissed it. "No," he said. And then he blurted, "Go to hell, Sheriff."

He knew it wasn't a wise thing to say to someone he needed to help him, and he regretted it immediately.

Sheriff Casey just nodded. "Nice," he said. "Real nice."

Then he drove off slowly, like a slither, into the late afternoon sun.

CHAPTER FIVE

Greg wore his exhaustion like a heavy coat weighing him down. He had slept poorly ever since returning home to an empty house. The visions or hallucinations or whatever the hell they were had ravaged his sleep and prevented him from giving his mind and body desperately needed rest. Tonight, he gave in to pills again, which he hated to do, but he couldn't face the next day with even more mental and physical deterioration.

This time he swallowed three sleeping pills with a glass of water. They came from a small bottle prescribed to his wife so long ago that they had expired, but he figured they would still do the trick – and they did.

He woke up nine hours later, stiff and disoriented in his bed. He recalled vague dreams of ghosts hovering above him, big eyes and twitching lips, distorted likenesses of his family. He remembered telling them, "You're not real," and his wife responding with a soft, faraway sob.

He firmly told himself it was the product of a deep sleep, just nightmares, even as a second inner voice persisted with: *Something's really happening...this can't just be my imagination.*

He had barely removed himself from the bedroom when the doorbell rang. It pierced him with a spike of panic – was someone delivering bad news in person?

He pulled on sweatpants and hurried to the front door, looking into the peephole as his hand froze on the doorknob.

Jesse Walton?

Jesse was the manager of the Engles Imperial Inn, someone he had known for many years. Prior to Greg's promotion, Jesse reported to him. He was a serious African-American man, tall and thin with a slim mustache. Greg immediately suspected that Jesse had been sent to check on him, being the company manager in closest proximity to Greg's home.

Greg opened the door and welcomed him in.

Jesse stepped inside, looking uncomfortable and searching for the right words. He wore his work outfit: a blue button-down shirt, dark tie and business slacks. "I'm sorry to disturb you, Greg. It's just that...."

"You've been sent here to find out why I'm ignoring the big boss?"

Jesse's head bobbed somewhere in the vicinity of a nod. "Well...yeah."

"Have a seat."

They sat in the living room. Greg knew his barefoot, unshaven, rumpled look concerned Jesse. "Sorry, I just woke up. I've had...one hell of a week."

"Mr. Peters asked me to come by," Jesse said. "To see what we could do...to help. He said you don't return calls, you're barely on email. He's... concerned."

"He's pissed," Greg said.

"Oh, yeah. That, too."

"Listen, I'll be straight with you. We've known each other a long time. I'm – I'm having a crisis."

"Oh," Jesse said. His voice was hesitant, compassionate. "I'm sorry, Greg."

"My wife and kids are gone. They left, and I don't know where they went. I can't get Janie to answer my calls or my texts, she's turned off her phone, or blocked me. The thing is.... I don't know if she's fine, or if something bad happened."

"God, Greg, I had no idea...."

"I haven't said much about it. I'm just...not in the right frame of mind right now. I've been waiting until I know more about what's going on. I finally got the sheriff's office involved."

"Shit. I don't want to bother you at a time like this. Is there anything I can do to help?"

"I don't know," said Greg, words swimming in uncertainty. "I just don't know anything right now. What to do, how to behave...."

"Are you okay if I tell Mr. Peters about it?" asked Jesse. "I mean, it will get him off your back. He's in the dark. He's speculating all sorts of crazy stuff, stuff that's not right."

"Yeah," Greg said. "That would be fine. You can tell him my family is missing. I just don't want to engage with him right now. You know?"

"Absolutely," Jesse said. "He's an asshole."

Greg smiled. It was the first time he had smiled in days. "Yes. You got it."

★   ★   ★

Greg arranged for a meeting with Susan Bergan later that day, returning to the Ridgeview Diner to share updates and continue their joint investigation. They occupied the same red booth as the day before, an unofficial headquarters. She wore a gray sweatshirt, jeans and brown leather ankle boots.

After a waitress in an apron poured cups of coffee, Greg called up photos on his phone.

The mysterious yellow eggs.

He handed Susan his phone and asked her to scroll through the pictures. "Okay, bear with me on this," he said, as she slowly advanced through them. "Maybe it's a coincidence, but whatever those are, I've never seen them before. I found them on my lawn. And, I'm sorry for trespassing, but I had to see for myself.... They were on your brother's lawn, too. And nowhere else."

"I've never seen anything like it," she said, using her fingers to expand one of the photos for a closer look. "You're sure you didn't see them other places?"

"I checked," he said. "I mean, it wasn't very scientific. Just a spot check around the area. I only saw them on my lawn and your brother's lawn."

She handed the phone back. "I'll go to his house and check it out. It's weird. I can't imagine a connection, though."

"The tinsel rain," Greg said. "Maybe it caused some kind of strange growth."

"So..." she said, trying to connect the dots. "Something discolors the rain, then something weird grows in the grass. Do you think this affected them, made them sick? I checked the hospitals."

"I googled those yellow things for hours," Greg said. "I came up with some possibilities, but they were all harmless. Moth eggs. Beetles. The photos...nothing was a perfect match."

"Unless they're not eggs at all...and some kind of weird excrement."

"What shits in yellow?"

"I don't know. A sick rabbit?" Susan laughed at her own response and shook her head. "Listen to us. What can this possibly have to do with people going missing? Maybe we're just desperate for clues and clutching at straws. So it rained. And we have yellow weeds or whatever this is. What can the sheriff do with that? He'll just laugh at us."

Greg thought about the ghostly images in his house. He had not brought the topic up again with Susan, but it fell into the same category: information he had withheld from the sheriff's office because it sounded so silly he might lose their trust in the other things he was telling them.

The waitress returned and asked if they were ready to order.

Greg had not yet looked at the menu. "I'm sorry – come back in five minutes." She returned her order pad to the pocket in her apron and left to check on another booth.

Greg glanced at his watch. It was eleven o'clock. "Do we order breakfast or lunch?"

"I know one thing," Susan said, studying the offerings. "I'm not ordering the eggs."

Greg's phone vibrated. He quickly looked at it.

Eryn Swanson, the local reporter.

He showed the name to Susan and then answered the call.

Eryn sounded breathless, excited. She led with, "Have you heard anything about your family?"

"Nothing," he replied.

"Okay, interesting," she said. "I just got word about another family disappearing. The mom, dad, kids – the whole clan, gone from a campsite in Engles. Also, an older couple, the campground attendant and maybe more. The Riverwoods Campgrounds at the edge of town. The tents, the RVs are all empty. No sign of anyone."

"Holy shit," said Greg.

"There's something big going on."

CHAPTER SIX

Terry Jenkins was a religious man, and he believed in heaven but he never expected it to take this form. Skimming the ceiling of his modest Engles, Indiana home, the sixty-six-year-old retiree watched his lethargic black Labrador, Blue, engage in a series of light naps. Every hour or two, Blue moved from room to room to find a fresh resting spot and break up the monotony. He sought out sunny areas of the carpet as the sun rays shifted their entry point through the windows.

Terry had tried to speak to Blue but his attempt at forming words resulted in small moans or sputtering, like a balloon losing air. Blue's ears would twitch, he would raise his head, but he never really extended his interest beyond a moment's consideration of a random sound disrupting the calm, like a rumbling truck outdoors or the chirp of a bird.

Terry also called out for the Lord, because he had many, many questions. But the Lord remained silent.

Number one on Terry's list of questions: *If I'm dead, why did my body get up and walk away?*

Number two: *And what exactly killed me?*

Hovering in the air without a physical form, unable to grasp a simple doorknob to leave the house, Terry was stuck with a lot of alone time to think.

In fact, his brain was as alert as ever. He just couldn't attach it to much of anything. His movements were slight, and he couldn't determine whether or not he was a contributor. It felt like swimming underwater, thick and sluggish, without a clean course of direction. Today his presence had drifted between four rooms, causing him to experience the house he had lived in for thirty-seven years in an entirely new perspective. In a sense, he was upside down. The ceiling was his floor, and the floor was his ceiling.

Blue lifted his head to unroll his tongue for a massive yawn and then sank back into a semi-slumber on the living room carpet.

"Blue," Terry attempted to call out again. It came out as a faint 'boo'.

Lord, what is happening to me?

Terry was in his first year of retirement from the gas company, where he served as an operations manager, accountable for teams that repaired the distribution network, a role he held for fifteen years, following an equally lengthy term in the meter reading unit. He was a widower, having lost his wife, Louise, to cancer five years earlier.

Terry's retirement had been sometimes lonely and mostly uneventful. He slept in. He watched ball games on TV. He read books from the public library. He delved deeper into his hobby, collecting model trains, and he had an elaborate setup in the basement, crowding the surface of an old ping-pong table. He had been looking forward to attending a convention of model train buffs in Ft. Wayne. He started a DVD collection of classic comedies: Laurel and Hardy, the Marx Brothers, Bob Hope.

The days comfortably blended into one another, unexceptional in a good way, without the stress of gas leaks and service disruptions and pipe replacement projects. All of that became someone else's problem.

But he would trade it in a heartbeat for *this* problem.

The first sign of weirdness came with the rain. A week ago, he had stepped out on his back porch to observe a light, unexpected rainfall. It had not been in the weather forecasts, which he watched twice daily on channel 5. It also didn't last long, just enough to give his lawn a good soaking.

His lawn needed it, but his growing reaction was concern, not satisfaction. The raindrops held an unusual color and texture. The rain looked silvery.

Was it tainted? He immediately suspected the industrial park fifteen miles away in the next county. Who knew what kind of garbage it was pumping into the atmosphere? The manufacturing complex hosted smokestacks and some kind of metals factory that was already under criticism for airborne lead. He became determined to write a letter to the editor of the *Engles Express*. But he had procrastinated and now he couldn't even hold a pen.

A day after the unusual rainfall, he encountered more weirdness. As he walked his dog, he came across clusters of tiny yellow eggs on piles of mud in several spots on his lawn.

He yanked on Blue's collar before the curious animal got too close. *Stupid dog would probably eat them.*

After securing Blue indoors, Terry returned outside with a shovel and paper sack, intending to dig out the foreign substance like weeds. He had a near-perfect lawn and wanted to keep it that way. He had previously battled an outbreak of ground ivy and thistle. Now that the majority of his daylight hours were spent at home – and not at work – he demanded an immaculate environment outside his picture window.

Terry sliced the shovel blade into the earth, just beneath the pile of yellow-speckled plop. He lifted the mess and deposited it into the sack. He cleared one area and advanced to the next, bringing the bag with him.

Hacking into the dirt, the shovel blade cut into a handful of the little yellow pods. He paused for a moment, watching as something black oozed out of the yellow. At first, it appeared to be tiny seeds, but then the seeds lifted and became bugs, accompanied by a startling, aggressive humming.

Terry instinctively swatted at them with his free hand, as if fending off flies.

Then the buzzing grew louder. He witnessed a swirl of black insects also rising from the paper sack.

He stumbled backward, dropping the shovel. He waved his arms and cursed. The bugs formed dense black clouds. *What is this? Do they bite?*

They looked like gnats.

Then Terry witnessed more spinning black clouds lifting from other areas of his lawn.

Holy criminy, it's a swarm.

Terry decided to retreat inside the house. He was certain he had some insect repellent, and he would blast this nuisance into submission.

However, as he quickly marched for his front door, the insects followed. They zeroed in on him, unifying into one big, black force. The buzzing intensified into an ugly, jagged audio assault. The noise entered Terry's ears, followed by the bugs.

They infested his inner ears, his nostrils, and his open mouth. They attacked the rims of his eyes.

Terry's view of his front door, just ten feet away, deteriorated as black specks overtook his vision.

Terry screamed, once.

Then the insects filled his throat.

Gagging violently, he stumbled into the door and groped for the handle. He found it and shoved the door open.

Terry fell inside the house, kicking the door shut behind him. Shaking uncontrollably on his hands and knees, he coughed up a black bile. The vomit sputtered between his lips in elastic, phlegm-like gobs, carrying little black particles. He wiped the substance from his mouth and chin.

His senses began to clear, and he tore at his clothes. He pulled off his shirt and pants, which were still spotted with clinging insects. He shoved them in the corner, quickly joined by his socks and underpants.

Blue watched curiously from across the room.

Naked, Terry gathered the clothes and quickly carried them to his fireplace. He tossed them on the crusty steel grate.

"You little buggy bastards."

Terry squeezed a can of lighter fluid on his clothes and drenched the black insects that stubbornly remained dug into the fabric. He opened the flue and ignited the pile with a handheld fireplace lighter with a red handle. An immediate ball of flames illuminated the room.

Terry mopped up his vomit with old dish towels and tossed them into the fire.

Watching everything shrivel, blacken and burn, he began to breathe more freely and feel under control again.

"I was attacked, boy," he told Blue, who sat on his hind legs, attentive and staying away from the fireplace.

Terry examined his arms and legs. They still itched with the memory of crawling bugs. He didn't see any lingering signs of them on his flesh. He didn't observe any unusual aberrations – no red welts or bumps from bites or scratches.

He waited until everything had burned to ash. Then he extinguished the flames. He didn't see a single bug.

He walked over to the front window overlooking his yard. He didn't see any hovering clouds of insects. Perhaps they had moved on? He pulled away from the window, realizing he was standing stark naked in plain view, probably not a good idea.

"Blue, I'm going to shower."

Terry entered his bathroom, reached into the shower and twisted the knob to release a blast of hot water.

He showered his wiry body for a good fifteen minutes with multiple applications of soap. He vigorously shampooed his thinned hair. He couldn't escape the sensation of those tiny gnat things covering his face and body.

What the hell were they?

He had never seen anything like it before, and he was well-versed in the insects and critters of Indiana, having lived in the state his whole life with a lot of time spent outdoors during his years in gas distribution.

After showering, he toweled off and got dressed in fresh clothes. He returned to the fireplace with a paper sack. He scooped the ashes and dumped them inside. Then he deposited the sack in a plastic trash bag and pulled the drawstrings tight. He brought the bag to a door at the side of his house, peered out the pane glass and did not see any airborne black spots. He quickly opened the door and dumped the trash bag near his garbage cans, then quickly scurried back into the house and shut the door. He dreaded the return of the swarm, buzzing and attacking like an angry nest of amplified bees.

All was silent.

Terry walked around the inside of his house, on the lookout for any stray insects climbing his walls or flying in his space. He found none. He stared through every window and didn't see a single dancing bug over his yard.

Blue followed him from room to room, tail wagging, oblivious.

Finally, Terry went to the kitchen sink, filled a tall glass of water and gulped it down. He feared he had swallowed a considerable number of the bugs. He wanted to flush the damn vermin out of his system. Some of them had already been vomited up, but he feared not all of them.

His stomach twitched just thinking about it.

Terry entered his den and plopped in his favorite chair in front of the television. He lifted the remote and skated across a few channels until he landed on a ball game. Blue curled up on the floor at his feet.

After an inning of baseball, the broadcast turned fuzzy. He couldn't remember the name of the teams or their cities. The score became abstract. The announcers sounded thick and sluggish.

Terry got the chills. He was freezing on the inside, feeling a hardening of his bones, while his skin perspired with fever.

"I gotta call Dr. Carlson," he said, rising from his chair. He advanced two steps and then crashed to the floor, without pain. His entire body felt numb and foreign. He squirmed and wiggled to sit up and return to his feet.

"This is bad," he said.

Terry entered his living room, where he still had an old-fashioned landline telephone. He owned a cell phone but couldn't remember where he had left it and rarely used it anyway, sticking to the familiarity of a simple touch-tone phone that had been a reliable presence in his life for nearly forty years.

He reached for the phone but only grazed it with his fingertips before collapsing again to the floor.

Unlike before, he could not get back up. His limbs became useless rubber. His stomach seized up with terrible pain. He gasped for air. His entire body felt angry and aflame.

Terry lost complete control over his physical movements. He began to vibrate, as if crackling with electricity. He became consumed with an overwhelming nausea. Every ounce of his being wanted to throw up, as if he had digested something very, very poisonous.

Terry experienced a rising bulge travel up his torso from his intestines to his chest to his esophagus. It blocked his airway, and he couldn't breathe. His eyes bulged. His vibrations intensified, flopping him like a fish out of water. His back arched unnaturally as his vision became blurred and distorted. He opened his mouth wide.

Terry vomited violently, expelling his inner being.

His eyes squeezed shut, and when they opened again, he was staring into his own ghastly face. How was that possible? He witnessed up close the grotesque, frozen expression of terror he was feeling inside. His lips stretched wide, stuck in a hideous grimace.

Like a camera moving in reverse, Terry's perspective of his own face slowly pulled back to take in more of the living room. It took him a moment to realize he was lifting up and staring down. His physical identity remained frozen on the floor, on its back, as Terry's point of view elevated to watch himself from the ceiling.

He tried to cry out and only emitted a thin, desperate squeak.

Blue began barking. He circled Terry's stiffened form on the floor and lifted his nose to sniff the air. He sensed something was wrong.

Terry watched helplessly, a floating cloud of consciousness above his own body.

Am I dead? Did I have a heart attack? Is this my soul?

He watched as Blue settled into a sitting position next to his owner, patiently waiting for him to wake up.

Terry tried to direct his movements, and it seemed to have no effect. He floated delicately, like a balloon, at the mercy of random currents.

All he could do was watch and think. He felt nothing, aside from the psychological horror that consumed him.

Why can't I just die in peace?

He remained a passive, shapeless presence in the house, a silent witness as the sun outside began its descent, darkening the room.

Blue wandered around a bit but always returned to Terry's body, sniffing it, even licking its face at one point, without receiving a response.

Twice the phone rang, and Terry was unable to answer it to beg for help from the caller. The ringing continued and then the caller gave up.

He thought about his son, Jeff, and daughter-in-law, Marcie, who lived nearby. Surely they would check up on him, eventually?

Who would take care of Blue?

He wanted to cry simple tears, but even that was not possible.

He thought about his deceased wife, Louise.

If he was now dead, would he be reunited with her? Did she go through this same separation of body and spirit?

As light drained from the house, he wanted to sleep. He craved unconsciousness. But he was not physically tired or physically anything.

He settled into a bland state of invisible existence, a mere observer, as if watching the world's most boring movie. Hours passed.

Then, in the middle of the night, it suddenly wasn't so boring anymore.

In a sudden jolt of movement, the body of Terry Jenkins sat up.

And Terry Jenkins watched it happen from across the room.

Blue rushed over, tail wagging.

Terry's physical being stood up on his feet, blank faced, ignoring the dog.

Blue sensed something was not right. The dog's temperament turned from affectionate to suspicious. He began to growl.

Terry's physical form ignored the animal. It took slow, shuffling steps toward the front door. Blue followed, keeping a watchful distance, rigid with tension. Moving stiffly and without emotion, Terry's body left the house like a sleepwalker. The door shut firmly, automatically relocking. Blue remained inside.

Terry's consciousness tried to comprehend this latest bizarre development.

Where did I go?

Blue returned to the living room. He paced anxious circles and finally settled down on the floor, ears still perked up, on alert for further happenings.

Terry wished he could follow himself. Was he dead or not?

He had lived a lifetime of normalcy in a small Indiana town, working a basic job at a local utility company, now widowed and retired, collecting model trains and following baseball, attending church on Sundays and keeping up with world events. He didn't drink much, never tried dope, but here he was hallucinating something terrible.

He was a good person, never in any trouble with the law, friendly with his neighbors, patient and calm. He was not deserving of some kind of divine punishment, like being pulled from his material presence and trapped against the ceiling while his body stalked off resembling a zombie in a horror flick.

He tried again to call out to Blue, desperate for any kind of response to validate that he still existed.

But the sounds Terry produced were small, easily ignored.

Nevertheless, he kept trying.

Finally, he produced a kind of moan that caused Blue to lift his head. Blue's response filled Terry with a small blossoming of hope.

I'm real.

★   ★   ★

Now a full day had passed, uneventfully, with nothing to do but reflect on all the strange events that led him here.

Daylight had returned to the house.

Blue had finished the remaining food and water in his bowls and needed replenishment. He also needed to go out. It was possible he had already relieved himself somewhere in the house. Terry had no way of knowing.

After hours of silence, Terry heard the sound of scuffling feet approach his front door on the concrete walkway.

Blue hurried over, tail wagging.

The doorbell chimed.

Blue began barking, loud.

Help, help, save me, I'm trapped, Terry tried to shout.

But he only produced a small, guttural groan.

Blue continued barking. The doorbell rang again.

Then Terry heard voices on the other side: his son and daughter-in-law.

It was hard to make out the words, but they were clearly wondering where he was, sounding worried. They switched from the doorbell to knocking on the door and trying the handle.

Then he heard something that filled him with hope: "...go back and get my key."

Jeff had a spare key to his father's house. It was rarely used, but he had one – it had been in his possession for a long time and came in handy many years ago, before Blue, when Terry and his wife Louise went on cruises and needed someone to check on the house, bring in the mail....

Jeff and Marcie's footsteps faded as they returned to their car. Terry heard the opening and closing of car doors, the start of an engine.

Blue remained sitting by the door.

Terry waited in fear and desperation for their return.

CHAPTER SEVEN

Greg and Susan met Eryn Swanson at the Riverwoods Campgrounds. The investigators had departed, leaving behind an intricate maze of yellow police tape roping off sections of the site, tightly wound across trees. The scene was desolate and frozen in time. Wind rustled the leaves and an occasional squirrel scampered around the tents and recreational vehicles.

A gray sedan sat idle near the entrance, crashed into a large oak tree, having swerved off the main path.

Eryn was a young and energetic reporter with short dark hair, inquisitive eyes and quick steps. She moved along the tape barrier, providing a succinct summary.

"This is how the sheriff found it," Eryn said. "At least seven people missing. They searched this whole area, all the trails. The state police are involved now. They spent the last day looking for clues."

Greg stepped closer to a stretch of yellow tape surrounding a camping vehicle.

"Stay outside the tape," Eryn said. "You don't want to add your footprints. The investigators will be back."

"This," said Greg, pointing.

Susan joined him at his side.

Greg pointed to a small mound of dirt, slightly darker in tone than the surrounding ground, speckled with split yellow eggs.

"Those things again," Susan said.

Eryn joined them to see what they were looking at.

Greg explained the sightings at his house and Susan's brother's house. He showed Eryn the pictures on his phone.

"So what is it?" Eryn said.

"We have no idea," Greg said. "I've looked around the neighborhood.

It's not widespread. It only seems to appear at places where people disappear."

Susan walked the perimeter of the secured site. She discovered another cluster of yellow spots.

Greg took more photos of the unexplained phenomena. Eryn followed him with curiosity. Susan remained several steps ahead of them, searching for additional evidence.

"Check this one out," she said.

Greg and Eryn caught up with her.

She pointed to a collection of yellow eggs that appeared plumper and luminescent. "These look different."

Greg leaned over the police tape, trying to get a closer look. "They are different," he said. "They're bigger, they're not creased. It's like.... They haven't hatched yet."

"So there's something still inside?" Susan pulled back with a grimace.

Eryn stared at the small, slick bulbs. "That's really strange."

"I'd love to know what the hell that is," Greg said.

"We can find out," Eryn said. "I have a contact at the Indiana DNR, Department of Natural Resources. They have a division focused on plants and insects, invasive species. There's a guy, his name escapes me, he's an entomologist. They have offices in Indianapolis. I have an appointment in the city tomorrow for another story. You know, maybe I can...."

Eryn turned away from the tape. She hurried over to her car, unlatched the door and leaned in. She brought out an orange-tinted, reusable plastic water bottle. She unscrewed the black cap and poured the water on the ground, jiggling the bottle to shake out the remaining drops.

Then she returned to where Greg and Susan stood at the police tape barrier.

"Okay, don't tell anybody," she said.

Eryn ducked under the police tape and took a half dozen steps into the investigation scene. She reached the unhatched eggs and bent down with the open-mouthed water bottle. She scooped the eggs inside, using the black lid to push them.

Once she had collected the eggs, she lifted the bottle and screwed on the cap.

"We'll have our answers tomorrow," she said, ducking again under the tape, returning to Greg and Susan.

Eryn searched the ground for a moment until she found a long stick. She picked it up and scraped away her footprint impressions in the dirt inside the investigation scene.

"Wherever these campers are…it will also explain what happened to my brother," said Susan, turning to Greg. "And your family."

"It's all connected," he said. "It's got to be."

"This might not be the last of it," Eryn said. "It could keep happening. It might be happening right now, somewhere else. They brought in the state police, and they could bring in the feds – there are vehicles here with out-of-state plates."

Then she mused, "It looks like I've got my page one story for next week."

CHAPTER EIGHT

Eryn Swanson couldn't sleep.

It was after midnight, well past her usual sleep time. She was an early riser. She did her best thinking and writing right after sunrise, with a cup of coffee and small plastic bowl of Greek yogurt. Her prose was more fluid and her head was less distracted in the early hours. It also opened up the rest of her day for interviews, story mining and pitches, and rewrites and edits on articles in progress.

But tonight she was too anxious to sleep. The missing persons story had gotten a lot bigger. More reporters would soon enter the picture, including that bitchy woman from the *Indianapolis Star*, Deena Blumfield. But Eryn was on it first and this was her territory.

The story could be the biggest of her career. Everything that had preceded it was ridiculously tame by comparison. A typical week's news might consist of a missing bike (not necessarily stolen), a small fire in a church basement (quickly extinguished), and disputes over zoning ordinances (neighbors arguing about fences). Such micro-drama.

When she finally almost drifted off, a pesky noise from somewhere in the room stirred her back to full consciousness.

"Oh for…" she muttered, pressing the ends of her pillow against her ears. It stifled the sound, but as soon as she relaxed and loosened her grip, the ugly disturbance resumed.

The buzz of a fly.

Eryn threw back the sheets and swiveled off the bed, landing her feet hard on the floor, uttering an expletive.

She could hear the fly but not pinpoint its location. The abrasive hum seemed to have left the bedroom and traveled into her small living room.

She opened a hallway closet, where she kept random essentials: a vacuum, broom, mop and bucket, alongside a stock of paper towels, tissues and toilet paper. A simple flyswatter hung on a hook. She grabbed it.

"Where are you?" she said, listening for the buzz, advancing into the dark living room.

She stood still for a moment, bare feet on a well-worn cotton rug. Just thinking about that tiny winged insect made her skin itch all over. She could hear the buzz again; it was definitely in this room.

Eryn reached over and gripped the stem of a tall floor lamp. She twisted the knob with a click, illuminating the room.

She faced one side of the living room and saw nothing, no flying specks, no spots on the wall.

She slowly turned her head and that's when the scene mutated.

On the other side of the room, a large section of the wall had turned black, like a big stain, and it was pulsing with life.

She realized it was coated with a dense gathering of black bugs, layers deep, wings twitching, climbing on top of one another.

Only one of the insects was airborne, and it soon settled into the larger, writhing mass.

Eryn dropped the flyswatter.

She immediately looked to the water bottle she had placed on a table earlier in the day, near the front door, next to a small stack of mail.

The container's black plastic top was partially disintegrated as if something had chewed its way through.

They've hatched.

She froze. She could sense they were watching her.

Do they bite?

Moving very slowly, she took one step back. She took a second step. Several of the fly-like insects detached from the wall, buzzing and hovering in the air.

She accelerated her retreat and knocked into the floor lamp. She spun around to catch it, but it was too late.

The lamp hit the floor with a crash, returning the room to darkness. The abrupt commotion ignited the army of insects. They immediately pulled off the wall and filled the air with a deafening explosion of angry buzzing.

Eryn screamed and ran for her front door.

She grasped the handle but didn't have enough time to disengage the locks.

Like a spray of hot lava, the swarm of insects pummeled her exposed flesh. They burrowed into the openings of her nightgown.

They attacked her eyes, nose, mouth and ears.

She swung her arms wildly at them, swatting blindly, and her screams turned into choking.

She felt the bugs all over her skin, but that wasn't the worst of it. She could also feel them on the inside of her body, crawling and poking in her throat, her lungs, her sinuses, her ear canals.

Then she could feel them canvassing her brain, like ants consuming a fallen apple, darting spasmodically in a crisscross patchwork of jagged paths, rapidly growing in numbers, chewing away at her consciousness.

Eryn fell to the ground and began to vomit. But instead of expelling the foreign substances in her body, she purged her own being in a long, squirming heave as the invaders took over.

CHAPTER NINE

Downtown Engles featured a basic Main Street of modest shops, a library, a post office and several restaurants cozily installed on a four-block stretch of classic architecture before blending into leafy residential neighborhoods. The major chains – grocery stores, fast food outlets, big box retailers – occupied a strip mall a few miles away, but Susan liked to endorse the locally owned businesses, even if the prices edged higher and the selections were limited.

She had just stepped out of Miller's Hardware with a paper bag of purchases, including light bulbs and bird feed, turning right for a stroll to her next destination, Sam T's Deli, to pick up a sandwich and chips for lunch, when something caught her eye and caused her to stop on the sidewalk.

She gasped and nearly dropped her paper bag.

Someone had taped a simple poster to a utility pole with a single word at the top in big, heavy lettering:

MISSING.

A smiling old man's face stared at her with kind eyes and gentle bemusement.

Beneath the photo, the text filled in the story:

Terry Jenkins, aged 66, missing from his Engles home, diabetic, 5 foot 8, short gray hair. If you have any information on his whereabouts, please contact Jeff and Marcie Jenkins.

There was a phone number at the bottom of the poster, and Susan immediately entered it into her phone.

Then she called Greg.

"We've got another missing person," she told him. "*Another one.*"

*   *   *

Greg and Susan met with Terry Jenkins' son and daughter-in-law in the living room of their small ranch home. They were joined by a large, sad-eyed, black Lab named Blue, identified by Jeff Jenkins as his father's dog. Blue settled on a scratchy, circular rug between the young couple, who were seated in hardback chairs, while Greg and Susan sat on a lumpy couch. Jeff wore a faded Harley-Davidson T-shirt, jeans and several days of facial stubble. He listened with a hard expression as Greg told his story and Susan followed, describing her experience.

When they were done, Jeff slowly shook his head. He struggled for words. "I don't...I don't see a connection. I mean, aside from them missing. People go missing for different reasons, probably happens all the time. We just got a coincidence 'cause it was in the same town."

"We think Jeff's father was in the early stages of...what's it called," said Marcie. She had long blonde hair with pink tips, a white sleeveless top and a blurry tattoo on one shoulder.

Jeff said, "Altzen-heimers. Dement-ya. Maybe. I don't know. He's a diabetic. He forgets stuff. He takes all these medicines. He's old, he's losing his marbles, a few at a time, you know? There was one time...he went on a long walk with Blue and kind of got lost and a neighbor had to bring him home."

"But by now," Susan said, "wouldn't he show up somewhere? Or at least someone would have seen something. It's a small town."

"You would think."

"I believe there has to be a link between what's happened to you, me and Greg. Something is happening to people in this area."

"So what, you think it's like a serial killer or something?" said Marcie.

"I don't know."

"Serial killer." Jeff rolled his eyes, and he sunk back in his chair. "C'mon."

Marcie said, "I saw it on the TV, they had one in Illinois, guy was just killin' random people, cuttin' 'em up and buryin' 'em in cement."

Jeff threw his hands in the air with exasperation. "Nobody is carving up my dad and burying him in a basement. You gotta stop watching that shit." Then he turned to Greg and Susan and said scornfully, "The other day, she said maybe he was kidnapped. Like, who's going to pay money for a broken-down, sixty-six-year-old man? What are they gonna get out of me? I got two hundred dollars in the bank. They want my motorcycle? I mean, did you guys get a ransom note?"

Greg shook his head.

Susan said, "I don't think that's it."

"We just wait," Jeff said. "We see what turns up. Sooner or later, we'll get answers. Probably different answers for all of us."

"We'll pray for you," Marcie said. "If you pray for us."

Jeff scowled. "That ain't gonna do anything."

Marcie said, "You don't know for sure."

Jeff gave her a look. Then he said to his visitors, "Listen, I gotta get back to my shift. This is my lunch break, and I thought you had some real information about my dad. No disrespect."

"None taken," Greg said. "Let's stay in touch. We'll text you our contact information. If you hear anything, a sighting, a clue, let us know and we'll do likewise."

"You got it," Jeff said. He stood up and led them to the front door.

"Good luck," called out Marcie.

Greg and Susan left the Jenkins' house. For a moment, they stood in the gravel driveway by their cars and contemplated their next move.

"Have you heard anything from Eryn?" Susan asked.

"Not yet. Supposedly she's in Indianapolis, meeting with that entomologist."

"We should go to his father's house," Susan said, turning back to Jeff Jenkins' home. "I'll bet we find more of those yellow eggs."

"Yeah, I was all prepared to talk about the eggs, but I got the impression it wouldn't be a very productive conversation."

"We don't even know what those eggs are all about or if they're connected...."

"And if it doesn't make sense to us...."

Then, in a moment of silence, Susan's face creased with worry. "What she said, about a serial killer. I mean, it's not totally far-fetched, is it? Do you think there's someone going around...."

Greg shut his eyes. He didn't want to imagine the possibility of violence toward Janie, Becky or the baby.

"No," he said. "That can't be it."

"There are a lot of sick people in this world."

"You can't think that way," he said.

"I know, I just…anything is possible. This whole thing is so strange, God, I swear, it makes me want to scream."

"I totally understand how you feel," Greg said. "Sometimes I—"

Susan's phone rang in her purse, a generic ringtone.

She quickly dug it out and glanced at the caller ID, which she registered with trepidation. "It's the sheriff."

She answered and pressed it to her ear. "This is Susan."

She listened. Her eyes grew large.

Greg searched her face for clues. Her expression appeared to freeze.

"I'll be right there," she finally said. "Thank you."

She hung up and stared at Greg for a long, uncertain moment, still stunned by the news.

"That was Sheriff Casey. He says they've found my brother."

CHAPTER TEN

Susan sped to the sheriff's office in her silver Hyundai, closely followed by Greg's blue Ford Escape. They parked in adjacent spaces in quick succession and hurried up the cement walkway to the front glass doors.

Inside, Rachel stood at the front desk, expecting their arrival. She quickly contacted Sheriff Casey on an old-fashioned intercom. He emerged from the back of the office and beckoned with a finger. "This way."

Susan and Greg followed him down a corridor and into a small break room, where Steve Bergan sat at a long table, eating slowly from a vending machine bag of Fritos. Deputy Billings stood nearby. He smiled and gestured to the no-longer-missing person.

"Steve!"

Susan ran over and leaned down to hug her brother's shoulders. He barely reacted to the embrace. He looked up at her with a small, pleasant smile. When she let go, he took a sip from a can of Pepsi.

She stepped back to study him. He appeared disheveled and unshaven, but unharmed. "Steve, where the hell have you been?"

When he didn't respond, she turned to the sheriff. "Where did you find him?"

"Side of the road, Tamarack Avenue, a few miles from the highway."

She turned back to her brother. "Steve, are you okay?"

"I'm okay," he said plainly.

"Something's not right," she said.

"I'm okay," he repeated.

Greg studied the scene. He had never met Steve before, but could tell this was an odd reunion. Steve's primary focus appeared to be finishing his Fritos.

"Steve, please tell me where you've been."

"Just around."

"No, you can't…it's been weeks. Why did you leave your house? Did you stay with someone? You weren't just…walking around all this time?"

"Walking around," he echoed, staring into the bag of Fritos he had emptied.

Sheriff Casey touched her shoulder. "Let's step outside a minute."

Her eyes grew wide with worry. She glanced over at Greg. He joined them in the corridor.

"He's been like that since we found him," Casey said.

"Just like that?"

"Ma'am, is he a little, well, retarded?"

She cringed at the crude language. "No. This isn't…he's not himself."

"I suggest you get him checked out at the hospital. He might have suffered a knock on the head, got amnesia. You said he drinks, maybe he injured himself. We didn't notice anything, no blood, but he could have a concussion, brain trauma, hit by a car, what have you."

"Oh my God," she said quietly.

"He's been cooperative," said the sheriff, offering a comforting tone. "We just can't get anything out of him. He doesn't appear to be… upset."

Deputy Billings joined the conversation. "What about a stroke? He's kind of acting like my grandpa after his stroke."

Susan shut her eyes for a moment, overwhelmed. She held up a hand to stop the speculation. "Let me talk to him some more," she said.

She reentered the room.

The other three filed in after her, quietly observing the interaction.

Steve remained seated, blankly looking across the room at nothing in particular. He barely blinked.

"You must be tired," Susan said to him.

He shrugged slightly. "Tired."

"I've been so worried. We've been looking for you. Where did you go?"

"Just around."

"Okay. Yes. You said that. Can you tell me more?"

"Not really."

"Do you know how long you've been away?"

"Away from where?"

"Your home."

He shrugged. He didn't look at her. He looked down at the table, like a bored little boy.

"Does anything hurt?" she asked. "Like your head?"

"No."

"We should have you checked out by a doctor."

"I just want to go home."

"We'll go to the hospital first."

"No. I want to go home."

"But we don't know if you're hurt. You're not acting right."

"*I'm fine*," he said with a forcefulness unlike his previous responses.

Susan looked over at Greg.

Greg didn't know what to say. He couldn't stop thinking about his own family. Would they reappear? Would they be like this?

"Well," Sheriff Casey said, "as far as I can tell, there hasn't been a crime committed here. He probably went on a B-E-N-D-E—"

"He's not a child," snapped Susan.

The sheriff halted, then continued, "—and suffered some kind of head injury that's affected his mental state. We're not doctors here. You best get him in front of one."

"I don't need a doctor," Steve said. "I want to go home." After a beat, he added, "Please."

Susan slowly nodded. "All right, Steve. I'll take you home. But I'm going to set up an appointment...."

"Home," echoed Steve.

As they walked Steve out of the building, Casey engaged Greg in a brief side conversation.

"I want you to know...we're still looking for your family."

"Thank you," Greg said.

"This should give you hope. People turn up, eventually."

Outside, Susan helped Steve into her car. He climbed into the passenger seat gingerly, studying the vehicle like a foreign object.

Sheriff Casey and Deputy Billings stood at the building's entrance, waving with forced, hopeful smiles.

Greg and Susan did not wave back. Greg stepped over to Susan before she climbed behind the wheel.

"You're still going to get him checked out?"

"Of course," she said. "Even if I have to bring someone to the house."

"Do you think…this cloud he's in…mentally…has anything to do with the eggs, the rain, something, like, poisonous?"

Susan frowned and shrugged in weary resignation. "Greg, your guess is as good as mine."

After she drove off, Greg sat in his car and made a phone call.

He tried reaching Eryn Swanson again.

After several rings, he got dumped into her voice mail. Again.

He swore and headed home.

*   *   *

Back at the house, returned to the awkward silence and empty rooms, Greg stood in the kitchen and decided to microwave a frozen burrito. Food had become meaningless to him, except as something to consume two or three times a day out of obligation.

He ate the burrito quickly, barely tasting it.

He was rinsing the dish in the sink when the doorbell rang.

He rushed to answer it, hopes heightened after the discovery of Susan's brother. When he opened the door, he faced Jesse Walton.

He refrained from groaning and said simply, "Hey, Jesse. What's up? Is Peters sending you after me again?"

"Can – can I come in?"

Greg noticed Jesse was trembling. "Yes, of course."

He brought him into the living room where they both sat down.

Jesse looked at the floor, dazed. He was sweating, maybe even hyperventilating.

"Jesse, what is it? Are you okay?"

"No."

"What...what's going on?"

"I don't even know how to say this. I haven't told anyone about it yet. I came here first. If you want to fire me, I understand."

"Fire you? For what?"

Jesse raised his head to look directly at Greg. His tie was loosened, his blue, button-down shirt had damp clouds of sweat.

"I...I lost my guests."

"You lost a guest."

"No! Guests. All of them."

"I don't follow."

Jessie paused, catching his breath, organizing his train of thought.

"All right," he said. "I'll start from the beginning. This morning, I went to the hotel. The desk clerk was gone. The staff, too."

"They quit?"

Jesse produced a pained smile. "There's more. The hotel seemed strange. Extra quiet, you know? And it took me a while to figure out... the whole place was empty."

"Empty?"

"I mean, we weren't very full, nothing like capacity, but we had guests."

"They all checked out?"

"I have no record of that."

"Okay, so no desk clerk, people just...walked out of the hotel?"

"Sort of, but it gets weirder."

"How?" Greg felt his skin prickle. This was quickly following a terrible pattern.

"I walked around the hotel, looking around, you know, and some doors were open, the guests were gone, but they left their things behind, with the doors unlocked."

"Then they're coming back?"

"All day, so far, nobody's come back."

Greg started to reply, but he couldn't find the words. He felt flush with a wave of panic. No, a tsunami.

"I lost my guests," said Jesse, and it looked like he was going to cry. "How does that happen? They're gonna fire me. They put me in charge of a hotel, and I lose everybody."

CHAPTER ELEVEN

The phone rang in Jesse's pocket.

He jumped a little in the chair, as if receiving a small electrical charge.

He extracted the phone from his wool pants pocket and looked down at the screen to identify the caller.

"Oh shit," he said, his tone collapsing into weary defeat. Greg waited for him to elaborate.

"It's Peters." Jesse sighed. He waited one more ring, slightly prolonging the agony, then answered.

"Jesse Walton speaking...."

Greg listened to one half of the conversation. The other side was represented by a shrill, tinny, faraway garble, words not discernible but clearly in the angry category.

"Yes, Mr. Peters," said Jesse. "I'm dealing with that right now.... I don't know...yes...Mr. Garrett? He's right here, I'm at his house."

Greg grimaced and waved his hands, not wanting to be pulled into the dialogue, but it was too late.

"What? Yeah, okay," Jesse said. "Sure. I'll tell him."

Jesse lowered the phone from his face and addressed Greg. "He wants to talk to both of us. Right now. On Zoom."

Greg sighed. He stood up to get his laptop and bring it into the living room.

A few minutes later, Greg and Jesse sat before the monitor, propped on a table, facing a furious and red-faced Carl Peters. He was a bald man with beady eyes and too much forehead.

"What the hell is happening to the Engles location?" he shouted. "We're getting calls, there's noise on social media, asking why we're closed. Guests with reservations are showing up to an empty hotel and there's nobody there to serve them. The guests who signed in, nobody can reach them. What the hell is going on?"

Jesse struggled to find words. "I...I don't know. The staff must have walked out and the guests...."

"Was there an evacuation? A gas leak, a fire?"

"No. I don't think so."

"You don't think so?"

"I don't know. I was going to call the police."

"No!" thundered Peters. "No calls to the police. Not until we know what's going on. If the media gets ahold of this, it could be a public relations nightmare. Your job is to protect the brand, Walton."

Then Peters directed his ire at Greg. "Garrett, this is your territory. It's under your watch. What the hell is happening?"

Greg opened his mouth but no words came out, just a drawn out, "Errrr...."

"Jesus, you look awful. Have you been drinking?"

"No. My family—"

"I know, I know. Your family left you. People deal with family issues every day, but they don't desert their jobs. It's called work-life balance. You have an obligation to the people who pay your goddamned salary."

"I understand. It's just that—"

"Every day that hotel sits empty, it's a hit on revenue. How can you abandon a core responsibility? Have you forgotten our mission statement, our brand values?"

"No, sir. Not at all."

"Then recite it."

"What?"

"Recite the company mission statement and our four core values. Right now."

"Really?"

"Yes, really."

Greg shut his eyes. His mind was muddled with exhaustion. He couldn't recall the company mantra through the fog, something about guests being family....

"Our...we...always..." he wandered, then gave up.

"You're fired," Peters said.

Greg felt a sudden jolt but couldn't identify the emotion – shock or relief?

"Oh..." Greg said, dazed. "Okay."

Peters immediately turned his burning stare to Jesse. "Walton. I'm personally coming out there to sort this out. I'm taking the corporate jet. My secretary will contact you with the itinerary. You will pick me up at the airport and together we will go to that hotel and get to the bottom of this nonsense."

"Yes, Mr. Peters."

"And while you're at Garrett's house, please do me a favor. Collect his laptop and any other property belonging to the company."

Jesse turned to face Greg and shrugged apologetically.

"Don't look at him, just do it!" Peters said.

"You can have your crummy laptop," Greg said, pushing in closer to the camera, suddenly overcome with anger. "Because I'm done with you, too."

Greg punched the screen, squarely in the center of Peters' face, cracking it. Then he slammed the lid shut.

★　★　★

"Jesse, you didn't lose anyone," said Greg, after Peters had been disconnected from the conversation. "There's something...bigger going on."

Jesse stared at him, perplexed. "Like what?"

"My family.... I still haven't heard from them. Not a word. They really just disappeared, vanished, and it's been happening to other people, too."

Greg told Jesse about the empty campsite and other missing persons in the community.

"I...I think this is all connected," Greg said.

"Like they just evaporated?"

"I don't know. One person came back...but he's not the same. Mentally, I mean. It's like he's got brain damage."

Jesse's eyes searched the room. "I don't know what to say. This wasn't in my job description."

THE INTRUDERS • 77

"Do me a favor. When you return to the hotel, can you tell me if you see, somewhere in the grass, little yellow eggs...like the size of a small jelly bean."

"I really have to go," said Jesse, inching toward the closed laptop. "You okay if I take this?"

"Of course. You heard the man, I'm fired."

"I'm sorry, Greg."

"I know I look a little crazy...I've had no sleep...and I sound crazier... but...."

"It's okay," Jesse said. "Whatever's going on...we'll get it figured out."

After Jesse left, Greg immediately called Susan.

"We've got more people disappearing," he told her. "An entire hotel."

"A hotel?"

"The Imperial Inn on Fairfax. I work with the manager. The building just emptied out."

"Where did they go?"

"Same story. No one knows."

"Like the campsite."

"How's your brother? Has he opened up about what happened?"

"No," she said sadly. "I tried, I really tried. Either he's acting dumb or he really doesn't know. I took him to his house, and I wanted to go in with him to talk some more, but he wouldn't let me."

"He wouldn't let you in?"

"He actually shoved me to keep me from coming inside. He pushed me, really aggressively, slammed the door on me." She sounded like she was going to cry. "That's not like him. He's a big guy, but he's gentle. His behavior is not the same. I don't know, the sheriff thought maybe he's on drugs. He refuses to see a doctor to get checked out. He's sick, I'm sure of it. Have you heard back from Eryn?"

"No." Greg paced through his house with the phone pressed against his ear. He was sweating, incapable of remaining still as panic pushed through his body. "I gotta...I gotta track her down. Find out about her meeting with the entomologist. Tell her about the hotel and your brother. Maybe she has new information. We've got to piece this all together so it makes… makes sense." He was breathless.

"Greg, are you okay?" asked Susan, sensing the overwhelm in his voice.

"Sure," he said. "I lost my job. I lost my family. I'm doing just great."

★   ★   ★

Greg spent the rest of the afternoon in search of Eryn Swanson.

He called her cell phone repeatedly and sent text messages.

He called the *Engles Express* and spoke with an older woman on the administrative staff, who said she hadn't heard from Eryn and her editor was actively trying to reach her.

Greg contacted the Indiana Department of Natural Resources next for the name and number of the state's entomologist. His name was Mark Seiber, and he was very polite on the phone but only deepened the mystery by telling Greg that Eryn never showed up for their appointment.

"I figured she got pulled into a story, you know how it is with reporters, always on deadline."

After the call ended, Greg became very worried.

As dusk began to settle in Engles, Greg looked up Eryn's address, hopped in his car and sped to her apartment building.

Eryn lived in a three-story brick building with eight units on each floor, a plain but well-kept property in a quiet part of town. When Greg arrived, he immediately saw her car in the parking lot, which gave him a surge of hope that didn't last.

In each missing persons case, including his own family, the car had been left behind.

Greg rushed into the small entry lobby and found her name on the panel of buzzers, apartment 22.

He buzzed, a long one, then removed his thumb and waited.

Nothing.

He buzzed several more times, staring at the little round speaker, hoping to hear her voice.

Nothing.

He glanced down at a bin used to collect bulk mail that wouldn't fit into the individual, locked mailboxes. It was filled with magazines, catalogs, advertisement flyers, newspapers. He sifted through the clutter.

Eryn's name was on a fair amount of it, indicating she had not retrieved her mail.

He resumed buzzing aggressively, losing all remaining hope that she would answer.

The lobby entrance opened behind him and a gangly teenage boy stepped in, wearing narrow-rimmed glasses and a scraggly goatee that insufficiently covered his acne.

The boy nodded a silent greeting and dug in his jeans pocket for a key.

"Hey," Greg said. "You live here?"

"Yeah."

"Do you know...she's in apartment 22...Eryn Swanson?"

He looked Greg over. "Yeah," he said slowly. "I think so. The reporter lady?"

"Yes, yes. The reporter lady. Can you tell me.... I'm trying to reach her. Have you seen her around?"

The boy stood there for a moment, holding his key, wrinkling his brow before producing a thought.

"Yeah. I saw her last night."

"Last night? What was she doing?"

"I was coming back from my girlfriend's place, it was like one in the morning. I was coming in, she was going out."

"Going out?"

"Yeah, we kinda crossed here in the lobby."

"One in the morning? Did she seem okay?"

"Well...." The boy twisted his lips, and he held his response for a moment. "What, you want me to be honest? She looked kind of spacey, kind of high, you know?"

"High?"

"I mean, I don't know." His eyes darted nervously. "I'm not an expert...."

"I'm sure you're not. Do you know where she was going?"

"She got picked up."

"Picked up? Like an Uber?"

"It didn't seem like an Uber. It was, like, a big white van."

"White van? Did you see who was inside?"

"Nah, the windows were dark. She just climbed in. It was her ride. That's it. That's all I know."

"Was there any writing on the van?"

"Just a white van. It was kind of beat up. There was like a big dent in the door. On the driver's side."

"Did she say anything when she got in? To the driver?"

"I didn't hear anything."

"Which way did it go?"

"I don't know."

"What was she wearing?"

"Just...clothes. I don't remember. What's this all about? Is she okay?"

Greg hesitated before responding with full transparency. "I don't think so."

CHAPTER TWELVE

Jeff Jenkins needed dog food for his father's dog, Blue, and rather than shelling out his own hard-earned cash for an overpriced bag of kibble at Walmart and standing in line with the other late-night bums, he chose to go to his father's house and grab the old man's idle stock. Besides, he didn't know Blue's favorite brand and wasn't in the mood to make choices from a crowded aisle of pointless options. It had been a long day at work, the clock was approaching beer and bed time, and the only reason he was making this nighttime trip was to stop Marcie's nagging: "We can't keep feeding him table scraps, he needs real dog food, just go get it."

Blue seemed totally content with Cheerios on a paper plate (who wouldn't prefer that to crappy pet food?) but fine, fine, *fine*, he would get the stupid dog chow just to shut her up. Then beer – no, *beers* – and bed. And then some sleep and back to work.

What a life.

As he pulled up to his father's house on his motorcycle, what he really wanted was to see some lights on to indicate the old man had returned from wherever the hell he had wandered off to.

But, no, the place was dark. Very dark, as in you could barely see the outline of the house. He told himself to turn on some outdoor lights to at least keep burglars at bay.

"Dad, you're killing me," he grumbled as he parked in the slim driveway.

He climbed off his Heritage Classic cruiser and popped the kickstand. He headed for the front door, fishing the house key out of his leather jacket pocket.

Since his father's disappearance, he had only been to the house during the daylight hours, and the complete darkness creeped him out. The nearest streetlamp was probably half a mile away. Jeff took small steps to avoid stumbling, and when he reached the door, he felt around with his hands until he located the keyhole.

"God damn it."

He finally unlocked the door, creaked it open and stepped inside, entering an even deeper blackness. His sight was completely wiped away. His hand ran along the wall.

Where the hell is the light switch?

Then something glistened in the room before him. At first it appeared like wisps of faintly illuminated smoke. Then it took on the form of his father's face and arm, as if projected on the ceiling.

What the hell!

His father's image flickered. Terry Jenkins stretched out his hand, reaching for his son. His mouth opened and then the most awful noise came out, a painful push of sounds, something between crying and strangulation.

"Dad?" said Jeff.

Jeff couldn't believe what he saw – his father had transformed into something ghostlike – as if his physical being had dissolved and become particles in the air.

Jeff yelled at the insanity, slamming his hands across the wall in search of the light switch, finally finding the bump and flicking it up with a sharp *click*.

The living room burst into light and color.

His father vanished.

Jeff searched the room. His eyes gravitated up toward the ceiling.

"Dad?" he said, softly this time.

The ghost, the smoke, whatever it was – all gone.

Jeff walked through the house, turning on every light he could find.

Each room was empty and still, untouched since his last visit.

His heart pounded hard in his chest. Was his mind playing tricks on him?

He cursed his teenage years – those dumb, bored weekends with Danny Kacheris and the other burnouts, experimenting with LSD and mushrooms.

Was this an acid flashback?

"I fucked up my brain," he muttered. It was the only logical explanation. He had a dent or a hole or something in his brain, causing tricks.

He continued to examine his surroundings. Where did the illusion go? Maybe the light scared it – whatever 'it' was – away?

One by one, he started to turn the lights back off to test his theory. Jeff returned to where he had been standing when he had the vision. He took a deep breath, returned his hand to the final wall switch, and then....

Click.

The room plunged back into pitch-black darkness.

After a moment, Jeff could see his father again.

He stared at the faint, transparent image that barely stayed in view, portions fading and then reappearing, never quite steady or complete. He saw his father's frightened, haunted face looking back at him.

His father's mouth moved but the sounds were barely audible from somewhere deep inside, wordless and desperate.

"Dad...is that you?"

The lips struggled and the eyes held open, wide. Then the image flickered, sputtering like a weak light bulb.

Jeff slowly pulled his cell phone out of his pocket. He turned on the flashlight app and pointed the beam toward his father, hoping for a better look.

The injection of light into darkness caused the specter to vanish.

"Where are you?"

Jeff stepped forward and waved the stab of light, penetrating the room's corners. He poked his free hand into the air to feel for something tangible he could not see.

The vision of his father was gone. Jeff's fingers probed the space around him, uninterrupted.

"It's the light," he said to himself. That explained why he had not seen his father's image the other times he had been to the house, in the daylight. This strange thing could only be seen in total darkness.

Jeff shut off the flashlight beam. He returned the cell phone to his pocket. His eyes readjusted to a total lack of light.

He stared into blackness.

The faint outline of his father returned, floating gently in the center of the room, never quite whole, offering glimpses: an arm, a foot, a face.

"How-how can I help you?" asked Jeff.

The response came in clicks.

"I don't know what you're saying."

The next sound was mournful, like the faraway wail of a wounded animal.

Jeff was shaking. He wanted to get angry. He wanted to cry. He wanted to embrace what remained of his father.

He stepped toward the vision and tried to reach up and touch it.

When Jeff's hand entered his father's space, the physical world wiped away any evidence of the ghost's presence.

Jeff quickly withdrew his hand.

He waited.

He watched the portion of his father that had been erased gradually recollect through the union of tiny, dust-like particles of illumination.

Jeff felt like he was going to barf.

This has to be a dream. This has to be a dream.

He desperately wanted to communicate with this weird thing that looked like his father. He wanted answers. How could this be happening?

And if this was really, truly his father's ghost…caused by his death….

Where was the body?

"Dad, I wish we could talk," he said. He tried to recapture eye contact. The damn image never stayed steady, pulsing in and out of view, floating and rotating in silence like some kind of birthday party balloon.

He thought about the absurdity of communicating with ghosts. Then he thought about his mother, who had believed in such things, clinging to ideas of an afterlife and always looking heavenward to acknowledge the silent presence of a dead relative or friend, and all at once it hit him….

The Ouija board.

His mother had owned a Ouija board, nestled in a stack of board games, brought out on occasion to 'speak' with deceased family members or, ridiculously, dead celebrities like John Wayne.

Even as a child, he found the whole Ouija board thing ridiculous and fake, but it lent itself to a lively party game, usually late at night after many hands of bridge and several rounds of alcohol.

His mother swore it was real, while his father just winked, went along with it, and said, "Who knows."

Jeff wondered if the Ouija board was still sitting on a shelf in the basement, dusty and forgotten since his mother's death five years ago. His dad didn't toss out her things, he just let them sit in memorial.

"Dad," said Jeff, and the one-way dialogue was feeling increasingly ludicrous. "I'm going to the basement to see if the Ouija board is still down there." He stopped short of adding, "Don't go anywhere."

Using the light on his cell phone to shine a path, Jeff moved through the small house. He reached the basement and descended the creaky, wooden steps into a familiar odor of musty decay. The basement was filled with forgotten storage – clusters of cardboard boxes, plastic buckets and shelving touched only by years of clinging spiderwebs.

He found the board games on a long shelf along one wall: Life, Battleship, Clue, Monopoly, Candy Land, Chutes and Ladders, Risk and others, representing a time before video games. The long, slender Ouija box sat there with the other oldies, sandwiched between Yahtzee and checkers. He slid it out.

The lid proclaimed 'Mystifying Oracle'.

He brought it upstairs.

In the living room, he set up the Ouija board on a squat coffee table, pulling up a chair. He needed light to see what he was doing, so he turned on a nearby floor lamp.

The presence of light disrupted the total darkness he needed to see his father, but he could sense him in the atmosphere, watching from above.

The Ouija board offered simple options: the letters of the alphabet, numbers, 'Yes', 'No', and 'Goodbye', all presented in old-time, carved wood-like letters.

Jeff placed the wooden, heart-shaped indicator on the board.

"I'm – I'm going to ask you some questions," he said. "Think about your answers. Send them to me, like a signal. Okay?"

He was met with silence.

He felt both frightened and ridiculous. He didn't believe in the occult or seances, but he also didn't believe in what he had already seen with his own two eyes.

Jeff lightly touched the fingers of one hand to the indicator. He was careful not to press it or push it in any way to steer the direction. He surrendered to passive contact.

Jeff hesitated in the stillness, then spoke, enunciating clearly, spacing out his words.

"Are you my father?"

Then he waited.

Nothing happened.

After nearly a minute, he began to lose hope. Then, with a jolt, there was a short tug beneath his fingertips.

Jeff gasped.

He watched as the indicator moved to a side of the board, dragging his soft touch with it. He maintained contact with the device as it slid in tiny puffs of movement, like breaths of air.

The pointer landed on: YES.

Jeff became overwhelmed with a sense of wonder, like he was a child again.

His mind swam with a barrage of new questions, and he sorted through them to quickly pick the next one.

"Are you in pain?"

After a long pause, the indicator moved on a horizontal path, stopping at: NO.

Jeff hurried to his next inquiry: "Are you dead?"

The indicator moved up into the spread of individual letters. Jeff watched closely, connecting the sequence of movements in his mind to spell words and form a phrase.

I...DONT...KNOW.

The answer struck Jeff with more confusion. He blurted, "Where is your body?"

I...DONT...KNOW.

Jeff contemplated his next question. He couldn't get real specific, it was all too strange. Finally he said, "What happened to you?"

I.

WAS.

STOLEN.

The reply stunned Jeff. He trembled under his skin. What the hell did that mean? *Stolen?*

"Stolen by who?" he said out loud.

The indicator glided very slowly under his fingertips. Jeff froze in shock when the movements stopped, producing an answer.

THE FLIES.

CHAPTER THIRTEEN

Greg awoke with a start. His neck hurt. He had fallen asleep in his car.

The early morning sun struggled somewhere from behind gloomy gray clouds. Sounds of activity emerged out of the stillness: the rolling of a shopping cart, the grumble of a truck on its way to the loading dock.

After a moment of disorientation, Greg reacquainted himself with his surroundings. He was parked on the edge of a large parking lot serving a supersized grocery store in Engles' largest shopping center. He had stopped here to rest, late at night, after hours of driving in search of the white van. Now it was dawn.

He was convinced the white van that took Eryn Swanson away was connected with his own family's disappearance. He had to find it.

It explained one of the mysteries of the missing persons: how people vanished from their homes, leaving their personal cars behind.

Someone had picked them up.

And taken them away.

The white van became an obsession.

He had driven around the Engles community and surrounding territories, eyes glued, looking for the vehicle. He couldn't stop.

He found numerous white vans and followed each one until he was satisfied they didn't fit the description: plain and unmarked, with a big dent in the driver's door.

There was one van in particular that raised his suspicions, old and beat up. He followed it until the stocky driver pulled over to the side of the road, hopped out and threatened to punch his lights out for stalking him.

"I understand, let me explain," said Greg quickly, stopped behind the van and eager to defend himself. "There's been a kidnapping involving a white van. My children—"

The thick-necked man immediately began to shout. "Kidnapping? I haven't kidnapped anybody! Jesus Christ!"

He threw open the rear doors of his van, and Greg's headlights revealed a broad array of electrician's supplies.

"I just got done with a job. You see anybody tied up in here? You're barking up the wrong tree, jackass."

"Sorry," Greg said quietly. "I'm good."

He later followed another white van to someone's driveway on a residential road. He advanced an extra block, parked, and snuck back on foot to get a better view of the vehicle from the sidewalk.

There was a minor ding in the driver's door, but nothing that could be classified as a 'big dent'. A peek in the man's front window revealed an innocent domestic scene: mom, dad, kids.

It made him sad, and he missed his own family. His insides ached.

He checked his phone for messages and found nothing useful.

He decided to go home, freshen up, eat something and then continue his search.

He kept reminding himself Susan's brother had returned, and that gave him hope. It also gave him deep concern. Steve had come back in a changed mental state, affected by something or someone.

Susan had sent frustrated email updates: *He won't talk to me. He's locked himself in his house. I still don't know where he went or what happened!*

He thought about the other missing persons cases and the future ones to come. Despite the sheriff's lackadaisical attitude, this was all going to explode any day now into a major crisis, led by the empty hotel. Just because the threat was unseen, undefined and unexplained didn't mean it didn't exist.

After an hour at home, he couldn't stay confined any longer and returned to the road.

He found more white vans, many of them obvious delivery vehicles with stenciled logos on the side for florists or plumbers. And no big dents in the driver's door.

He traveled the main roads – some of them several times. He canvassed side streets in residential neighborhoods and two-lane highways in wide-open rural areas. The skies stayed gray and dreary, matching his mood.

He entered miles of Indiana farmland and the deeper he advanced, the fewer cars he saw. He ultimately hit a dead end on a dirt road that stopped at a simple farmhouse surrounded by acres of corn. He saw a small flatbed truck, tractor and plow parked at random angles across the side lawn.

Greg stopped short of the driveway entrance and began to make a large, sweeping U-turn to retreat the way he came.

Just as he was getting his car pointed in the right direction, a sudden *smack!* startled him and caused him to slam the brakes, kicking up a cloud of dust.

He sat still for a moment.

What was that?

Then there was another *smack!*

He stared forward at a wet, greasy stain on his windshield, like a droplet of dirty water.

He looked up, looking for the source of the drip and seeing only sky.

Then he heard the rustling of leaves. He watched as more raindrops began to fall. It quickly became heavy.

But now the rain wasn't touching his car.

Greg watched in awe as a powerful downpour engulfed the farmhouse, stopping short of the road.

It was the most focused rain he had ever seen, a precisely placed square perimeter that covered the home and the immediate yard, a few hundred feet at most, halting abruptly outside of its target.

"Oh my God." He studied the rain and its strange, silvery coloring.

It was the same phenomena his wife had described in a text. The same thing that Susan's brother had alluded to over the phone.

He studied the isolated, unmoving rain pattern in total fascination. No further drops landed on his car, aside from the first two. He was not the intended recipient.

By the time he realized he should take a picture with his phone, the rain stopped.

It wasn't a gradual drop-off from downpour to drizzle. It was as if someone – or something – had squeezed off a valve.

The area returned to an eerie stillness and silence, like nothing had happened. The skies remained as gray as before. A mini storm had raged and quickly retreated. Evidence of the outburst remained: the grass was soaked, and murky puddles appeared in the dirt driveway.

Frightened, Greg's eyes returned to his windshield and the two grayish stains where stray drops had struck.

Impulsively, he squirted windshield wiper fluid and wiped the spots clean.

He flooded his windshield with more and more fluid, a ridiculous amount, and continued wiping, just to be sure.

Whatever it was, he didn't trust it.

This was something weird and toxic.

He knew he had to warn the people inside.

Greg opened his car door and hopped out on stiff legs, hobbled by hours of driving.

He hurried to the front door, stepping around the discolored puddles that were quickly absorbed into the earth.

There was no bell, so he knocked, hard, on the wood. The door was weather-beaten and flaking paint. The entire house looked brittle and neglected, barely surviving from another era.

The man who answered appeared equally worn. He was large, hunched and wearing denim overalls. His face was a map of wrinkles surrounded by graying hair and a heavy beard.

His eyes immediately thinned with suspicion.

"Yes?" he said in a coarse voice.

"My name is Greg Garrett. I live in town. I need to warn you, there was a heavy rain around your home just a minute ago."

The look of suspicion deepened, but Greg kept going. "This wasn't any ordinary rain. It's tainted with something that makes people – I know this sounds crazy – but something happens to them and they can't be found. There's been—"

"What do you want?" asked the homeowner, interrupting with impatience.

"I – I just want you to know, something serious is happening. I—"

"Why are you on my property? There's no reason for you to be here."

"I've been driving all over, there's a—" Greg stopped in mid-sentence.

The white van story wasn't going to make any sense. He needed a tighter explanation. "There's...like a pollutant in the rain. Every time there's a rain like this, something bad happens."

"Do you know how crazy you sound right now?"

"I – I can only imagine. But this is—"

"I want you off my property. And you better not come back."

"Who is it?" cried out a harsh woman's voice from somewhere inside the dim house interior.

"Some fool not making any sense. Environmental stuff."

"Tell 'em we don't want any!"

The man smiled insincerely. "We don't want any crazy today, thank you," he said. He started to shut the door.

Greg stuck his hand out to prevent it from closing.

The man's eyes widened, angered by the action. Behind him, a scrawny teenage boy appeared and said, "Who is it, Pops?"

Without turning to face him, the man said, "Son, get my shotgun. We have a trespasser who doesn't understand the English language."

The boy obediently departed to follow his father's instructions.

"Please listen—" said Greg.

"No, you listen. Get your hand off my door or I am within my rights to—"

Greg removed his hand from the door.

"Now don't let me see you around here again. Drive on out of here and go bother someone else, you understand?"

"Yes," said Greg quietly.

The door slammed shut.

Greg slowly walked back to his car, head down, feeling queasy, staring at the ground, wondering....

How long before the yellow eggs?

CHAPTER FOURTEEN

Jesse Walton pulled up his Toyota Corolla to the front curb of the Imperial Inn Engles with the vice president of hotel operations in the passenger seat. The VP wore a black suit, blue tie and big scowl. Jesse felt embarrassed about the age and condition of his car, even after a quick car wash and interior cleaning before picking up the boss of his fired boss at the Indianapolis Executive Airport.

Jesse had never met Mr. Peters in person before and the forced, close proximity in his small car, coupled with his sky-high anxiety, made Jesse so distracted he feared he would run a red light or worse. Peters was in a foul mood, and Jesse let him lead the conversation during the drive, answering his questions the best he could.

"You didn't contact the police, right?" Peters had asked the moment he climbed into the Toyota.

"No, you said not to."

"Not until I know what we're dealing with. I've got the head of PR on standby. You canceled all the reservations for today?"

"Yes. Just like you said. We're closed until further notice. There's no staff, so—"

"And you still haven't heard from any of them?"

"I've been going through the phone tree, calling nonstop. Nobody's picking up."

"Did anything happen to upset them? Cause a walkout or a strike?"

"No, sir. I have no reason to believe they were upset about anything."

"And no utility trucks in the area? No fire trucks, no gas leak, no electrical outage? No police cars?"

"It's been quiet."

"How many guests?"

"Well, we weren't very crowded. Definitely less than half capacity. Being a weeknight and all...."

"Is it possible they were all here for the same event, a wedding or a conference, and left on a bus, and they got hung up and just didn't get back to their rooms?"

"I'm not aware of that. It's possible. I mean, there wasn't a group discount, so if it was organized...."

"Do you know how stupid this looks?" Peters said. "An entire hotel evacuated and we don't know why?"

"Yes. It's crazy."

"It's under your watch, Walton. Just remember that."

Peters' demeanor didn't get any warmer for the rest of the drive.

As they walked up to the hotel entrance together, Jesse prayed he would see someone – anyone – inside.

But they stepped into an empty lobby.

"Hello?!" called out Peters in an angry, unwelcoming tone.

No one responded.

The phone at the front desk buzzed in a persistent rhythm. It was the only sound in the big space. Jesse looked at Peters, who waved his arms in an exasperated gesture.

"Well, answer it!"

Jesse hurried behind the counter. He picked up.

It was a woman trying to reach her husband.

"Can you check his room? He's not answering his cell phone. I'm worried sick. I've been calling for hours. Doesn't anybody work there?"

"I'm sorry, ma'am," said Jesse, noticing Peters glare at him, with an expression that read, *Don't say anything stupid.*

"We'll check his room and call you back," Jesse said. "That's no trouble at all."

He hung up and then the phone rang again with a hard buzz.

Another family member trying to locate a guest. A male voice this time.

"Did she check out?"

"What's the name?"

"Danforth."

"Ah...no. According to our records...."

"Great. She won't answer my calls. That bitch is having an affair. I knew it!"

"Ah...I don't know anything about that."

After Jesse hung up, Peters told him, "Stop answering the phone. Let's take a look around. We're going to go room by room."

As they entered the long corridor of units on the first floor, Peters sighed and turned to Jesse.

"Let's do this. You start on the ground floor. I'll go up to the top floor. I'll work my way down, you work your way up, we'll meet somewhere in the middle. It'll be faster. If you see anybody, or anything that looks unusual or suspicious, you call me. Got that?"

"Yes," Jesse said. "Absolutely."

Then Peters looked down at the multi-colored, multi-patterned carpet at his feet.

"Jesus, this carpet is filthy. Get it cleaned, would you?"

★   ★   ★

Carl Peters almost always simmered with a layer of anger under his skin, just from dealing with the irritations of his day-to-day life and job. He took medicine for his blood pressure and paced the treadmill on occasion, but it didn't seem to calm him down. As each day wore on, his bubbling tension typically boiled over rather than subsided, and today was a whopper.

He was royally pissed off. He was a corporate vice president forced to leave his big city high-rise to stroll the common grounds of one of the low-performing hotel shacks out in the sticks, a job that others beneath him were hired to do, but incompetence rendered them useless in the critical moments they were supposed to manage.

He felt satisfaction in the firing of Greg Garrett, and before the day was over, he was pretty certain that Jesse Walton would be shitcanned, too.

The hotel had been evacuated, and the clown overseeing the hotel had no idea why or where anyone went. Peters had worked at Imperial Inn Incorporated for twenty-plus years and this was a first.

Even the CEO was dumbfounded. His biggest request to Peters: *Keep this out of the papers!*

Peters knew it was best that he and Walton had split up to search the hotel separately, because Peters couldn't guarantee that his interaction with Walton wouldn't spiral into a profanity-laden rant. And that would be the gentlest of his desired outbursts because corporate protocol prohibited him from kicking an employee squarely in the ass.

Peters reached the end of the corridor and faced the silver, fingerprint-smudged elevator doors. *Isn't it someone's job to clean this?* He pressed the orange-rimmed Up button with a jab of his thumb.

He listened to the abrupt lurch and hum of machinations to lower the elevator to the ground floor. It only took about fifteen seconds, but his impatience kicked in after five.

The elevator doors pulled apart, revealing an empty car.

Peters stepped in.

He pressed for the top floor and turned to face the doors as they slid shut.

With a small jolt, the elevator began its journey upward. The lighting inside felt muted, as if bulbs needed changing. Another checkmark against the hotel manager.

Peters folded his arms across his chest and waited to be delivered to his destination. As he ascended, he heard the elevator emitting strange, abrasive buzzing sounds.

What the hell is that?

It was not a noise that elevators were permitted to make.

Great, mechanical problems on top of everything else?

The more he listened, the more curious the sound became. It didn't seem to be coming from the pulleys and gears.

Bzzzzzzzzzzzzzzzzzzzzzzzzzzzzzzzzzzzzz.

The fluorescent light above?

Peters rolled his head back to stare into the elevator ceiling.

The ceiling was writhing and twitching with a thick layer of black insects.

"What the—!" shouted Peters, jumping at the sight.

He was familiar with the common pests of the hotel industry: bedbugs, flies, gnats, roaches, spiders.

But what the fuck was this?

It was an ugly swarm, throbbing at the top of the elevator like a single living entity.

Peters quickly jabbed for the next floor. As if activated by his panic, the flies began dancing in front of his face. He frantically punched at all the elevator buttons and they lit up in succession.

When Peters opened his mouth to scream for help, the bugs poured inside, forming a long, black, tube-like shape that pounded into his throat and lungs with a single-minded intensity.

Peters spun madly in the elevator, banging on the four walls, boxed in with nowhere to go. He kicked and swatted at the attacking insects, throwing his fists in random directions. He continued the crazed dance until the elevator floor rushed up to greet him. His physical being had collapsed, useless and unresponsive, as his brain went into overdrive with the most electrifying fear he had ever known.

The bugs covered him with a feeling like being swallowed in sand. They not only coated his entire being, they *owned* him....

★   ★   ★

Jesse Walton entered the guest rooms on the first floor one by one, experiencing the same drag of discomfort and confusion each time he encountered idle luggage, unmade beds, scattered personal items and no people.

"Helloooo..." he called out as he walked across the rooms, ending his searches with a glance into empty bathrooms.

The longer this mystery lingered, the more awful he felt, guilty and responsible, even though he had no idea what he had done wrong.

His only crime was not being present when whatever happened happened.

In fact, some blame could be directed to corporate for not investing in a security camera network. The company was a notorious penny pincher, allegedly so they could keep room rates low for the thrifty consumer, but profits seemed to channel primarily to stockholders and executive compensation.

Nobody was well paid, so maybe something caused the staff to quit en masse, but it felt very odd they would do so without saying anything. The staff seemed to like Jesse; he treated them with dignity and respect.

Yet his calls to staff members remained unanswered, as if they were giving him a colossal silent treatment.

As he investigated the final guest room on the first floor, finding abandoned guest belongings but no guests, Jesse checked his cell phone for any messages he may have missed.

Nothing. No calls, no texts. That included a lack of communication from Carl Peters from the floors above. That was fine. Most of the words directed his way by Peters were angry and humiliating.

Peters had already fired Greg Garrett, and Jesse felt it was only a matter of time before he lost his own job.

And that was fine. He didn't like working here anymore. He really wanted to run away from this entire ugly, bizarre mess.

Jesse walked over to the elevator and pressed the button. He waited for the doors to open, facing his own clouded reflection in the time-worn metallic sheen. He feared his search of the second floor would produce similar results. But maybe he would uncover a clue, any clue, to submit for Mr. Peters' approval.

The elevator landed on the ground floor with a thud. The doors slid open.

Jesse took a half step forward to enter and immediately skipped backward, nearly tumbling over his own feet.

"Oh, *shit!*"

Carl Peters' body was crumpled on the floor of the elevator, covered in a mass of small winged insects. They clung to his skin and clothes, discharging a harsh, grating buzzing sound. Their tiny, constant movements created the illusion that Peters was vibrating.

Jesse turned and fled.

As his steps pounded down the hall, he heard the collective hum of millions of insects. It did not grow dimmer with distance.

The swarm was coming after him.

Jesse saw the housekeeping supply room up ahead, its door slightly open. He slammed his way inside, striking the door with his body, then spun around to slam the door shut.

His eyes immediately traced the outline of the door for any unsealed spaces. He spotted a thin crack along the bottom, leaking in light from the corridor.

He grabbed towels from the linen shelf and jammed them against the narrow opening where the door didn't touch the floor.

Jesse could hear the frantic sound of the insects, buzzing like a furious, collective anger. What were they? Where did they come from? Had they really stung Mr. Peters to death? Is this what chased everybody else out?

Jesse kept his eyes on the doorframe. In one hand he clutched a wrapped roll of toilet paper, not much of a weapon, but something he could squash bugs with if any wiggled into the room.

He froze still, except for the shudder of his chest from heavy breathing, rising and falling.

The buzzing from the other side of the door diminished a little bit.

Maybe they were moving on?

Jesse slid his free hand into his pocket. He took out his cell phone to call for help. To hell with protecting the corporate brand. This was an all-out emergency.

His thumb pressed the 9 in 911.

Then a small, black winged insect landed on the screen.

Then another insect landed on his phone. And another. And another.

Jesse let out a long, withering gasp.

The bugs appeared before his eyes in growing numbers, a sprinkling of black spots against the illumination of the screen, quickly obscuring the touchpad numerals. They landed on his hand and wrist.

Jesse heard a rising hum…coming from behind him.

He turned to see a steady flow of black insects spilling into the room from an air vent.

He moved to close the vent but it was too late.

A succession of insects struck his eyes.

His sight began to chip away toward darkness.

Jesse screamed and dropped his phone. He dropped the toilet paper roll. He clawed at his face.

He felt the squirming, crawling bugs scratch across his skin, slipping beneath his clothes. It felt like fire.

Jesse blindly fumbled for the door handle to flee the supply room. After smashing his hand into the wall and shelving units, he found the door, then the handle.

He threw open the door and spilled into the hotel corridor.

A huge black cloud awaited him.

CHAPTER FIFTEEN

Jeff brought Marcie to his father's house the following night to witness and validate the old man's eerie, intangible presence. He couldn't bring himself to use the word 'ghost', even though that's exactly what it felt like, something ridiculous out of a children's storybook that didn't fit with his world of hands-on labor and earthly possessions, where everything existed to be seen and grasped in obvious physicality. His wife tagged along without question, a wise choice and one learned over the years.

They arrived at dusk, and Jeff explained, "It has to be total darkness or you can't see him." Marcie nodded and allowed a small "yes", while wondering about her husband's state of sobriety when he saw his father floating around the house.

Did he stop at Bucky's Bar on the way over?

Jeff quickly moved through the house to shutter and shade every window and deny the entry of the outside light, which was already dimming. The large picture window in the living room was not cooperating, covered loosely by a weak pull-down shade that permitted big cracks of bluish gray when he required all black. He immediately took to correcting the matter.

Jeff searched out a large blanket, hammer and nails. He dragged a chair over, standing on it precariously, and hung the blanket over the window, pounding it aggressively in place, wall plaster be damned.

The thick blanket completely shut out the light.

Then he set up the Ouija board on the low coffee table in the center of the room.

Marcie looked down at it with a queasy look on her face.

"He can't talk, this is the only way," Jeff said. He had spent the previous night asking questions and receiving short, usually cryptic answers.

He wanted to learn more, and he needed Marcie to watch and confirm his sanity. This couldn't be a one-time fluke. It had to happen again.

Today he had skipped his usual post-shift beer in his favorite chair to keep a clear head. The prior night's visit already felt like a sketchy dream. This morning, in the ordinary daylight, he had settled back into the routine of his job, repairing car engines at Murph's. Without missing a beat, drab reality rushed back in, pooling like cement to secure him firmly in the familiar drudgery.

But he knew his experience the previous night was not a figment of his imagination. He simply wasn't that creative.

"It has to get totally dark to see him," Jeff told his wife, who fidgeted nervously with her bracelets. "But we can try to communicate with him first, with this." He knelt down in front of the Ouija board.

She watched with apprehension as he started his line of questioning.

"Dad, I'm back. Marcie is here. Do you see us?"

His fingertips touched the indicator, which did not move. The entire room became still, like a painting. Marcie remained frozen in place.

Nothing happened.

"Sometimes it takes a while," Jeff said.

She nodded absently.

"Dad. Do you see us?" he repeated.

After a minute, the indicator began to move.

Jeff's eyes widened. Marcie watched from the other side of the table.

The indicator landed on YES.

"I'm not doing this, I swear," Jeff said.

When Marcie didn't respond right away, he insisted, "I mean it, Marcie. I'm not pushing it. He is!"

"Okay," she said, watching.

"Are you in the room with us?" Jeff called out.

After a short hesitation, the indicator tugged to a response.

YES.

"Ask him if he's a ghost," Marcie said.

"Shut up," said Jeff. Then he mulled it over and asked, with a slight tone of sarcasm, "Are you a ghost?"

The indicator moved. It landed between YES and NO.

Jeff waited for additional movement.

There was none.

Jeff took a deep breath. "Okay. Okay. Last night, you said something took...took your body. We need to find your body. Do you understand? Is it somewhere around here? Can you tell us?"

The indicator moved again.

NO.

Jeff looked over at Marcie, to monitor her reaction. She offered a crooked smile and a shrug.

"What, you think this is bullshit?"

"I didn't say anything. I don't know anything."

"You think I'm moving it? You want to put your hand on it?"

"No," she said immediately.

Jeff grumbled. "I used to think this stuff was bullshit. My mom believed in it. I always thought she was pushing on this thing to make up the answers."

"We should call those other people," Marcie said.

"What other people?"

"That came by our house. About the other missing people. Maybe this happened to them, too."

Jeff considered it for a moment. He was hesitant to bring anyone else into this circle of crazy. "Maybe."

"Ask him if he's hungry," Marcie said.

"Shut up." Jeff looked around the room. "It's getting darker. We should be able to see him soon."

Marcie's eyes looked upward toward the ceiling. She fidgeted with her rings.

"If I told anybody at the shop about this, they would laugh in my face," Jeff said.

"I'm not laughing."

"Yeah, how do I know? Maybe you're laughing at me on the inside."

"Please stop it."

"Don't tell me to stop it. In front of my dad."

She pursed her lips shut.

Jeff rolled his eyes at her. He returned his focus to the Ouija board and a new question.

"Dad. Next question. Last night, you said something about…flies. What did you mean, like bugs?"

After a short pause, movement:

YES.

"Flies, like in the air? Little, buggy, flying things?"

The indicator remained in place. YES.

"Did you get…bit by something?"

In the thinning light, the indicator moved across the board, stopping at a sequence of letters.

IT. WAS. A. SWARM.

"It was a swarm," Marcie said.

"I can read," snapped Jeff, studying the board. "It still doesn't make sense. It's getting harder to see. But keep the lights off. Let's – let's wait for him to appear."

Jeff stood up from the Ouija board. He looked around the room.

Marcie joined him in glancing into the deepening shadows.

Her cell phone buzzed in her pocket. She pulled it out and held it to her face.

"It's Shari. Texting about doing lunch."

"God damn it, put that away! No light!"

She quickly stuffed the phone in her pocket.

The room was getting darker by the minute. They could barely see one another, becoming faint outlines of black against black.

"Dad?" said Jeff.

"Mr. Jenkins?" said Marcie.

The couple moved closer, brushing against one another. Marcie took Jeff's hand.

"I'm scared," she said.

"I am, too, baby."

A faint wisp of light appeared like a strange projection in a corner where the wall met the ceiling.

"Do you see…?" whispered Jeff.

"I do, I do." Marcie grasped his sweaty hand tighter.

The trace of light wavered, defining nothing, simply pulsing like a faint source of energy.

"Keep watching," Jeff said.

The illumination seemed to stretch and expand in slow fits and starts, as if emerging from another dimension. The developing form was not yet human in appearance, details still blurred and incomplete.

Jeff and Marcie watched in awe.

All of a sudden, like an expanding balloon, Terry Jenkins' face appeared, eyes wide and mouth huge in a horrible expression of anguish.

Marcie screamed.

She pulled away from her husband and began running blindly for the door.

Jeff immediately went after her, grabbing her by the shoulders and pulling her back in a tight embrace. "Don't go! Marcie, don't!"

"I'm scared!" she wailed. "I can't stay here!"

"I know, I know." He held her close, trying to settle her down. "We need to stay. It's my dad. I told you – he's with us in this room. We have to help him."

She slumped into her husband's arms and began to cry.

"It's okay, it's okay," he said, turning her back toward the room. "He's not going to hurt us. We have to communicate with him – to find out what's going on."

Marcie looked at the floating, partial image of her father-in-law. Choking back tears, she said, "I'm sorry. I'm sorry I ran away, Mr. Jenkins. I'm so afraid...."

They watched as his likeness continued to fill in, like a puzzle being assembled before their eyes.

"Can he talk?" Marcie said, seeing Terry's mouth continue to move without making a sound.

"Not words," Jeff said. "Sometimes...sounds."

The specter of Terry Jenkins was mostly assembled now, losing and regaining elements as it shifted positions above them.

"You see it then?" Jeff said. "You see exactly what I see?"

"I do. It's just like you said."

"So I can't be crazy?"

"Unless we're crazy together."

"That's not possible."

"This is amazing." Marcie began to calm down from her hysterics. She stared at the unique display of light and human form that did not remain still. The being's movements flickered, sometimes stronger, sometimes weaker, like a small fire determined to keep burning.

"Dad, we see you. We know you're real."

"We'll get you help," Marcie said.

"Anything you need. We're just very...." Jeff finally landed on a word. "Confused."

"Can you talk? Can you say anything?" Marcie said.

The face of Terry Jenkins tried to expel words, straining hard, but could only push out low sounds like escaping air mixed with moans.

Marcie started to cry again and pulled closer to her husband.

"We can communicate with him through the Ouija board," Jeff said. "But then we need light to see what we're doing, and he goes away."

"Can...can you touch him?"

"I tried. I couldn't. But maybe...."

TAP TAP TAP.

A sudden noise interrupted their exchange. Followed by silence.

Marcie trembled in Jeff's arms.

"What – what is that? Where's it coming from?"

TAP TAP TAP.

"What the hell." Jeff let go of his wife. He began to turn in a circle, disoriented and searching. "Dad, is that you?"

TAP TAP TAP.

"It's not coming from in here," Marcie said, voice trembling.

"Is it outside?"

TAP TAP TAP.

"It sounds like...someone's knocking at the door."

TAP TAP TAP.

"Shit. You're right."

"Who—?"

"How the hell would I know?" He slowly moved across the room, feeling in the dark with his hands. "I have to turn on the lights."

He found a light switch and the living room exploded into brightness, requiring a moment for their eyes to adjust.

Terry Jenkins was gone. The Ouija board sat on the table. Jeff looked at Marcie. Her eyes were puffy and red from crying.

TAP TAP TAP.

"Whoever it is...maybe we can show them...what we're seeing," Marcie said.

"Maybe," Jeff said, and he began walking to the front door. "But who the hell would show up here at this time of night?"

TAP TAP TAP! More aggressive now, impatient.

"All right, all right! What do you want?"

Jeff threw open the door—

—and faced his father standing in front of him.

Marcie screamed.

Jeff let out a shout. He quickly found words. "Dad? Is that you?"

The man looked exactly like his father, wearing his father's clothes. It was uncanny. It had to be?

"Yes," responded the figure at the front door. Jeff recognized the voice immediately.

"Oh my God," Jeff said. "You're here. But you were just – we were just—"

"I'm coming in," said Terry Jenkins.

"Yes. Of course." Jeff stood to one side, and his father entered his house. His expression was curiously bland, barely acknowledging his son and daughter-in-law.

Jeff closed the door and examined his father. He wanted to embrace him but he appeared stoic and remote. Jeff had an avalanche of questions. "Where were you? What happened? You've been missing for more than a week. What's going on?"

"Missing," repeated his father, without much meaning, just a simple echo.

"He doesn't sound well," Marcie said, studying him.

"Dad, are you okay? Did you have a stroke or something? We'll call a doctor."

"He needs his medicine," Marcie said.

"No," said Terry Jenkins simply. He remained standing still for a moment, looking around the house. He gave a long stare to Marcie, then Jeff. Then he advanced forward. He took a turn and entered the kitchen.

Jeff and Marcie exchanged shocked glances.

"What the hell," said Jeff quietly.

"If this is your dad, then what's that thing in the living room?" Marcie said, gesturing toward the ceiling.

"I have no fucking idea," Jeff said. His brain felt ready to overload from so much confusion.

Sounds of rattling utensils could be heard coming from the kitchen.

"Dad, do you want us to fix you something to eat?" asked Jeff.

"Come sit down," Marcie said. "I can make you something. What would you like?"

She took a single step toward the kitchen.

Terry Jenkins emerged with a large steak knife.

"What's that for?" Jeff said.

In a million years, he never would have anticipated what happened next.

His elderly father took two steps forward, eyes focused and unblinking, and thrust the sharp blade into Jeff's chest.

Jeff let out a large gasp. Then he gurgled.

Terry Jenkins continued to chop the blade into his son in repeated, mechanical thrusts. Marcie screamed, loud and continuous.

Jeff dropped to the floor in a growing pool of his own blood. Then Terry turned and faced Marcie.

She knew she was next.

Marcie wanted to escape out the front door, but her path was blocked by a demented father-in-law with a big knife.

She ran back into the living room, desperate to move quickly without being caught. She snapped off the living room light to plunge her pursuer into darkness.

Marcie maneuvered as soundlessly as possible in the pitch black, sucking back her gasps, walking softly on the carpet. She listened for the movements of Terry Jenkins to stay away from him. His footsteps were heavy and slow, and she circled the room, maintaining a consistent distance. She could hear him banging into furniture and grunting in anger. It sounded like he dropped the knife.

She waited until she sensed a clear path to the front door. Then she made a run for it.

She almost succeeded, but she slipped on a loose throw rug and fell wildly into the pitch black, hitting her head hard on a closet door.

Deep inside, she knew she had blown her only chance.

Tough, firm hands grabbed at her almost immediately, and as much as she kicked and screamed, there was no hope to break free.

She tried to rise from the floor, but she was pushed back, a knee in her sternum, and then thick hands wrapped around her neck, old but unusually strong and supremely committed....

$$\star \quad \star \quad \star$$

The wisps of Terry Jenkins' specter jerked along the ceiling in anxious fits, watching the scene unfold in helpless terror.

The sixty-six-year-old man witnessed himself murdering his son and daughter-in-law with no means of stopping the action, trapped in passive observation.

Terry's expelled consciousness tried to scream, shout, object, but could not. The only sound he could produce was a low, mournful wail that pushed into the house with great emotion but no physical presence, coldly ignored by his zombie-like replica, who finally loosened the grip on Marcie's throat and let her drop lifelessly to the floor.

The physical version of Terry Jenkins flipped on the lights, and his intangible, floating double dissipated from view. With two corpses stiffening on the ground, the house became very quiet and still.

Terry Jenkins in the flesh stared down at his violent accomplishments. The other Terry Jenkins could only express himself through tiny movements on the Ouija board, moving the indicator so slowly that it remained noiseless on its quest to form words to convey the feeling of the moment.

HELP. ME.

FORBIDDEN PLANET

179 SHAFTESBURY AVENUE
LONDON

MID: XXXX1573
TID: XXXXXXX36
AID   A000000031010
VISA CREDIT

VISA

**** **** **** 7105
CONTACTLESS   PAN. SEQ 0
SALE

CARDHOLDER COPY

PLEASE RETAIN FOR YOUR
RECORDS

AMOUNT   £0.99

NO VERIFICATION USED

Thank You
15:24:54 07/10/24

AUTH CODE:03747D

worldpay

MIX
Paper from responsible sources
FSC® C147551
www.fsc.org

worldpay

MIX
Paper from responsible sources
FSC® C147551
www.fsc.org

#5/11/9030 - 284   07/10/2024/15:34

5878154	1	0.99	0.99

THE INTRUDERS
PINKERTON BRIAN,

Total   @   0.99

No of items 1

Your payment
Credit Card/Debit Card   0.99

VAT %	Net	Gross	VAT
0.000	0.99	0.99	0.00

Your assistant is: Liam

Get FP on your phone!
Available for iOS and Android now - FREE

FORBIDDEN PLANET
MEGASTORE
179 SHAFTESBURY AVENUE
LONDON WC2H 8JR
TEL 020 7420 3666.
ForbiddenPlanet.com
COMPANY REG NUMBER 1356755
VAT NUMBER 991 2914 93

#S/17/9030 - 284   07/10/2024/15:34

5878154	1	0.99	0.99
THE INTRUDERS			
PINKERTON BRIAN,			

Total   1   0.99

No of Items 1

Your payment
Credit Card/Debit Card   0.99

VAT %	Net	Gross	VAT
0.000	0.99	0.99	0.00

Your assistant is: Liam

Get FP on your phone!
Available for iOS and Android now - FREE

CHAPTER SIXTEEN

Greg awoke to the sounds of a new day in progress: a neighbor's puttering lawn mower, the chugging of the weekly garbage truck advancing down the block.

He didn't want to look at the clock. He knew it was nine or ten, or perhaps eleven. He had fallen asleep with the lights on again, quickly pounded into a deep sleep with a handful of prescription sleeping pills and a helping of vodka. He knew it was a horrible habit, but the panic and stress that burrowed into his bones needed a time-out after ravaging him for so long. The collapse into a serious unconsciousness allowed him to reset for another day of fears about his family, sorting through a bizarre puzzle of clues that strained his already fragile mental state.

He entered his kitchen, feeling numb and rubbery, and fueled himself with a pot of coffee. He gradually came back to life.

He remembered he had a noontime lunch appointment with Susan to continue their search for answers. He needed to tell her about witnessing the strange silvery rain firsthand at a farmhouse across town. She continued to try to get information out of her uncommunicative brother about his mysterious absence.

Greg checked his cell phone with a heavy sigh.

More calls from work – this time from the CEO himself, an extremely rare occurrence. He didn't want to listen to the messages or call him back. Imperial Inn was no longer his problem. Being fired brought certain privileges.

Greg did worry about Jesse and chose to contact him instead.

Jesse didn't answer his phone.

Greg looked at the clock. He still had ninety minutes before meeting with Susan. He made the choice to drive over to the local Imperial Inn to see what was happening, because he feared the worst. He couldn't abandon Jesse. The rest of the corporate clowns, yes, but not Jesse.

Greg had fallen asleep in his clothes – too many sleeping pills too quickly was the culprit. He peeled them off and tossed them into the bedroom. He took a shower, shaved, brushed his teeth, dressed in a fresh outfit and hopped in his car.

He drove to the all-too-familiar, flat-roofed, orange-and-white building known as Imperial Inn Engles. The front entrance was lined with cars from the sheriff's office.

"Oh boy," Greg said.

He parked in the rear of the lot, away from the other vehicles. He turned off his engine and surveyed the scene. The lot was medium full. He spotted Jesse's Toyota Corolla. He felt a pang of discomfort.

Then he observed Sheriff Casey standing just outside the sliding doors to the lobby entrance, talking with one of his deputies.

Greg climbed out of his car. Jesse's frightened, bewildered words played back in his head.

"I lost my guests."

Greg strolled up to Casey, who turned and recognized him immediately through mirrored sunglasses, without a smile.

"Mr. Garrett," he said.

"What's going on?"

"That's what we're investigating."

"I need to go inside. One of my coworkers is in there."

"Nobody is in there," Casey said. "And that will include you. It's a secured site. This hotel is roped off until my men can give it a thorough inspection."

"So what happened? Let me guess. More people disappeared."

"They vacated their rooms. I'm sure they're somewhere."

"Like the people from that campsite?" Greg shot back.

Casey considered this with a slow smile. "Yes. Exactly like that." He paused for emphasis and added, "Those campers all came back."

Greg froze. This was new news. "They—?"

"Every one of them. The family with the two boys, the older couple, the attendant, all the rest. Just like your friend's brother."

Greg said, "Just like him in what way? Behaving like they have brain damage?"

"This is not your investigation," Casey said.

"I want to talk with them."

"They're still undergoing questioning. I don't need your interference."

"I'm part of this. Whatever happened to them – it happened to my family."

"Maybe and maybe not."

Greg gave him a long, cold stare. "You're a real piece of shit."

"Yep," said the sheriff, turning his back on Greg and walking away. "This conversation is over."

★   ★   ★

At Ridgeview Diner, in the red booth in the back, Greg told Susan about the return of the campsite occupants. "He wouldn't tell me anything more than that. Everybody's back and they're being questioned."

"Maybe they'll get better answers than they got out of my brother."

"Or the same."

"Steve still won't talk to me. I call, I've gone over and banged on the door. It's like he wants nothing to do with me. That's not him. Even when he was going through his darkest period, he didn't shut off like that. We could talk."

Greg stared down at his BLT, which had two bites in it. He was no longer hungry.

"Listen," she said to him. "There's some good in this. If they've returned, there's a lot more hope for your family."

"I suppose. There's still so much to process."

Greg's cell phone buzzed on the table near his plate. He glanced at it. The CEO. He ignored it.

"Okay, so I need to talk about the rain."

"You said you saw it?"

"Yes. I saw the rain, and it was definitely different. It had a weird look to it, and it was focused just on the farmhouse, the immediate lawn around it, then nothing. It barely made it to the road."

"So what does it mean?"

"I don't know. But if the pattern follows…those yellow things will appear…and then people will disappear."

"Did you see any yellow spots?"

"No. I had to leave. I tried to talk to the homeowner, but he was having none of it. I'm sure I sounded nuts. I was babbling. As if I can make any of this sound rational…."

"And still no word from Eryn?"

"Nothing. The white van – what the kid told me – that's all I've got to go on. Another thing that doesn't make sense."

Susan took a pen out of her purse. She wrote a sequence of words on a napkin. She studied it, then rotated it upside down and pushed it toward Greg to look at.

Rain > yellow eggs > van > disappearance > reappearance > sickness.

"Yeah, that sums it up," Greg said. "Kind of insane, but that's it."

"So, this farmhouse, if they're at stage one, a whole lot more is about to happen," Susan said.

Greg nodded.

"Then we have to go watch. We've got a case study unfolding right now."

"Go back? The old man said I was trespassing and threatened to shoot me."

"I'll talk to him."

"Good luck with that."

"We'll come up with something." Then a rare grin emerged from her tired face. "I did some acting in high school."

★   ★   ★

Susan slowly walked up the long driveway concocted out of gravel, dirt and weeds, trying to examine the lawn without being obvious or coming to a premature halt before she reached the front porch of the old white farmhouse.

Greg waited in her car a short distance down the road, staying out of view while keeping an eye on her.

A simple stone path connected the driveway to the bottom step of the porch. Susan took one last glance at the front lawn – *were those yellow eggs or dandelions?* – and approached the front door.

The wooden floorboards of the porch creaked with age. A small scattering of leaves had reached the seats of weathered wicker chairs. The nearby picture window was clouded over with dust and the harsh reflection of sunlight. If someone was peeking out at her, she couldn't see it.

Susan knocked, firm, short and polite.

She took a deep breath and quickly recalled the key messages of a script she had composed with Greg back at the diner.

Just like high school drama class. Remember your lines.

She gripped a clipboard, her only prop, with a phony form bearing an important-sounding masthead she created in Microsoft Word.

The door swung open with an aggressive pull from inside the house. A large man in his fifties – looking beaten down and toughened by the years – scowled by way of a greeting. He wore a faded flannel shirt, tucked in tight behind a chipped leather belt.

They probably don't get many door-to-door solicitors way out here, thought Susan. She brightened with her best smile and replaced his hard silence with a cheery greeting.

"Good afternoon, sir. My name is Britney Bell. I'm with the Indiana Department of Agriculture. How are you today? I'm your regional partner from the agency of pest detection and plant disease, and we're in Engles today to track a potential threat to your crops."

The man stared so intensely that Susan feared he would look right through her charade. His face and neck were etched with deep lines, none deeper than the two creases between his eyes that conveyed well-worn animosity.

She kept going: "It's new vermin to these parts, malus cimex." It was a crude attempt at making up a Latin term but sounded legit when spoken quickly. "We require an official sign-off that you are not impacted."

The farmer remained unimpressed. "Ma'am, there's nothing wrong with my crops." He said *Ma'am* with the hard punch of enunciation usually reserved for profanity.

She continued smiling. "That's wonderful to hear. Then my visit will be very short. I just need to conduct a quick inspection of the grounds, and then I'll be on my way."

"No," responded the man without hesitation.

"But, sir...."

"Not necessary."

She shifted her feet. Time to travel down the 'Refusal' side of her talking path.

In a tone of not-so-mild suspicion, she said, "I'm sorry. I don't understand. Do you have something to hide?"

"'Course not."

"I mean, I can call my boss back at the agency, but why drag this out?"

"My crops are in perfect condition." He thumped his chest with a knotted fist. "I should know. I'm out there *every day*."

"That's fantastic. Then this will probably take less than ten minutes. Thank you!"

His shoulders sagged. His refusal was not getting through.

She kept going. "Please, sir. My boss, he's something of a hard-ass, and he's going to make me keep coming back, again and again, until we get this done." Now she pouted, delivering sad eyes and playing a part she didn't really like, a vulnerable and defenseless female.

But it worked.

She softened, so he softened. She stopped short of a trembling lower lip.

He lowered his ire to a weary grouse. "Oh, Jesus almighty. Make it quick. You have ten minutes. This is private property. I can have you arrested just for standing on this here porch."

She quickly and graciously accepted the opening. "Yes. Ten minutes and not a second more. Thank you. Honestly, sir, we're just looking out for your welfare."

This last line was truth, but in ways the old farmer could not fathom.

Susan left the porch in a measured stride, holding the clipboard to her chest, feeling the continuance of his probing eyes.

She stepped into the lawn and made a gradual circle, head hung low for a careful inspection, nodding occasionally to send a signal back to the man in the doorway that everything looked good, no cause for alarm.

Then she heard a sound that filled her with some relief: he shut the front door.

She glanced over and no longer saw the grumpy farmer, although he could have resumed watching her from behind one of the dirty windows, and it would be hard to tell.

The lawn was healthy looking but a tad overgrown, and she didn't spot the first nest of yellow eggs until she had practically stepped into them. She immediately halted and stiffened, allowing a small gasp. She repositioned so her back was to the house, tucked the clipboard under one arm and took out her cell phone.

She snapped a couple of photos of the eggs and texted them to Greg.

The eggs looked plump and ripe; likely still hosting whatever waited inside.

She purposefully didn't dwell too long in one spot or send any visual cues back to the farmer that she was alarmed about anything.

She found another clump of swollen yellow eggs closer to the side of the house and took a quick, nonchalant picture.

Then she advanced to the backyard, which transitioned after a hundred feet into a wide and deep cornfield. There was a lopsided toolshed, a rusted swing set from another era for children who had no doubt grown up and moved on, and a dirt path to a big, old-style wooden barn that housed all the farming equipment.

In the backyard, she found two more collections of fulsome yellow eggs, not creased or deflated like the ones she had seen at the campsite. She thought back to the simple narrative she had composed on her napkin and the need to add to the sequence:

Plump eggs > hatched eggs

She took more photos casually, expressionless, and stole a couple of glances to the rear of the farmhouse.

She didn't see anyone watching from the windows.

She checked the time before depositing the cell phone back in her pocket. She had used up eight of her ten minutes.

She didn't want to go over her time allotment and bring the farmer out of the house.

Greg had said something about a shotgun.

She stopped to stare a moment into the cornfields, watching the stalks sway gently in the breeze, producing a lush whisper. Were the yellow eggs restricted to the lawn or had they infected the crops?

Then, for a split second, she witnessed something that caused her to open her mouth to scream – but she held it in.

Something moved in the cornfield. It was big, hulking and hairy. The cornstalks concealed most of it, but there was no doubt it was a living, moving creature with a human shape. It was impossible to define through the corn.

Susan continued to step around the backyard, doing her best to act as if she had not seen anything. She didn't want the creature to know she was aware of its presence. When she was brave enough to look back in its direction, the strange figure was no longer visible, having sunk further back into the corn.

Susan left the farmhouse. She retreated down the driveway to the road, picking up her pace as she got closer to her car. She climbed into the driver's seat, slammed the door and locked it.

"I received your photos—" said Greg from the backseat, lifting his head.

"Ssh!" she said.

He went silent.

She stared at the farmhouse for a solid minute to make sure nothing was following her.

Then she said, "I saw something."

"The eggs?"

"No. Yes, there were eggs on the lawn, but there was something else in that cornfield."

Greg looked out the car window.

"Like a person – or a thing – it was hiding in there, watching me."

"What did it look like?"

"I don't know. Big. Tall. Hairy face."

"Bigfoot?"

Susan was not amused. "Damn it, Greg, I'm serious. My heart is *pounding*."

"Let's go see," Greg said.

"Really?"

"We can't leave now. Everything is a clue. We'll be careful."

"Careful how?"

"I don't know," Greg said. "For one, we don't want the farmer to see us, so we'll have to go around the other side of that barn to get to the cornfield, so we're out of his view."

"I'm not afraid of him, I'm afraid of *it*," Susan said.

"Maybe this thing took my family. Took away your brother. And brainwashed them or something."

"God," said Susan. "This is only getting weirder."

"We can't just drive away."

"I know. I'm not going anywhere."

"I wish we had something to protect ourselves with."

"I don't have any weapons in this car."

"How about a spare tire?"

"A what?"

"You have a tire iron?"

"Probably. In the trunk, under the floor."

"I'm going," Greg said. "You don't have to come with."

"Stay in the car? To hell with that."

"Then leave the doors unlocked. So we can get in quick, if we have to run back."

"That doesn't sound reassuring."

Greg opened the door to the backseat. He climbed out.

Susan emerged from the driver's side moments later.

"Bigfoot," she muttered.

"Yep," Greg said, and he felt himself giving in to the absurdity of it all. "I can see the tabloid headlines now. 'Bigfoot Stole My Wife and Kids'."

CHAPTER SEVENTEEN

Greg and Susan stepped through the rows of dry cornstalks that stretched high above them, weaving their way slowly to minimize the sound of their approach. Greg advanced first, gripping the tire iron to defend against any sudden threats. Susan grasped her cell phone, ready to snap pictures of anything extraordinary.

What they discovered was neither threatening nor extraordinary.

A fat, bearded man in his twenties stood tucked in the thicket of cornstalks, close to the edge of the farmer's lawn, calmly eating from a bag of salsa-flavored Doritos. He wore a green cap perched on wild hair, sloppy clothes and muddy gym shoes. A half-full backpack clung to his spine, zippered halfway shut, decorated with a series of goofy patches with the random creative zeal of a high school student.

Greg and Susan halted and exchanged glances.

One of the patches depicted a flying saucer icon; another appeared to show a Storm Trooper character ringed with the affiliation '501st Legion'; and a third was a *Doctor Who* logo.

"Excuse me," Greg said.

The fat man turned with a startled jump of his shoulders. His eyes were big and frightened. He wore a pair of binoculars around his neck like a bird watcher. His baseball cap featured the cartoony image of a green alien head with bulging black eyes.

"Take it easy!" responded the fat man, arms held out defensively, noticing the tire iron in Greg's fist. "I'm just on a walk. I'm not doing anything."

"Yeah, you are doing something. You're spying on that house," Susan said. "It's obvious."

The fat man appeared deflated and said nothing.

"Look, we don't live there," Greg said. "But we're worried about the people that do."

"You know them?" said the fat man.

"No. Not really," Greg said. "Do you?"

The fat man shook his head.

Greg said, "How about you start with what you're doing here, and then we'll tell you our story."

The fat man's pudgy fingers fidgeted. He attempted an explanation but his words were so guarded they became jumbled. "I'm with.... I represent.... I write.... I have a blog. I'm just doing research. Nothing interesting. I go places...and I have things I write about. My readership is small. It doesn't matter. It's a hobby. I write about eclectic topics. I get curious...about things. I've always been curious. My mom used to say...."

"So what brought you here?" said Susan, impatient.

"A tip?" He answered in the tone of a question.

"Okay," Greg said. "You're not being very clear. I think we can get to the point." He looked at Susan. "How about we start?"

She shrugged, then nodded.

He proceeded. "My name's Greg. This is Susan. We live in Engles, but not around here. Both of us had family members disappear. Other people have disappeared, too."

The fat man listened with interest. From his expression, Greg's words made an immediate connection.

Greg continued, "Right before my family disappeared, it rained. On our house and lawn, and nowhere else. It wasn't a normal rain, it had a shiny, silver texture. The same thing at Susan's brother's house. And then I saw it rain here, the same thing, a short rain, only on this farmhouse. It glittered like tinsel. I contacted Susan and—"

The fat man finished Greg's sentence. "You wanted to see if the people who live here disappeared."

Greg paused, staring at him. "Well...yes."

The fat man let out a big sigh, relieved to move forward with his own truth. "*That's why I'm here.*"

Susan said, "How do you know? What do you know?"

"I don't know!" said the fat man. He pointed to the sky. "I just know that something up there..." And his finger descended to aim toward the farmhouse. "...is causing people down here to disappear."

"Did you lose someone, too?" Susan asked.

"No," said the fat man. "I don't even live around here. I'm from Grand Rapids, Michigan."

"Michigan?" Greg said.

"My name is Zeke Gorcey. This – this is my specialty. Sort of. In an amateur kind of way. Wait. I can show you." He shook the backpack off his shoulders. He unzipped it wider and pulled out an iPad.

"This'll just take a second...."

After a few minutes, he handed the tablet to Greg and Susan. Greg took it and Susan looked over his shoulder.

"You've heard of storm chasers? I'm a UFO chaser," said Zeke.

They studied his web page. A cartoony masthead decorated with aliens and spaceships proclaimed, 'Out of This World: Unexplained Phenomena in Our Earthly Presence'. The headline immediately underneath dealt with a possible alien sighting at an old railyard in Amarillo, Texas.

"Okay," said Zeke quickly as they scanned the post. "That one might have been a fake. But I check every lead because, eventually, one of them is going to be real. And I think this one, what we have right now, is...."

"Real," Susan said, looking up from the tablet.

"Maybe," Zeke said.

"We're in the middle of something very weird," said Greg. "I'm sure you deal with a lot of kooks and crazies, but this one has substance."

"No," Zeke said. "I don't deal with kooks and crazies. They're all sincere in their own way. They've seen something that's not normal. And that's what we have here: Not normal."

"We should go someplace and talk," Greg said, looking back toward the house. "That farmer is very protective of his privacy, and he has a shotgun."

"The old dude is in for the day," Zeke said. "I'm pretty sure about it.

Besides – I can't leave this spot. If something happens, and we leave this spot, I'm not doing my job."

"This is your job?" Susan asked. She handed back the tablet.

"Okay, hobby. I need more advertisers to make a full-time living at it. But my following is growing. Twitter, Instagram. If I can crack this case...."

"Wait, wait," Greg said. "So if you're not from around here, how do you know so much?"

Zeke hesitated.

"Swear to secrecy?" he said. "If I tell you, then you have to tell me everything you know. Information for information. No holding back."

"Of course," Greg said. "I *want* people to listen. I have the opposite problem. The sheriff...."

Zeke sputtered his lips. "Bppp! The sheriff. Worthless. Forget him. Okay. It's this. I have a contact in a federal agency. It's a small group headquartered in Seattle. They don't get any publicity, on purpose. But they're responsible for investigating atmospheric irregularities."

"Climate change?" Susan said.

"No," Zeke said. "Things in our atmosphere that don't belong because there's no scientific backing that they should exist."

"Like...?" said Greg.

"Okay, in simplest terms, UFOs," Zeke said. "I'm not saying that's what this is. But something foreign entered our stratosphere and caused some kind of abnormal cloud formations that released some kind of substance and then immediately dissipated. Quick, on a small scale, barely detected. But it was noted."

"You mean..." Susan said, absorbing it all. "So – so there's an acknowledgment somewhere that this is *real*?"

"I wouldn't go so far as to say 'real', but worth investigating."

"And the missing people?"

"You bet that's got attention. Because in each instance of a missing person, it was preceded with this anomaly, this unexplained smudge on a radar. That's why I'm here. I heard there was another flash or formation, right here, and I got here as soon as I could."

"But who's giving you all this information?" Susan said.

"Right!" laughed Zeke. "I'm not supposed to have it, don't you think? Well, I have my ways."

"It doesn't sound like a very secret agency," Greg said, and as his tone turned cynical, Zeke jumped to more admissions.

"I know a guy," he said with a confident grin. "We go way back. We grew up together watching *The X-Files*, *Twilight Zone*. He joined the agency two years ago. It was a lifelong obsession. He actually works there!"

"But isn't he sworn to secrecy?"

"Oh, yes. Of course."

"He's not doing a very good job."

"Like I said, I have my ways," Zeke said. "I know how to get to him."

"Blackmail?" Susan said.

"Money?" Greg said.

"Neither," Zeke said. "Listen, you want to know my real job? Where I make actual, real money? I'm one of the biggest collectors of sci-fi memorabilia on the planet. *Star Wars*? Check. *Star Trek*? Check. *Stargate*, *Battlestar Galactica*, *Terminator*, *Predator*, check, check, check, check! My handle on eBay is scificlassix with an 'x'. If you can't find it anywhere, I probably have it. For a price. I've been collecting since I was seven years old."

"So…?" said Greg.

"So my contact is an even bigger sci-fi geek than I am. That's how he got his dream job at the agency – he lives and breathes this stuff. But it pays shit, it's a small department, gets no respect, expense reductions all the time – you can imagine, right? They're probably one budget cut away from being eliminated entirely. So I'm his dealer. I feed his addiction. We trade. Merch for tips."

"So what did he get for this tip?" Susan asked.

"Original *Star Wars* Han Solo action figure, limited edition variant, from the first production run, before they fixed his hair color. Still in the box. Mint."

Greg responded with a slow blink. "Okay."

"Not a big deal to you," Zeke said, "but for him – total ecstasy. Fanboy orgasm."

"So where is this agency?" Susan said. "Are they coming?"

"Sure," Zeke said. "But, you know, it's the government. Slow as molasses. To make the trip, there's paperwork to be filed, layers of bureaucracy to go through, cost analysis, the usual bullshit. God only knows when they'll truly get started on this case. Plus, they're in a bit of a pickle. Their last investigation – they spent four weeks in Hawaii responding to some colored lights in the sky. I guess it ran up quite a bill, and the lights were just satellites that weren't correctly recorded into the international database."

"We need them out here investigating," Greg said. "Can I contact someone? I'm an eyewitness. We have people still vanishing."

"You gotta be patient," Zeke said. "We're not supposed to know this agency even exists. Until they get their act together, the three of us, we're it. We got here first. We don't have to wait for any approvals or budgets or deal with some government protocol. That's why I only report to me."

"So what do we do now?" said Susan to both of them.

Zeke gestured beyond the corn. "It's a stakeout. We watch the house."

"The three of us?"

"Well, we can trade shifts, so we can get some sleep. I have my Jeep Wrangler parked about a half-mile away. There are blankets in the back."

"Lovely," said Susan.

"I've told you everything I know," Zeke said. "What about you guys? You say you actually saw this rain cloud?"

"I didn't, he did," said Susan, looking at Greg.

"I don't really remember the cloud. Just the rain. It all happened so fast." Greg then shared the remainder of his story. Zeke nodded, listening intently, until Greg made a reference to the yellow eggs that appeared in the grass when people went missing.

Zeke interrupted. "Wait, wait. What? Eggs?"

"Well, I don't know what they are. Small, yellow…. We can show you, they have them right here in the grass around the farmhouse."

Zeke pulled a small notebook and pen out of his breast pocket and began scribbling. "I haven't heard anything about yellow eggs. This is new. I just knew about the satellite pictures and the missing persons reports. Holy shit. Another element. Eggs!"

"If you get closer, you can see them," Susan said, pointing toward the farmhouse.

Zeke immediately pushed his hulking frame several steps through the dry stalks to the edge of the cornfield. Unlike Greg and Susan, his footsteps were loud and crunchy. He squinted.

"They look like dandelions," he said.

"They're not," said Greg, behind him.

Zeke placed the binoculars to his face. After a long silence, he said, "Yeah.... Those don't look right."

"I think that's what made my brother sick," Susan said. "He hasn't been the same since."

"Do you think I could interview your brother?" Zeke asked.

"You can try," Susan said. "But he won't even talk to me."

Just then there was a thumping noise coming from the farmhouse.

Zeke, Greg and Susan could see a gray-haired woman – the farmer's wife – opening a window. The late afternoon sun was radiating extra heat, and it was likely the old farmhouse didn't have central air.

The threesome in the corn immediately pulled back to avoid being seen.

"How many people do you think live there?" asked Zeke in a low voice.

"I'm not sure," Greg said. "I know there's a teenage son. The house isn't that big – I suspect it's the man, the wife and their kid."

Zeke returned to scribbling on his pad.

Susan continued to stare through the cornstalks at the farmhouse. It turned quiet again with a soft breeze.

Then she broke the silence with: "What the hell is that?"

The three of them looked into the backyard where several small clouds of black bugs began forming above the grass. Each cluster grew in size and darkened with density, hovering and pulsing like a unified entity.

"This can't be good for the crops," muttered Zeke.

"This is not normal," Greg said.

"It's strange how closely they stick together," said Susan. Then: "They're on the move."

The clouds of insects streamed across the yard toward the house. As they advanced closer and consolidated, they appeared to take the shape of a long black missile.

"Holy shit," Susan said.

In a deliberate, straight path, the swarm entered the house through the opened window.

Zeke began scribbling madly on his pad.

"Do we warn them?" asked Susan. "I mean, that's a lot of bugs. Is this part of—?"

"It's so weird, it has to be," Greg said.

Then, from inside the farmhouse, the screaming began.

CHAPTER EIGHTEEN

As soon as the screaming started – multiple, tangled screams from a man, woman and boy – Greg pushed his way out of the cornfield and rushed toward the house. The sounds were so horrific he couldn't remain still.

He ran across the lawn, feet pounding the grass, until he reached a tattered screen door. He threw it open, twisted the knob on the interior door and pushed.

He entered chaos.

The first person he saw was unidentifiable because they were coated from head to toe with clinging, black insects, obscuring flesh and clothing. It looked like they had been dipped in tar. The wobbly individual remained on two feet – just barely – digging frantically at their face with clawed hands. The only exposed humanity consisted of two horrified, enlarged eyes and an open mouth that screamed with the kind of agony reserved for severe burn victims or worse.

Greg instinctively reached out to the figure but only grasped air as the victim collapsed to the ground – alongside another fallen person buried under a frenzy of burrowing bugs. This second individual had moments of clothing briefly revealed – a blue floral pattern, a dress – the wife.

The cries coming from another part of the house sounded like a teenage boy.

Greg didn't have to run to him. The boy came staggering into the room, blindly, engulfed in a quivering mass of winged vermin. He knocked over a small table and lamp and crashed to the floor. The impact of his fall loosened some of the bugs back into the open air.

Greg's moment of paralysis ended as he witnessed several stray insects flutter in his direction. He let out his own scream and dashed back to the door.

As he emerged from the house, he nearly knocked over Zeke and Susan, who had caught up with him but not yet stepped inside.

He gave them a single, direct order: "*Run!*"

They didn't wait to ask questions.

Greg ran as fast as he could around the farmhouse and back toward Susan's car, which was parked a little ways down the road.

Susan followed close behind. Zeke huffed and puffed several paces slower, weighed down by his backpack and his own personal bulk.

Greg allowed himself one quick glance back – and his worst suspicions were confirmed.

A swarm of bugs was coming after them, moving at a steady pace.

"Don't slow down!" hollered Greg.

He reached Susan's Hyundai and opened a series of doors for himself, Susan and Zeke. He waved at the other two frantically.

Susan arrived, jumped behind the wheel and slammed her door shut.

Zeke was still chugging down the center of the road, red faced and gripping the straps of his backpack. His green cap flew off his head.

The swarm was catching up with him.

"C'mon!" screamed Greg.

Zeke made it to the car and dived into the backseat, legs dangling. Greg shoved the rest of him inside and shut the door. Then he jumped into the front passenger seat.

He closed his door just as the first few insects smacked against the window.

"Check the windows, close the vents!" Greg shouted.

Susan started the engine. She quickly ran her hands across the dashboard, closing every air intake.

"Oh shit!" Zeke said from the backseat. He squirmed to upright himself, noticing a thin slit where one of the windows did not fully reach the rubber trim at the top. "The back window!"

Zeke jabbed at a button in the door.

He accidentally lowered the window several inches.

"*No!*" screamed Susan.

He quickly reversed the direction, and the window sealed shut just as a smattering of bugs reached the glass.

"Incredible," Zeke said.

"Check everything," Greg said. "Is there any other way they could get in?"

"I don't know," Susan said, quickly looking around. "I don't think so." She checked again to ensure the air was off. The engine puttered quietly.

"What did you see inside the house?" Zeke asked.

"Those bugs.... It was like they were eating those people alive."

Zeke fumbled in his pocket for his pen and small notepad.

"We gotta get them help." Greg quickly dialed 911 on his cell phone. Susan kept a watchful eye on the modest but growing gathering of insects congregating outside the car.

"There's been a home invasion, three people in critical condition!" Greg shouted into the phone, deliberately leaving out the details of a bug attack or anything else that might create skepticism that would delay a response. He provided the address and emphasized, "Send the sheriff, send ambulances – it's a life-or-death situation here right now!"

He hung up as they started to ask about his identity. "That should do it," Greg said, staring at his phone. "Whatever this is, the shit will hit the fan. The paramedics will get involved, medical professionals, scientists...."

"Oh no," Susan said.

Greg looked up.

The insects kept coming. A growing mass had attached themselves to the car, filling portions of the windshield.

From the backseat, Zeke took out his camera to take pictures.

"Let's move, let's get out of here!" Greg said.

Susan activated her windshield wipers, spraying the bugs and swiping at them. It helped – and then it didn't.

The bugs became more aggressive and their numbers continued to grow.

Susan lurched the car forward. She pulled on the wheel to start a U-turn to leave the dead-end road.

"Holy shit," Greg said.

More bugs. Huge black swarms began arriving from the farmhouse, coming straight at them.

"Drive fast," Greg said. "Please drive fast."

Zeke took nonstop pictures, gasping excitedly.

Susan repositioned her car and slammed down on the accelerator.

The black clouds of insects also increased their speed, encompassing the car on all sides.

"This is fucked," Zeke said, more astonished than petrified.

Visibility through the windshield diminished as more bugs attached themselves and stayed in place. The open areas of light constricted into smaller holes as blackness took over the glass.

"Shit, I can't see!" Susan said. She worked the wipers at full speed, but they became slower and obstructed as the thickness of bugs held on.

"Keep spraying the fluid," Greg said.

"I'm trying – they must have clogged it."

The interior of the car appeared to go from day to night as the swarm choked the light from the windows.

"I can't see, Greg. I really can't see!" Susan said. "I'm going to have to slow down – damn it!"

Then, as if completing the final holes in a jigsaw puzzle, the entire windshield went dark.

Susan hit the brakes, and the car went into a long skid. Even without visuals, the change in terrain became apparent, from rough road to grassy field. The rickety sound of splintering twigs of brush gave way to the *pow* of a larger obstruction – a tree, most likely – and the vehicle lost complete control. It struck several more firm objects, crunching metal on both sides, and then there was a light, floating feeling that lasted for just a second or two—

—culminating in a heavy splash.

The inside of the car filled with shouts and screams. The vehicle began to sink blindly into water – tipping back with a lurch, still darkened on all sides by the layers of black insects.

"We have to get out of here!" Greg said, fumbling for a grasp on the door handle.

The car became fully submerged and promptly hit a marshy bottom. A cracked window burst on Susan's side and water began pouring into the car.

"Get out now!" shouted Greg.

"But those things—"

"We're going to *drown* in here."

In the backseat, Zeke had unlatched a door, and he was pushing on it with all his might.

Susan lifted herself through the open window, slicing her hands on broken glass. She fought her way against the rising rush of water and exited the submerged car. Greg quickly followed, battling the water flow. He sucked in a big gulp of air and entered the murky waters. He didn't shoot to the surface – he immediately grabbed the door handle to the backseat. As Zeke pushed from the inside, Greg pulled from the outside, using all his strength, teeth clenched, exhaling bubbles from his nose.

Finally, the dented door opened wide enough for Zeke to slide out. Greg pulled on Zeke's shirt and outstretched arm, peeling off his backpack.

Within tweny seconds, Zeke was outside the vehicle. Both men kicked upward, rising the short distance to the surface.

Gasping for air, they bobbed and paddled their arms, quickly finding footing in the shallow pond. They joined Susan, who was coughing on her side in the marshy grass.

The car was fully underwater – taking the bugs with it.

"Where are they?" Greg said, and the others fully understood what he meant by 'they'.

"The bugs went down with the ship," Zeke said, still panting.

"Look," Susan said.

A dark, paste-like substance floated on the water, like an oil spill. The insects had lumped into a collective, inactive mass.

"Is that what's left?" she asked.

"I don't know," Greg said.

Zeke stared at the pond, forlorn. "I lost everything. My notes. My pictures. My food."

"*No, God damn it!*" Susan suddenly shrieked, leaping to her feet and smacking at something on her cheek. After a long moment of alarm, she stared at the small dark smear on her hand. "I think…I think that was just a regular mosquito."

"Let's get the hell out of here," Greg said.

"We can go get my jeep," Zeke said.

"I want to get as far from here as possible," Susan said.

"I need to start my next blog," Zeke said. "Whatever this is, it's spectacular."

As if punctuating his statement, the sound of multiple sirens could be heard rising in the distance.

For a moment, the three of them stood and listened. It was a welcome arrival.

CHAPTER NINETEEN

Greg, Susan and Zeke watched the whirlwind of activity at the farmhouse, staying hidden behind the pine trees across the street to avoid being seen.

A team of paramedics emerged from the house with three limp bodies on gurneys. Their rapid movement to flashing ambulances indicated the victims could still be alive.

Several members of the sheriff's office strolled the interior and exterior of the residence, looking for clues in a clinical, impassive manner. Sheriff Casey appeared to walk in aimless circles, seeming confused and annoyed.

"Should we go talk to them?" Susan asked.

"No," answered Greg and Zeke in unison.

"Screw Casey, he's been no help," Greg added. "We need to take this higher. Besides, if he sees us here, it'll just make him suspicious. He might lock us up."

"I have to agree," Zeke said. "This is a job for the feds. They'll be here."

"When?" Susan said.

Zeke shrugged.

The trio stayed in place until the ambulances left the scene, sirens activated, and the sheriff and his deputies returned inside the house.

"Let's go get my Jeep," Zeke said, "and get out of here."

"Sounds good to me," Greg said.

"Hold on for a sec," Zeke said. He suddenly darted forward into the road, exposing himself in the open.

Greg started to say, "What the hell..." and then realized what Zeke was doing.

He was retrieving his green cap with the alien patch.

Zeke grabbed it and hurried back with a smile, returning the cap to his head. "Okay, now we can go."

They advanced deeper into a heavily wooded area. They stepped cautiously, eyes on the lookout for any clouds of bugs. After a ten-minute hike, they emerged from the brush to reach an isolated roadway of dirt and weeds flattened by occasional tire tracks. The quiet countryside surrounded them.

Zeke's well-worn Jeep Wrangler sat in a patch of dead grass. The bumper and back window were decorated with an eclectic collection of stickers with science fiction fandom imagery and slogans.

One said: 'We Are Not Alone'. Another claimed: 'The Truth Is Out There'.

"Sorry about all the junk," Zeke said, clearing the backseat by shifting clutter into the rear cargo area: half-eaten junk food, tabbed binders of research, assorted camera and computer equipment. He carefully inspected the vehicle's interior floor and ceiling.

"I don't see any of those things," he said. "Do you?"

"Whatever they are, they seem to stick together," Susan said.

"When you're that small, it's strength in numbers," Greg said. He told Zeke, "I recommend you run your Jeep through a car wash, just to be safe."

"Yeah," Zeke said. He stepped back from the vehicle and crouched to take a look under. "It's the last thing I want to find in my beard."

"Gross," Susan said.

"We need to get out of these wet clothes," said Zeke, standing up. "How about this. I'll take you home, so you can get cleaned up. Then we'll regroup in a couple hours. We'll get this thing figured out, lay all our cards on the table. Sound righteous? Let's exchange phone numbers."

Greg pulled his cell phone out of his pocket, then stared at it blankly. "It's dead. Soaked."

Susan frowned. "Mine went down with the car. Great."

"And mine's in my backpack at the bottom of the pond," realized Zeke. "Okay. We'll need to get new phones. Put that on the immediate 'to do' list. I'm staying at the Finch Motel, just off the highway. Let's all meet there at six o'clock. I'm going to try to connect with my source at the agency, trade some intel for intel. Then the three of us will have one big powwow to share every scrap of information we know."

Susan nodded, weary, red hair wet and tangled.

Greg said, "We still have a lot to cover. There are things we haven't told you yet."

Zeke nodded, and his eyes sparkled with enthusiasm. "This isn't going to be a blog. It's going to be a bestseller."

★   ★   ★

As Zeke dropped off Susan in front of her house, she asked, "So what do I do about my car?"

"Nothing," Greg replied. "Let's not get anybody else involved right now. Not insurance companies, not the sheriff's office."

She stood in her driveway looking back at the two men in the Jeep. "Okay. Great. So how am I supposed to get around without a car?"

"I don't know," Greg said. "A rental?"

She rolled her eyes.

"I'll be your driver," Greg said quickly. "I'll pick you up at five-thirty for our meeting tonight."

"Meeting," she repeated back at him. "What is this, a committee?"

"Sort of," offered Zeke. "We're investigators of unexplained phenomena in Engles, Indiana. We're like the Winchester brothers on *Supernatural*. Or *Stranger Things*."

Susan was not amused. "Fine," she said. She glanced around, hoping she wouldn't see any neighbors watching her. "I look like a drowned rat. My hands are cut up. I'm exhausted. I'm freaked out. I need to go."

She went inside.

Zeke drove on to Greg's house next.

As Greg climbed out of the Jeep, Zeke reminded him, "Okay, see you at the Finch Motel at six." He added, "I know, not the greatest place. I tried the Imperial Inn, but I couldn't reach anyone there to make a reservation."

"Yeah...I can speak to that," Greg said. "We have a lot to talk about."

"Bring all the clues and evidence you have," called out Zeke as Greg shut the car door.

"Will do." Greg waved as Zeke backed out of the driveway. The Jeep Wrangler disappeared down the street.

Greg stepped up to his front door, fishing his house key out of his pocket. He wiped it on his shirt and inserted it into the lock. He was so tired he could barely stand.

"Mr. Garrett?"

Greg froze for a second, then turned. The voice was familiar and startlingly close.

He faced Eryn Swanson.

She stood on the walkway behind him, appearing seemingly out of nowhere. Had she been waiting for him by the side of the house? She wore a simple white blouse with jeans and red shoes. Her short hair was pulled back and pinned up in a professional presentation. She held her reporter's notebook. A large handbag hung on one shoulder.

"Eryn?" he said, flooded with a new rush of emotions: relief, anxiety, confusion. The feelings collided with his already frail state of mind.

"I've been wanting to talk with you," she said with a frozen smile. She didn't blink

"Oh. Sure." Greg stared at her for a moment. He couldn't put his finger on it, but she looked odd. Then again, he knew he looked ridiculous in soaked, dirty, torn clothing.

"Are you okay?" he asked. "Where have you been?"

"I have so much to tell you," she said. The tone in her voice did not fluctuate. "Can I come in?"

"Well, yes. Of course. I have a lot to share with you, too." He repeated, "Where have you been?"

"Working on my story," she said, like it was the most natural answer in the world.

"All right. Well, okay. Please come in."

Greg opened the door, and Eryn followed him inside.

He gestured to the living room couch. She walked directly to it, sat down, crossed her legs and smiled.

Greg sat in his big chair, grimacing because he knew he was making it filthy, but that was the least of his concerns right now.

He stared at her for a moment, and she didn't speak, still offering a frozen grin.

She hadn't asked about his unusual appearance. He decided to lead the questioning to break the silence.

"What do you know? What have you learned?"

"So much," she said. He waited for an elaboration. There was none.

"Did you have the eggs analyzed?"

"Yes."

"What did they say about them?"

"Everything."

Greg said nothing, and the empty response hung in the air. Staring at her vacant, complacent expression, he was struck by the similarities of her behavior to the demeanor of Susan's brother after he had reappeared.

"You're not right," he finally said.

"No," Eryn said sweetly. "I'm afraid you're mistaken. It's you. You're not right."

"What do you mean?" Greg asked.

"You're a disruptor."

Greg started to laugh but it caught in his throat. She stared at him with the same thin smile, dead serious.

"I...don't think...you're the same person," he said slowly, watching her reaction.

She casually placed her handbag in her lap. She unzipped it and reached inside.

She brought out a snub-nosed revolver.

Greg gasped. "Hey—!"

The gun fired just as Greg leapt out of the chair. The bullet pierced the cushion with a puff of stuffing. She fired at him twice more as he ran across the room. He reached a table lamp – the closest weapon of any kind – and grabbed its thick base and flung it at her.

He scored a direct hit. The heavy lamp hit the side of her head, stunning her, and she dropped the pistol to the floor.

Greg dove for the gun.

Eryn scrambled for it, too, but when it became apparent he would get there first, she kicked him hard with a pointy red pump. Still gripping the gun, he made a grab for her ankle. He briefly caught it, and then she pulled loose and ran.

Eryn raced out of the house, slamming the front door behind her.

Greg remained on the floor, panting with panic, still getting his head wrapped around the events of the past ten minutes.

"What. The. Hell."

Holding the gun, he stood up and walked to a window. He looked out at his lawn. He didn't see her.

He quickly locked the front door.

Greg instinctively reached into his pocket for his cell phone. He had to call Susan. He had to tell her what had just happened. A strange variant of Eryn had showed up after a long disappearance. A pattern was developing. And it was getting dangerous.

He tried calling Susan, but his phone was dead. Of course – he had forgotten. It was waterlogged. Ruined.

He swore and threw the phone across the room as hard as he could.

Eryn's handbag remained on the couch. He walked over and rifled through it.

Nothing unusual. Her ordinary things. Hairbrush, makeup kit, lipstick, gum, credit cards, some cash, keys, *Engles Express* business cards, and a little packet of tissues.

No phone.

Her reporter's notebook was on the floor. He picked it up. He flipped it to the first page.

There was a single, handwritten word: GREG.

He turned to the next page. It was identical. Blank, except for his name in big, block letters. GREG.

He continued to peel through the sheets in the reporter's notebook. Every page was the same.

GREG.

GREG.

GREG.

GREG.

GREG....

CHAPTER TWENTY

He watched out the window for a long time. Would Eryn return? What had happened to her? What was happening to all of the people who disappeared and then reappeared? Where was his family?

His heart wouldn't stop pounding. His clothes, already wet and dirty from the plunge into the pond, now felt warm and sticky, this time from fresh sweat.

He walked into the bedroom and peeled everything off until he was naked. He needed to cleanse himself in the shower, put on new clothes and eat something. His hair was wildly askew like a madman's. He looked as crazy as everything that was happening around him. It was time to regroup and find a foothold of sanity in this circus of the surreal.

Before entering the shower, he placed the snub-nosed revolver on top of the toilet tank, within a quick reach if there was an unexpected intruder.

He soaped himself vigorously, looking for any evidence of tiny insects. He found none, but they continued to play tricks with his mind every time there was a random itch.

After the shower, he quickly got dressed in clean jeans and a fresh polo shirt. As he was buttoning the shirt, the doorbell rang.

He froze, barefoot on the carpet.

Had Eryn returned? Or was it someone else?

He grabbed the gun and hurried into the living room, where one of the windows allowed a sideways glance at the front step, when he angled himself just right. He peeked from behind a curtain and glimpsed two people he did not expect to see. He lit up with a fresh jolt of anxiety.

Carl Peters and Jesse Walton.

The pair didn't see him watching from the window. They faced the front door in their business attire, stiff and stoic.

They rang the bell again, followed by a hard knock.

Carl Peters shouted, "Open up, Greg. Let me in. All is forgiven. You're rehired! At double, triple the salary."

Jesse added, "Yes. He means it. You are the man!"

Peters proclaimed, "At Imperial Inn Corporation, we value our employees. Let's align our synergies and shift paradigms to break down silos."

Both of them sounded weird, reciting empty lines in a hard monotone. It reminded Greg of Eryn and of Susan's brother. It wasn't difficult to draw the conclusion that these two had met the same fate.

Peters shifted gears from conciliatory to demanding. He called out, "Open the door. You are in defiance of corporate compliance. You are obligated to respond to your employer in a timely manner."

Greg refused to be intimidated.

He saw Jesse walk over to the garden of daylilies and allium that Janie had nurtured to life over the past several months. Jesse pulled a red brick out of the small border that separated the garden from the lawn.

He clutched the brick like a weapon and returned to Carl Peters' side at the front door. He continued to force a hard smile.

"That's it, I'm out of here," Greg said under his breath. He maintained a grip on the gun and shoved his feet into a pair of loafers.

Staying away from windows, Greg moved through the family room to the door that led to the garage. He entered the garage as quietly as possible and headed to his car.

In rapid succession, he climbed in, shut and locked the car door, started the engine, opened the garage door with his remote and threw the car in reverse.

By the time he had backed out of the driveway and onto the street, Carl Peters and Jesse Walton were running after him. Jesse still held the brick.

Greg took a split second to jab the remote and close the garage door. As he did so, Jesse threw the brick. It struck the back window and cracked it.

Greg shifted gears and accelerated forward.

Jesse and Carl Peters ran after the car, fully committed to the chase, almost close enough to touch the back bumper before the gap began to widen. The sight of plump, old Carl Peters sprinting robotically down the street in his executive wool slacks, business shirt and tie, and Gucci black leather shoes was absurd.

But Greg wasn't laughing.

He gave the duo one last glance in his rearview mirror – they weren't slowing down, despite the increased futility of their foot pursuit – and then took a hard right onto another residential street, leaving them out of view.

The gun sat in the passenger seat, a last resort if things got really ugly.

Greg drove directly to Susan's house.

He parked in her driveway, locked up the car and brought the gun with him, wedging it halfway in his pants pocket. He rang the bell and pounded until she opened the door.

"Greg—"

He advanced into the house quickly and shut the door. "We have to talk," he said.

"Yes, yes we do," she said, and she was smiling excitedly. Greg noticed she was cleaned up, wearing fresh clothes with her red hair pulled into a ponytail. She held her purse as if preparing to leave. "I heard from him!"

"Who?"

"Steve. He called me on the landline. You know how he's been avoiding me? He wants to get together now."

"Wait – what?"

"He said he regrets his behavior. He's not been feeling like himself. But he's feeling better now. Greg, he asked me to come over. He wants to help figure out what's going on. Isn't that great?"

"Don't go," said Greg firmly.

"I've already called for a cab."

"Cancel it!"

"Come on, Greg, this is what we wanted – for him to engage with us and fill in some holes. There's so much he could tell us."

"I don't think...." Greg struggled with his words. "I don't think we can trust him."

"What do you mean?"

"Something's not right."

"And that's why we need to talk to him. To learn." She looked at her watch. "The cab will be here any minute."

"No!" Greg said. "You're not going."

"What's wrong with you?" She looked ready to burst into tears. "I can't take this anymore. All this not knowing. I'm going to lose my mind if I don't—"

"He might try to harm you."

She gave him a long stare. "He would never do that."

"What if I told you Eryn was just at my house?" He pulled out the gun. "And tried to kill me with *this*."

She jumped back a step from the gun. "Don't point that thing near me. What's wrong with you?"

"You're not listening. She called me a 'disruptor', whatever that is. She wasn't herself. She was different. Like your brother."

"My brother is better now. I need to see him."

Greg told her the full details of his encounter with Eryn, followed by the two visitors from his workplace. "Do you want to see the crack they put in my back window?"

"No," she said. "I want to see Steve." Then she broke into a sob. The tears flowed and her eye makeup ran. The weight of everything had finally caused her to crumble.

Greg gently embraced her. She hugged back.

He said, "We'll just…wait, until we know more."

"I can't – take – this roller coaster," she said in a broken rhythm. "He's gone, he's back, he's sick, he's well, he's dangerous…."

"Here's what we'll do," Greg said softly. "When the cab gets here, I'll pay the driver and say we don't need them anymore. Then we'll go get new mobile phones. Are you hungry? I'm starved. We'll get something to eat. Then we'll go see Zeke. The three of us will put our heads together, and we're going to solve this thing from top to bottom. He said there's a federal agency coming…."

"The UFO chasers?" Susan said with scorn, raising her face to look up at him. "Come on, Greg, he's just grasping at straws like the rest of us.

This isn't UFOs, there's something poisonous in the air, in the rain, I don't know, radiation, affecting these people."

"Maybe," Greg said. "Maybe. But whatever it is, we'll figure it out. I promise you, Susan. We will."

In that moment, drawn close, they looked into one another's sad eyes. Neither said anything. Then Susan tipped upward and unexpectedly kissed him. The connection felt right and desperate. He answered with his own release of passion. Everything else fell away. They kissed until a taxi sounded its horn at the front of the house.

Gently, they pulled apart. Greg continued to look into Susan's eyes. He found her attractive but had never put a conscious thought into a moment like this. Neither of them spoke about what had just transpired. It was a flash in time, a rush of adrenaline, an impulse of two lost souls.

"I'll...go talk to the driver," Greg finally said after the second honk of the horn, longer and more impatient.

Susan nodded.

Very slowly, they withdrew from one another's arms.

CHAPTER TWENTY-ONE

Zeke had covered the walls of his motel room with large sheets of paper with single word headings. Working with Greg and Susan, he filled them out with every scrap of information the trio possessed in an attempt to shape a cohesive narrative.

The room became a command center for their investigation, although one with limited technology and cramped clutter: an unmade bed, clumps of dirty clothes, scattered junk food wrappers, grease-stained pizza boxes and lots and lots of paper.

"Are you kidding?" Zeke had said earlier, when confronted about his sloppy data collection. "I'm not putting any of this in the cloud."

The room's soundtrack hummed not with music but the steady drone and crackle of an old-fashioned police radio scanner to capture any new developments from the Engles sheriff's department.

Zeke had cleaned up, somewhat, and wore an XXXL *Starship Troopers* T-shirt and faded pair of jumbo khakis. His large beard and long hair appeared extra frizzy, on the verge of giving him the appearance of a big bear or werewolf.

The three of them had spent the better part of two hours in an intense dialogue, filling the big sheets with notes, and now they stood back and reviewed their collective input. Parts of the jigsaw puzzle had come together but large gaps remained.

"Okay," Zeke said. "Let's look at this from start to finish." He kicked past an empty McDonald's bag and stepped in front of sheet number one, at the start of the long wall across from the bed. Bland framed art prints and mirrors had been removed and placed on the floor to allow for one big canvas for note-taking.

"*Radar*," said Zeke, reciting the heading at the top. He then summarized the scribbles below. "We know, from my contact at the agency, there's some kind of meteorologic anomaly taking place. I haven't seen them, but apparently we have irregular radar images. I could probably get copies in exchange for a complete mint set of 1977 *Star Wars* trading cards. But the question remains – is this condition organic or do we have a potential foreign entry into our atmosphere?" This final consideration gave him cause to smile.

He added, "You would think the agency would jump on that element given their classification, but you'd be surprised – most of them are cynical and have no imagination. Too many false alarms on the books, they've been burned. It's easier to dismiss something than really probe at it."

"So are they going to help us?" Susan asked.

"We're going to help them," Zeke said. "They'll be here soon. We'll meet with them and go over everything that's on this wall."

Zeke kicked dirty socks out of his way and stepped in front of the next big sheet of notes composed in a thick black marker that had probably bled onto the wallpaper behind it.

"*Rain*," he said. "In conjunction with the unusual radar patterns, we have eyewitness accounts of a strange rain, something untraditional and unexplained. Brief, discolored and boxed in to only reach small areas. Is the source natural or man-made? Or something else? And from the rain, we get...."

He took a couple of steps and stopped at sheet number three.

"*Larvae*. The little yellow droppings, the puffy bulbs, that appear to be byproducts of the rain. I was all over the Internet before you got here, and there's nothing that's a fit, in terms of producing that kind of result. Yellow larvae are not unusual. There's the Clonorchis sinensis, a worm parasite, but this is no worm. There are members of the beetle family – the Colorado potato beetle, the cucumber beetle, the Mexican bean beetle and the ladybug, but that's not what we saw, it was more like rabid horseflies."

"It was definitely no ladybug," Susan said.

"I researched flying insects and there was nothing this extreme, this consuming, anywhere in the world. What we experienced was absolutely abnormal."

He moved to stand in front of the next sheet, labeled *Insects*.

"So what do we know? They are hyperaggressive. They attack as one single, unified force. They cover the skin."

"They enter the body," Greg said. "I saw those things...." He stopped to grimace at the memory of the attack in the farmhouse. "They were pushing into their eyes and ears, pouring into their mouth and nostrils...."

"Stop, we get it," Susan said. "I'm going to throw up."

Zeke stared at the *Insects* sheet. His eyes lowered to where he had written: *Hodges Family*.

"This is where we have fresh, real-time evidence," he said. "That family was viciously attacked, and they're in Engles Community Hospital. I have their names. Like I said when you got here, I was able to talk to one of the doctors for a few minutes in the lobby."

Earlier, Zeke had shown Greg and Susan his collection of fake press credentials that he used to gather research for his blog: CNN, *New York Times*, Reuters, Fox News and others. The doctor had been reluctant to talk, but agreed to share a few things off the record, as an unidentified source. Somehow Zeke generated an aura of authority to get more than a straight 'no comment'.

"We know that the three of them are totally unresponsive, hooked up to life support, in a – quote – coma-like state. And the strange part: no evidence of bugs or bug bites. It's more like they just went into shock and shut down."

"Do you think the doctor's holding out on us?" Susan asked.

"He seemed genuinely confused. He called it unprecedented. Some state medical experts are on their way, so we should learn a lot more."

Zeke stepped over to the next sheet, crunching a Subway soda cup. "Now we come to *Disappearances*. This is where the narrative doesn't exactly flow. I will send this list to my contact at the agency to see if it syncs up with the unusual radar activity."

The sheet listed the names of all known disappearances: Greg's family, Susan's brother, Jeff Jenkins' father, Eryn Swanson, the Imperial Inn guests and staff, and the campsite occupants. Eryn's name was circled with an arrow pointing to the clue: *White Van.*

Zeke had added the name of Clay Mueller, a local 'runaway' teenager. While Clay's story had not made the news or become a police report, Zeke had discovered it in an online forum for paranormal experiences, where the boy's mother claimed to have experienced visions of the boy's ghost in the house, late at night. She was a single mom, alone.

This had been a huge revelation for Greg, who eagerly retold the story of his own encounters with ghost-like images of his missing family. "Thank God, I'm not the only one," he had told Zeke. "We have to talk with his mother."

"We will, in due time," Zeke said.

On the next sheet, *Ghosts*, it listed the names of Greg's wife and children, followed by Clay Mueller.

Since the sightings early in the disappearance of his family, Greg had not encountered the ghosts again, and he had been ready to write it off as his own head games until Zeke had shared the information on the runaway teen's reappearing 'apparition'.

The next sheet listed names under the header *Reappearances*: Eryn Swanson, Steve Bergan, Jesse Walton and Carl Peters, along with a reference to the people from the Riverwoods Campgrounds. In large letters, at the bottom, Zeke had written: *ODD BEHAVIORS.*

They stared at it for a moment.

"People are reappearing but what about my family? Why not them?" said Greg.

"They will," Susan said. "Don't lose hope. They're out there somewhere."

"Yes, but in what kind of mental state?" said Zeke.

They advanced to the final sheet with the header: *Violence.*

They had previously discussed Eryn's attack on Greg, and the subsequent confrontation with Carl Peters and Jesse Walton. Susan was still upset – but understanding – about the need to stay away from her brother, in case the pattern continued.

"I'm guessing the more we know, the more we become a target," Zeke said. "Something has gotten into the heads of these people, and they don't want us asking a lot of questions."

Zeke stepped back to review one of the middle sheets in the sequence: *Insects*.

"Whatever is altering these people starts right here. Everything else follows – disappearances, reappearances, ghosts, violence. I believe the Hodges family is our critical link right now, the bridge to what's really happening. We need to find out more. Tomorrow, I'll go back to the hospital. I'll get dressed up, use fake government credentials to go deep. I'll interrogate the hell out of the doctors, the nurses, the staff. I'll be a pest until I get every last bit of information I can."

Greg nodded. Standing shoulder to shoulder with Susan, he gently put his arm around her. She leaned into him.

Greg said, "I feel like we're close...but to what?"

CHAPTER TWENTY-TWO

Nurse Irma Knudsen was two hours into the midnight shift at Engles Community Hospital, quietly checking on patients to monitor any changes in their condition and alert the physicians as needed. She preferred working when the floors were dark and quiet, without the tension of visiting family members or the bustle of meal deliveries and cleanup. Despite the difficult condition of some of the patients, she found the overall atmosphere relaxing, with voices kept low and interactions at a minimum. The reduced presence of management was another perk. The extra pay for working 'nonstandard hours' didn't hurt either.

Her body was well adjusted to the flip-flop in sleep schedules and finding seven to eight hours of slumber during the daytime, shutting out sunlight with heavy shades and turning off the ringer on the phone. She was single – recently broken up with a noncommittal boyfriend, no regrets – and lived independently and worked independently, which suited her just fine.

The intensive care unit had received three family members earlier that day. A father, mother and teenage boy. They required extra check-ins. These patients had lapsed into 'quiet, steady comas', according to Dr. Robbins, and the catalyst for their condition was unknown, although there was speculation they had been exposed to something on their farm, perhaps a dangerous pesticide, or eaten something with a noxious effect. She had checked on them several times and observed their relaxed faces and unmoving bodies, hooked up to ventilators and various intravenous lines.

As she walked the tiled floor alone toward the father's room for the next glance at his monitors and positioning on the bed, there was an abrupt noise, like a thrashing, that immediately stood out against the silence.

Nurse Knudsen accelerated her pace to the patient.

She discovered Frank Hodges standing up at the side of his bed, firmly tearing off the wires, tubes and adhesives that clung to him.

"Stop!" she ordered, her first word spoken out loud in over an hour, and he immediately looked at her.

His eyes had a cold, dead look, ringed with age, and his entire face appeared slack, mouth dropped open without a statement.

The slight, pulsing beeps on his cardiac monitor now streamlined into a single, alarmed tone. He swatted at the device with the back of his hand as if it was the irritating buzz of a circling mosquito. It tilted out of position and continued to pierce the air with a continuous electronic alert.

"You have to get back in bed!" she told him. "I'm calling the doctor." Everything was on the floor: his ventilation tube, the blood-oxygen clamp, the connection to his IV drip, his catheter.

She took additional steps in his direction, hoping she could guide him back to bed. It was wishful thinking.

He approached her, while giving the heart monitor another strike, this time sending it off the cart and onto the floor with a crash. He grabbed another obstacle in his path – the pole with the IV bag – and threw it across the room with considerable force.

She started to retreat, but he reached out and clutched the front of her nurse's uniform, and in a flash she was slammed into a cart of towels and utensils, spilling with them onto a floor puddled with fluids.

Nurse Knudsen screamed.

Frank Hodges reached the door. As she shook away the stars from the hard fall, she heard a male voice shout, "Stop right there!"

She didn't know if it was a doctor or security, but the next sound she heard was a scuffle and then someone letting out a tight squeak of pain.

As Irma rose from the floor, she could see the struggle framed in the light of the corridor. She witnessed the patient choking Dr. Markum, a fit man in his twenties reduced to a dancing puppet at the grip of the barefoot, tubby, fifty-three-year-old farmer in a hospital gown.

The sight was surreal, and she screamed again for help.

Dr. Markum dropped unconscious to the floor. Frank Hodges

continued his path forward, heart monitor wires dangling from his chest. He disappeared down the hall.

Nurse Knudsen followed, stunned.

She stopped and knelt before Dr. Markum, who was out cold. She looked out into the hallway and saw Frank Hodges joined by his stoic wife and teenage son, also torn free of their ICU equipment and still wearing their pale hospital gowns.

They didn't say a word to one another.

They stepped into the elevator together.

As the elevator doors shut them out of view, Nurse Knudsen rushed in the opposite direction down the hall, head still spinning, until she reached a nurses' station. It was unoccupied and sterile, cleaned by the night crew hours earlier. She grabbed the phone and called security.

Still panting and in pain, she told the voice on the other end that three patients were trying to leave and one of them had gotten violent and that Dr. Markum needed medical help immediately outside room 305. Her words were rushed and became a semi-coherent scramble, so she slowed down and repeated everything a second time.

She was pretty sure the voice on the other end was Buzby, the security guard usually stationed at the front desk and reading thriller novels from the library.

"Got it," he said. "You said they're – oh, hey, I see them now. I'll—"

Then she heard the drop of a phone receiver, and his voice became a shout directed at someone else.

"Yo! Hold on! You can't leave. All of you, listen up—"

Nurse Knudsen stayed on the line, listening.

Buzby's voice became more distant and muffled as he confronted the Hodges family. She couldn't make out the exact words, but he was yelling at them to stop.

Then she heard him shout with increased urgency, releasing a rare exclamation of profanity, followed by a sudden burst of shattering glass.

Nurse Knudsen screamed and dropped the phone.

She ran across the hall to a stairwell, pushing on the thick bar across the door. She hurried down the steps, using the banister for balance, still dazed from her fall and the overall dreamlike events unfolding during this traditionally serene hour. Her hard nurse's shoes smacked the linoleum with echoing pops.

She reached the ground floor. She ran to a limp body in a blue uniform sprawled motionless in a spew of broken glass.

"Buzby!"

Buzby was laid out at the former site of a clear glass partition at one side of the security desk in the front lobby. He was bleeding.

She looked up and out the front entrance. She could see the slow, steady pace of three figures in thin hospital gowns stepping off the curb to enter the drop-off lane in front of the large, dark parking lot, their silhouettes visible against the glare of outdoor lights.

They weren't hurried or acting panicked or excitable. They moved in unison, without acknowledging each other, with single-minded focus.

A white van pulled up. The back door slid open, with an empty row of seats waiting in the shadows.

The Hodges family climbed in, casually, as if they were headed to a picnic.

Several more members of the overnight staff quickly arrived to the lobby from different assignments around the building.

"Holy shit!" one of them exclaimed.

"Call the police," said Nurse Knudsen, leaning on the ground, gently checking Buzby's cuts. Buzby stirred, blinking away blood that rolled from his forehead to his eyes. "Get the paramedics," she said.

A pair of paramedics arrived beside her in their familiar white tops and dark pants. "We're right here, ma'am."

The white van drove off into the night.

CHAPTER TWENTY-THREE

After hours of analyzing every scrap of information they possessed between them, Greg, Susan and Zeke hit a dead end. They were exhausted, barely able to think straight anymore in conjunction with the disjointed storyline stretched across the wall in a furious scribble. They decided to call it a night with plans to regroup in the morning.

Greg drove Susan home from the Finch Motel. Taking a series of long, rural roads, they encountered only a few other pairs of headlights in the dark. They remained silent for most of the drive.

Greg insisted on accompanying Susan into her house to make sure everything was safe. He brought the gun.

Once inside, she flicked on lights and immediately noticed the blinking answering machine. She played back a message and listened to it with Greg.

It was her brother, Steve.

"I missed you, sister. Is everything okay? Maybe we can get together tomorrow? I have a lot to tell you. Please call me."

It ended with a beep, and after a long pause, she said, "That's his voice. But it doesn't sound like his words. He doesn't talk that way. 'I missed you, sister'?"

"You can't let him get near you," Greg said.

She nodded, frowning.

They stood close to one another, and Greg couldn't help thinking about their earlier kiss as he looked into her solemn face.

He suggested, "I can stay here with you."

"No. It's okay."

"You can come back with me."

"You're married."

He took a small step back. "That's not what this is about."

"I'll be fine."

"Keep the windows and doors secure. Don't let anyone in. If anything happens, call me immediately."

"Of course."

Tired and confused about everything, including their relationship, Greg resorted to a simple smile. Then Susan leaned in and gave him a small hug.

When they pulled apart, Greg said, "Tomorrow we'll get you your own gun."

"I can't wait," she said in a flat tone.

She walked Greg to the door. He said goodbye and returned to his car. He heard the front door click twice behind him – latch and bolt. He stood for a moment on the driveway, observing his surroundings. The night was ordinary and still, decorated only with the faint rhythm of crickets under a luminous moon.

His eyelids wanted to shut. He knew he needed to get home quickly, before he risked falling asleep behind the wheel.

Greg drove across the neighborhood, traveling a series of residential streets, each one spotted by grainy streetlamps and void of any people or activity. He came upon a small, familiar park with a modest collection of children's playground equipment wrapped in a web of concrete walking paths. Something caught his eye, and he turned to look.

Greg saw the dark shape of a person standing in the park.

He immediately slowed to a stop for a better look. The car hummed quietly. He stared into the shadows. There was an adult and someone smaller, perhaps a child. The adult held something close.

He studied their movements. The child ran to a swing set and climbed on a swing. The adult stood nearby and shifted their position, revealed by a faint reach of moonlight.

It was his wife, Janie.

She held a baby, Matthew.

Becky rode the swing. She began to pendulum back and forth in a steady rhythm, legs folded back, then kicked forward, repeating the motion as she reached higher above the ground.

Greg turned off the engine. He turned off the headlights.

They did not turn to look at him.

His eyes welled with tears.

They were not dead. They were here, alive.

It made no sense that they were lingering at this park in the middle of the night, innocently, as if it was a Sunday afternoon.

But the strangeness of the circumstances was eclipsed by his relief over their physical return. He opened the car door and stepped out into the street.

They still did not turn to look at him, even when he shut the door with a small slam.

"Janie," he said in a quiet, surprised voice, mainly to himself. Then, as he took steps toward them, he turned it into a frantic cry.

"Janie! Janie!"

She still didn't look at him. It was like shouting at a movie. He quickened his pace. His ears filled with two sounds: his feet hitting the pavement and the relentless *creak...creak...creak* of Becky on the swing set.

"*Janie!*"

He reached her, and she finally turned her head and looked at him. She smiled pleasantly, holding baby Matthew. She was dressed in one of her simple daytime dresses. Her expression was mundane, not at all surprised to see him.

Greg immediately feared: *Brain damage, like the others.*

"Janie...." He was panting now from the short sprint. "Janie... what's...what's...are you okay?"

For a long moment, she simply looked at him. The swing set's incessant creak grew more abrasive, cutting into the air.

"I'm fine," she finally said, barely blinking.

"The baby?"

"Matthew's fine. Becky's fine."

"Where – where have you been? You need to see a doctor. There's something happening. People disappear, they get sick...."

She expelled a mild laugh. "I'm not sick. I feel just fine. We're all fine."

"No...no. You feel fine, but...what are you doing here?"

In a plain, matter-of-fact tone, she said, "I lost my house key. I've been trying to get home to see you, sweetheart. Every time I go, you aren't there."

Greg said, "I've been...running around, trying to find you."

"You didn't need to do that."

Greg turned to look at Becky on the swing. She was locked into a hypnotic rhythm that did not deviate, a perfect half-circle. *Creak... creak...creak....*

She called out, "Hi, Daddy."

He waved. "Becky! Are you okay?"

"I'm fine, Daddy!"

Fine. The same word Janie kept using.

He turned back to face his wife. "Are you sure she's—"

In that instant, Janie lunged at him. It was an abrupt motion, a blur in the dark, and he wasn't prepared. She pulled a knife from the swaddle of blankets covering baby Matthew. She punched the blade forward. Greg instinctively twisted away but not quickly enough to avoid impact.

The knife cut into his side, just below the rib cage.

He yelled and staggered back from the sting, almost falling to the ground. He could feel immediate wetness from the blood escaping his wound.

She remained still, smiling pleasantly, holding the baby in one arm, a bloody blade in the other.

Greg could now see Matthew's small, placid face peeking out of the blankets.

The baby's eyes glowed hot red, as if pulsing with some kind of demonic charge.

"Daddy!" cried out Becky. "Come push me on the swing!"

He turned to look at her, then just as quickly turned back. Janie took a step forward, knife held firm.

He thought about the small pistol in his pocket. But he couldn't imagine firing a bullet into his wife.

"I'll get you help..." he told Janie.

"But we're fine," she said. She took another step forward. He took a step back.

Greg's sight was becoming smeared with tears. This was just like his encounter with Eryn, and the return of Jesse Walton and Carl Peters.

He placed a hand on his side, in his blood. It was soaking into his shirt.

"Hold me, Greg," pleaded his wife.

Greg fled. He ran back to the car. He jumped in, slammed the door shut, locked the locks, blasted the headlights on bright, and started the engine.

He quickly looked to see if she was coming after him.

She remained standing where he had left her. Not moving. Just staring, like a statue. On the swing set, Becky continued her smooth glide through the air, back and forth, like a metronome.

Crying, Greg gunned the car forward and left them there. He sped all the way home, taking sharp turns that bumped over curbs, roaring the engine through silent streets, blood leaking on the vinyl seat.

He reached his house, opened the garage with the remote, drove inside and promptly shut the clattering door behind him. He turned off the engine. He left the vehicle and hurried into the house, double-locking the entry.

He entered the bathroom and tore off his shirt to inspect the cut on his side. It was bleeding less and didn't appear to puncture any organs, just a hunk of flesh. He grabbed medical supplies out of a cabinet. He cleaned the wound and bandaged it. Then he turned off the bathroom light.

He moved through the house and turned off all the lights, until he was consumed in total darkness.

Then he went to the living room. He peeked out the big picture window from behind a curtain to get a good look at the front yard and street.

Greg was overwhelmed with paranoia. He tightly gripped the gun. *Who would come after him next?*

The neighborhood appeared calm, immersed in a deep sleep. The homes across the street sat in oblivious, dark silence. His mind and body were beyond exhausted, yet he was lit up by a fresh shot of adrenaline. There was no way he would close his eyes right now, not for a second.

He feared he would see Janie, Matthew and Becky approaching the front door any moment. Ringing the bell. Knocking. Janie calling out his name. Becky calling out for Daddy. Matthew crying out for comfort.

He knew he needed to call someone. The sheriff? Zeke? Susan?

He calculated it would take about twenty minutes for Janie to walk from the park to the house on foot, with the children in tow. When no one showed up after thirty minutes, he left the window to check that his wound wasn't bleeding through the bandage. He moved through the pitch-black living room and reached for a light switch, then stopped. His hand froze in midair as he glimpsed faint light and color skimming the corner where the wall met the ceiling.

At first, it appeared to be a strange projection, almost like a kaleidoscope pattern, but the more he stared, faces emerged: eyes, nose, mouth.

"Oh my God," he said.

The images became his family: Janie, Becky, Matthew.

The ghost-like visions had returned.

He pointed the gun at them, fully aware of the absurdity of such a defense. They appeared before him in increasing clarity, hovering slightly above his head.

"How did you get inside?" he said. "What *are* you?"

At the park, Janie's expression had been blandly pleasant, relaxed and undisturbed. But now she appeared fraught with emotions, grimacing and wide eyed with a look of terror and despair. Her lips moved to talk but the only sound that came out was a low, guttural moan. Becky floated nearby, looking tearful and lost. Then he heard a raw, piercing sound and immediately recognized it from the first night he had arrived home to an empty house.

Matthew's infant cry.

It sounded distorted, as if choked by a malfunctioning tape deck. It was both human and unlike anything Greg had ever heard before.

The noise twisted in painful knots. It caused Greg to reach again for the lights.

He snapped on the overhead light fixture and the images vanished, wiped clean.

He looked around the room to see where they had escaped to. He called out their names.

It was as if their presence was controlled by the light switch.

He turned off the lights, plunging the room back into complete darkness. Within seconds, they reappeared.

He immediately recognized why his sightings of these images had been so sporadic. They could only exist in a total absence of light.

"Oh God," he said. Their faces appeared desperate, pleading for help with minimal means to communicate. Their bodies were rough sketches fighting for life, occasionally displaying arms and hands, while their heads created a more defined presence, blurred one moment and hauntingly detailed the next.

"Are you the same thing that's out there?" he asked.

Matthew's wail amplified. Becky said something that sounded like, "Daddy." Janie said something that resembled, "Help us."

"I want to help you," Greg said. "I don't know how. I don't know what you are...."

Greg put down the gun on the coffee table. He took out his phone. "I'm going to get some people who can help...who'll believe what I'm seeing...."

He dialed Zeke.

Zeke answered after six rings.

"Are you awake?" Greg said.

"Of course not," Zeke said. "I went straight to bed after you guys left. Shit, what time is it?"

"You need to come to my house right away."

"Do I really?"

"The ghosts are here. *Right now.* You need to see this."

There was a long pause on the other end. It concluded with, "Holy shit. Are you serious?"

"After all we've been through, you have to ask that? Listen, I'll call Susan. Pick her up on your way over. I need both of you here to witness this. I-I just realized…you can only see them in total darkness."

He looked for the images of his family and immediately became alarmed they were no longer visible.

Then he realized the light from his phone had snuffed them.

"*Get here right away,*" Greg said. He hung up and turned off his phone, returning it to a black screen.

After a few minutes, his family reappeared.

"Unbelievable," he said softly.

He reached up and tried to touch one of the images but it was like stroking air. "I believe in you," he said.

CHAPTER TWENTY-FOUR

Greg, Zeke and Susan sat on the floor in the middle of Greg's living room in total darkness, watching the flickering images of Greg's family hover above. Susan was stunned into silence. Zeke was shocked into nonstop talking.

"Are you real?" he asked Janie Garrett. "Can you hear us? How did you get this way? How do you float? Oh my God, I am so spooked right now, and that term is totally appropriate. This is evidence we're not only physical beings, we exist on a whole other level. Ma'am, are you a ghost, a spirit, a soul, an optical illusion or—"

Finally, Susan spoke up. "Stop bombarding the poor woman like this. It's too much. She can't keep up. One question at a time."

"It's not that easy," Greg said. "She can't talk."

"Can't talk?" Zeke said.

"She tries...but it doesn't sound like speech. It doesn't come out right. You can't hear the words."

As if to demonstrate, Janie's mouth moved but could only produce a low, anguished moan.

Susan watched closely. Then she had an idea.

"I think I can help," she said. "I can read lips a little. I have a cousin who's deaf, who has trouble with speech. So I follow his lip movements. Zeke, ask her *one* question."

Zeke nodded. He searched a moment for the main thing he wanted to know. He finally settled on: "*What the hell happened?*"

"Go slow, honey," Greg told Janie. "We'll try to follow."

Janie's image could not sustain a consistent visual, fading and reappearing like a flashlight beam with weak batteries. Her face stretched and constricted with surreal distortion.

Zeke lifted his iPad to take a photo.

"Don't. The flash will make them disappear," Greg said.

"I can do it without—"

"Any light from your tablet will cause them to dissolve. I know, I've tried."

Zeke attempted a photo anyway. "I have to capture this."

"No," Greg said, but it was too late.

As soon as Zeke fumbled for the camera app and tried to frame the wispy images, they disintegrated. He took a picture of total darkness.

"See?" Greg said.

"How – how long until they come back?" Susan asked.

"I don't know," grumbled Greg. "Minutes. Hours. Never."

"Fascinating," Zeke said. "It's as if the light steals their energy."

They sat together in total darkness, waiting for Greg's family to reappear.

"I'm so tired I'm delirious," Susan said. "This could be a dream, for all I know."

"Should I make coffee?" Greg asked.

"I don't need it," Zeke said. "I've never been so wired."

"I'll be all right," Susan said. "I don't want to move. Let's just stay here and wait."

After several minutes, Greg spotted a blurry smear of light in a corner of the room, near the ceiling. He nudged the others.

Becky's face came into view. Her eyes were big and scared.

Then, suddenly, much closer, Janie's image blossomed out of the darkness, causing Susan to jump. Baby Matthew followed soon after, small and pink, seemingly relaxed and at peace.

"Janie," Greg said. "We can only see you in total darkness. We don't have a lot of time. When the sun comes up, we're going to lose you. We need to find a way to communicate and learn what's happening so we can help. We're going to let you talk and just listen. Even if we can't hear you, we can try to read your lips. If you go slow, enunciate everything very carefully, we can try to catch what you're saying."

Janie's brown eyes stared with sadness. She appeared to possibly nod, but her unstable form made it hard to discern.

"Susan, let us know what you see," Greg said.

"Interview of the century," Zeke said. "No pressure."

"Janie," said Susan to the incomplete image of a scared woman roughly her own age, flickering like a candle flame feeding off oxygen. "Just tell us...from the beginning...what happened?"

At first, Janie's face just stared. *She looks on the verge of tears*, thought Greg. Becky and the baby remained on either side of her, rarely straying too far, remaining close to their mother as if held there by a magnetic force.

Then Janie's lips moved. A slight murmuring noise came out. Greg worked hard to ignore the sounds, focused on the words she tried to shape.

Susan translated: "We were attacked by bugs. Bees...or flies. Flying...in the backyard. It was a big swarm."

"This is working," Zeke said softly.

"Keep going," Greg said.

In slow, short sentences, Janie described what happened and Susan studied her lips to translate.

"Becky wanted to play...in the backyard...in her playhouse," Susan said, following Janie's words.

Greg could picture the scene immediately. He knew Becky was very fond of her plastic outdoor cottage. It was five foot by five foot with red, green and yellow candy-land colors distinguishing the roof, door and window shutters. Greg and Janie had bought it for Becky's fourth birthday. She had moved some of her more durable toys into the toy house, and Greg had added a small wooden chair picked up from a neighbor's garage sale.

Susan continued to repeat Janie's statements aloud: "I told Becky to go play...and I would come out in a few minutes...with the baby."

Greg felt queasy, dreading what would follow. He kept quiet, and Susan continued to be the only voice in the room, relaying everything Janie mouthed to them.

In broken phrases, brought on by the trauma of describing what happened next, Janie said that when she stepped into the backyard, carrying Matthew, she did not see Becky but assumed she was in the playhouse.

The plastic door and window shutters were closed, and she immediately worried it would be too hot inside the playhouse, and she should open it up.

She walked across the lawn, calling out Becky's name, but Becky didn't respond.

When Janie opened the small door, she screamed and almost dropped the baby. The interior of the playhouse was covered in a thick, black layer of winged insects. Becky was motionless on the floor, and the bugs were attacking her face: eyes, nose and mouth.

At this point in the story, Greg could see Janie cry, and her sobs did not sound like the crying of a regular human being, it was twisted and echoey, like some kind of moan from a wounded animal.

Greg felt tears running down his cheeks.

When Janie was able to resume her words, she described putting the baby down on the grass and squeezing into the playhouse to grab Becky. She brought out Becky in her arms, feeling the small stings of bugs all over her skin.

She fell to the grass with Becky, screaming for help. When she screamed, bugs entered her mouth and made her choke.

She knew she had to carry Becky and Matthew into the house as quickly as possible.

She reached for Matthew.

He was completely blackened, covered by the insects. It was as if they were feeding on him.

She managed to carry Becky in one arm and the baby in the other. The three of them were covered in bugs. She didn't even think about the pain. She just wanted to get inside the house.

She made it into the back porch room and closed the sliding door. The bugs quickly covered the glass from the outside, turning it into one big, black shivering blanket.

At this stage, Janie said her memory became fuzzy. She took the children into the bathroom and turned on the tub to try to soak the bugs off them.

She remembered lying semi-conscious on the bathroom floor with Becky and Matthew next to her, listening to the tub fill with water, reaching the upper rim....

Then she described a floating sensation, observing the bathroom from the ceiling. Becky and Matthew appeared to float with her.

But the three of them also remained on the floor. It was like they existed in two places.

Janie said she watched herself get up from the floor, turn off the bathtub faucet and drain the tub.

She remembered crying out her own name.

She recalled watching herself pick up Matthew and take Becky by the hand and leave the bathroom.

She heard them leave the house through the front door. She never saw their physical counterparts again.

Greg said nothing about seeing the three of them at the park. He couldn't share his own story yet. But parts of it were starting to follow some bizarre logic.

Janie described her current condition. She said she was able to control some movement over time in her floating state. She had tried communicating with Greg when he returned home from Minnesota, but couldn't do anything but frighten him.

Everything I experienced was real, thought Greg, remembering every moment of those nights, haunted by their images. *I'm not crazy. None of this is crazy. It's happening for real, right now, in front of us.*

Susan said to Greg and Zeke, "This must be what happened to my brother Steve. That means he's trapped in his house like this…a phantom, all alone."

"Unbelievable," said Zeke.

The room fell silent as they absorbed everything they had just heard. No one spoke. Then:

THUMP THUMP.

The silence was broken by an unexpected noise, firm and abrupt, at the front of the house.

Someone was knocking on the front door.

Greg rose to his feet. Susan gasped. "Now what?" Zeke said in disbelief.

Greg cautiously moved through the dark to a big picture window. It was covered by a curtain. He pulled back a small opening to peek through. He glimpsed someone standing patiently at the front door.

He turned back to the room. His eyes looked upward toward the ceiling, where Janie hovered in a quivering wisp of light and color.

"It's you," he said.

CHAPTER TWENTY-FIVE

Zeke jumped up so quickly that he nearly fell back down. The rotund giant found his balance and staggered to the front window to join Greg. He yanked back the curtains with a big tug, allowing light into the house and erasing the ghostly images of Janie, Becky and Matthew.

"Oh my God, you're right!" he said in a tone more fueled by awe than fear.

Susan stood up from the floor. "Are you saying she's out there…and in here?"

"That's exactly what I'm saying," Greg said. "This is what's happening all over Engles. It's like people are splitting in two."

"I have to talk with her," Zeke said.

"No!" said Greg, but it was too late. Zeke was already opening the front door. He stepped out of the house.

"Don't let her in!" Greg shouted at Zeke.

The front door closed behind him.

"She has a knife!" Greg yelled. Susan joined Greg at his side, and he turned to her. "God damn it, he knows what happened. She stabbed me earlier tonight. I told him, she's not well."

Greg promptly retrieved the snub-nosed revolver from a nearby table. He held it as he observed the scene through the window from an awkward angle. He saw Zeke standing on the front steps, talking with Janie, who smiled pleasantly, holding the baby in her arms. Becky stood silently by her mother, looking up at them sweetly.

"What are they talking about?" Susan asked.

"I don't know," Greg said. "Stupid asshole, he's probably interviewing her."

"She doesn't look mad, she looks happy."

"Right – that's how she fools you."

Zeke continued to chat animatedly with Janie, who gently rocked Matthew in her arms. She didn't look like a threat in that moment, cradling the baby. Zeke was quite a bit bigger than Janie, who barely reached five-foot-four in heels.

"What's going on, what's going on?" murmured Greg anxiously. "I don't like this."

"Greg, look!" Susan said with alarm. "Look at Becky."

Becky's hands had been behind her back as she stood silently alongside her mother. Now she slowly brought one arm into view, and Zeke didn't see it.

Becky had the knife.

"No!" screamed Susan.

Greg pointed the gun at his daughter but pulling the trigger was impossible. He began to hammer on the window glass with his free hand, rattling it loudly. "Zeke! Zeke, look out!"

Zeke turned his head and pulled toward the source of the noise. As he did, Becky thrust the knife toward his chest.

The first strike missed, but Becky immediately stabbed the knife again and caught Zeke in the forearm. He screamed and had no qualms about punching the little girl, sending her flailing back into some bushes. Janie began clawing at Zeke with her free hand, holding the baby so lopsided that it looked like he would topple to the ground.

Susan shouted, "Greg, look at the lawn!"

From out of the darkness, three more figures approached the house in steady, measured steps.

Greg recognized them. "That's Jesse and Carl Peters and, and holy shit—"

"It's Eryn!"

"We have to get Zeke back in the house." Greg rushed to the front door and opened it, gripping the gun.

Instead of Zeke, he faced Janie – or at least what used to be Janie. She stood at the bottom of the steps, clutching the baby with angry, clenched fists. Her face had changed, gnarled into an ugly, vicious sneer. Her eyes blazed with demonic fury. Behind her, Becky was climbing out of the bushes.

Greg saw Zeke running away from the house, big legs pumping hard. Eryn started to chase him but couldn't catch up. The fat man could move fast when his life was at stake.

Zeke raced down the street and disappeared into the night.

"Great," muttered Greg.

From the bottom step of the front porch, Janie growled at Greg, who stood framed in the doorway. She started to advance up the porch stairs. Becky was behind her and had retrieved the knife.

Greg slammed the door and locked it.

Within seconds, Janie was banging on the other side – not the measured knock of several minutes ago, but a wild, beast-like pounding and scratching. The noise quickly amplified. Greg could hear additional hands smacking the door, attacking it with raw fury.

"Honey, please!" Janie shouted. "I'm your wife. Love me!"

Then he heard Carl Peters: "I'm your employer. Trust me!"

Eryn's voice followed: "I'm a journalist. Believe me!"

"Not a chance in hell!" Greg hollered back at all three of them.

Susan stood close. "Now what?"

"I don't know," Greg said.

"What about Zeke?"

"He's gone. The big guy can really move."

"We can't stay here," Susan said. "We have to leave."

"I know."

All of a sudden, the noise at the front door stopped. Susan and Greg looked at one another. Everything went quiet. Too quiet. "What does that mean?" whispered Susan.

BANG BANG BANG!

Susan let out a startled shriek as hands began smacking the picture window just inches from her face. It was Janie and Becky, staring through the glass with wild eyes and gnashing teeth.

Greg and Susan scrambled to another part of the room, out of view.

"What are we going to do now?" asked Susan over their banging.

Greg pulled out his phone. "I'm calling the sheriff."

"How long is that going to take?" Susan said. The violent pounding continued to shake the window. "The sheriff is on the other side of town. By the time they get here, we'll be dead meat."

In a loud burst, the front picture window shattered.

Greg shouted, "Quick – my car!"

He led Susan through the family room to a side door that connected with his garage. As soon as he opened it, he saw Jesse and Carl standing at his SUV with the hood propped up. They were tearing up the engine's wiring, one step ahead of him after his last getaway.

They looked up from their handiwork and grinned at Greg.

"Son of a bitch," he said, realizing they had broken in through a garage window.

He pointed his gun at them. "Stop! I have a gun! Move out of here!"

Neither looked particularly concerned. Jesse held up the remote he had taken from inside the car. He proudly pressed the big white button. The garage door behind him began to roll open.

"Uh oh…" Susan said.

A small crowd waited to enter. More people had descended on the house – including many faces Greg didn't recognize. He realized they must be other missing persons – from the hotel, from the campground – united as one force. Eryn stood with them.

"I don't have enough bullets for all that," Greg said.

As the garage door thudded to a halt, fully open, the mob advanced forward.

"Disruptor!" exclaimed Eryn, pointing at Greg.

"Ah, shit," Greg said.

He jumped back into the family room with Susan and slammed the door. He locked it.

"We'll have to go out the back," he said. "We'll cut across some yards. Run like hell. Get some help."

They quickly moved through the house, reentering the darkened living room. The ghostly images of his family reappeared, swirling in a cyclone-like frenzy, blurred and distorted into horrible, deformed visages of his loved ones.

Something lunged from the shadows and grabbed Susan. She let out a big scream. Greg immediately hit a switch and flooded the room with bright light. He saw the flesh-and-blood version of Janie attempting to choke Susan. The baby lay on the couch, squirming. Becky stood by silently with the knife.

Greg shoved Janie away from Susan. He pointed the gun at her. He glanced over at Becky. She remained expressionless and motionless, as if drugged.

"I don't know who or what you are," he said to Janie, as Susan backed away, catching her breath. "But I won't hesitate to use this gun if you try to hurt us."

Janie's face studied Greg. Then she underwent a dramatic transformation from crazed aggression to a soft, pitiful look of sorrow. Her voice trembled delicately, as if on the verge of tears.

"Greg, honey, we don't want to hurt you. We love you. Don't we, Becky?"

"I love you, Daddy," said Becky. Her eyes watered, as if on cue.

Greg watched, bewildered by the abrupt change of tone.

"I don't...believe you," he said carefully. After a long moment of silence, he said, "Becky, give Daddy that knife."

"But, Daddy, you have a gun," Becky said.

"Becky's right," Janie said. "We need a knife to protect ourselves from you."

Greg could hear continuous, violent pounding on the door to the family room from the garage. The mob would be inside soon.

"I'm not fucking around," Greg said. "Hand over that knife before you stab someone else. You don't know what you're doing. Something has taken over your minds."

In an instant, Janie's face hardened, returning to cold evil. "You're not going to shoot us," she said. "You're not man enough to do it. You've never fired a gun in your life."

"Don't try me, Janie."

She said, "Becky, darling, come to Mommy. You know Daddy won't hurt us. Bring Mommy the knife. We're going to make sure Daddy gives us that bad little gun. It's tiny. It looks like a toy, doesn't it?"

"Becky, don't move," Greg said firmly.

Susan said, "Listen to him, Becky."

"Why should I listen to Daddy?" Becky said. "He's never home anyway."

That last statement stunned Greg. It was a sudden, unexpected shove into a previous, very real drama, that had haunted him long before any of this surreal madness began.

Baby Matthew started crying on the couch.

"It's only...temporary," Greg said, suddenly disoriented, lost in time and space. "Daddy...has a job to do."

The baby's cry quickly elevated to a shrill howl. It felt like it was directed toward him.

Janie said, in a simple tone, without feeling, "He's a bad Daddy. He needs to go away. Let's cut up Daddy into little tiny pieces."

"Okay, Mommy," Becky said with cheerful enthusiasm, as if invited on a play date.

"*Don't do it*," Greg said. The gun remained in his sweaty grasp.

Outside, an abrupt and persistent car horn sounded. It quickly grew louder.

Greg remained frozen, eyes on his wife and daughter.

"Your car?" Susan said.

"No, I don't think so," Greg said.

"Then...what?"

The car horn blasted louder, closer.

Then, adding to the chaos, the door from the garage to the family room collapsed with a crunch. A sudden burst of voices and footsteps entered the house. The mob was coming.

Big, powerful headlights beamed directly into the living room through the front picture window, temporarily blinding everyone.

Susan stared into the light through the curtains. Then she realized: "It's Zeke!"

Zeke's Jeep Wrangler slammed into the wooden front porch with enough force to rattle the entire house. Susan nearly fell over.

"Let's go!" hollered Greg. He grabbed Susan's hand and ran for the front door.

Janie and Becky ran after them, joined by Jesse Walton, Carl Peters and Eryn Swanson.

Greg and Susan pushed through the front door and the Jeep was waiting for them, pressed against the half-demolished front porch. They scrambled inside and activated the locks, just in time.

A cacophony of slapping and pounding hands struck the windows almost immediately as the mob piled against the vehicle.

"Hold on!" Zeke shouted.

He threw the Jeep in reverse and several people rolled off, landing in the debris of the smashed porch steps.

Zeke thrust the Jeep forward. It tore across Greg's front lawn and bounced over the curb and onto the street.

Within minutes, they were blocks away, out of reach of the small army of crazed attackers.

"What the fuck!" shouted Zeke, and Greg and Susan did not disagree.

CHAPTER TWENTY-SIX

Greg woke up in a moment of blurry disorientation and found an arm draped across his chest. He slowly recognized the inside of Zeke's motel room, where they had retreated after escaping the strange, zombie-like horde at Greg's house. Greg was sprawled on the bedsheets in his clothes with Susan next to him, still asleep. She had absently – or, not? – landed an arm on him, and he felt her close warmth.

Morning light streaked into the room. Zeke stood at the wall, writing on one of the big sheets.

Under *Disappearances*, he had added the Hodges family to the list of names.

The police radio was back on, volume turned low to be considerate of his sleeping guests. Zeke had insisted on dozing in the big chair so Greg and Susan could share the bed. He wore a *Twilight Zone* logo T-shirt and boxer shorts designed with toy robots. His baseball cap was perched on his head again, featuring the sewed-on patch of a green, cartoon alien face.

Greg sat up and Zeke noticed him.

"You're not going to believe this," Zeke said, marker in hand.

Susan stirred at the sound of Zeke's voice. She rubbed her eyes. "Believe what?" she mumbled.

Zeke gestured to the police radio. "The entire Hodges family – in the hospital, supposedly in comas, right? In the middle of the night, they just got up and left."

Greg's posture immediately straightened. "Left?"

"Yeah, and not without a fight. They hurt some people on the way out. A nurse, a doctor and a security guard."

"Holy shit," Susan said, fully awake in a matter of seconds, running a hand through her tangled red hair.

"I had some really weird dreams last night…but nothing as weird as the reality I'm waking up to," Greg said. His memory retrieved the sequence of events of the past twelve hours. "Jesus Christ, I stuck a gun in my wife's face…my daughter…."

"It's not really them," Zeke said, studying the next three sheets in the sequence: *Ghosts, Reappearances, Violence*. "Something is taking over these people, like a parasite. It's inhabiting their bodies. It's pushing out their true identities. It's supernatural. This is the real deal."

"When will that agency get here?" Susan said. "The one that investigates this kind of thing."

Zeke turned to face her. "I've been trying to get ahold of my contact. I've been sending him updates. He hasn't responded to my latest messages, but days ago, he assured me they were on their way. They need approvals up the chain, it's probably in somebody's inbox, you know how that goes. Government bureaucracy. That's why I'm here, getting shit done while the official response is stalled somewhere in Seattle. Just means more for me. I've been capturing all of this and writing it down. This has blockbuster written all over it. I'm going to be on the *New York Times* bestseller list."

"Great," murmured Susan. "We'll see you on the talk shows. In the meantime, I feel lightheaded. I think it's because I'm starving."

Greg looked down at the small red stains on the bedsheets, leakage from his stab wound. "We need food and we need fresh bandages. Zeke, how's your cut?"

"Grazed me, I'll be fine. But I could use some nourishment, too. There's a truck stop with a convenient mart, just up the road. A short walking distance."

"Good," Susan said. "They'll have coffee." She went in search of her shoes.

Greg stood up from the bed. "I'll go with Susan. Zeke, what can we get you?" He figured Zeke wanted to stay back and keep listening to the police radio.

Zeke gave it some serious thought, then recited: "Cheez-Its, Hostess Cupcakes, a Kit Kat bar, Jack Link's extra spicy jalapeno beef jerky, Mountain Dew. Please and thank you."

Greg hesitated for a moment, then shrugged. "Sure."

Greg slipped on his shoes and followed Susan outside into the crisp, morning air. The sun was making a groggy appearance behind cloudy skies.

"Are you really going to get him all that junk?" Susan asked as they walked across the parking lot toward a grassy hill that led to an area of gas stations and fast food restaurants.

"I guess."

"He's going to die of a heart attack."

"It beats getting murdered by your own family."

"You've got a point."

They reached the top of the hill. Greg surveyed the scene. "The truck stop's probably the only place open right now. Those restaurants look closed." He spied McDonald's, Wendy's and Taco Bell.

"How's your wound?" She could see it bleeding in a few small spots through his shirt, creating dark stains.

"It doesn't hurt as much as knowing who did it," Greg said, and with that the conversation concluded. They reached their destination.

They entered Happy's Stop N Shop with the jingle of a bell. The unshaven, balding man at the counter didn't look particularly happy. He looked up to glance once and then returned to distracting himself with his cell phone. The low murmur of country music played overhead.

Greg gathered the items Zeke had requested – all were in stock in plentiful quantities.

Susan's eye caught a display case of knives. The collection ranged from folding pocket knives to razor-like, self-defense daggers to large hunting blades with smooth wooden handles and sheaths.

"We need more to protect ourselves," she said. "All we have is your gun."

He stood by her side, and they studied the offerings. "I don't think I have more than a couple of bullets. It's not going to save us against all of them."

She pointed to one of the pocket knives, three inches of steel with a sleek, black handle with a grooved grip and quick-release trigger.

"That one," she said.

"Okay," Greg said with a small, nervous exhale. As a kid, fishing with his father, he couldn't even bring himself to gut a bass. His father had frowned and made him watch the act up close 'to get over your sensitivities'.

Susan moved to a nearby rack of additional self-defense items encased in plastic bubble packs: handheld pumps of pepper spray and tear gas, and keychains equipped with panic buttons for unleashing loud, shrill alarms. She grabbed one of each.

Greg said nothing.

They advanced to a small selection of medical items, and Greg picked up fresh bandages and antiseptic.

Susan found yogurt and a questionable banana. Greg took several granola bars.

As they collected their final items, Susan gave Greg a small nudge. He looked up and followed her gaze.

A strange-looking man in a red cap and faded flannel shirt stood nearby, staring at them with blank eyes.

Greg looked back at Susan.

"Do you think...?" she whispered.

"I don't know. He could just be some tired guy passing through town."

"Or he could be one of *them*."

As Greg and Susan made their way up the aisle to the counter, the stranger turned and continued to watch them.

At the front entrance of the convenient mart, a plump woman stepped inside, triggering the bell. She looked odd: hair frazzled, no makeup, and an equally dead stare. Greg looked at her until their eyes connected and he turned away.

He muttered, "Shit, I don't know if I'm just being paranoid or...."

Greg and Susan spilled their merchandise on the counter. The balding, stubble-faced clerk began to ring it up.

He also gave them strange glances.

Greg had the snub-nosed revolver in his pocket. He let his right arm dangle loosely near it. How quickly could he draw and shoot? Accurately?

His heart began pounding.

The clerk broke through his stoic demeanor with a sudden grin at the sight of the knife, pepper spray, tear gas and 'supersonic sound blaster' keychain.

"Looks like you're expecting trouble," he said with a chuckle.

"Yeah, well, maybe," Susan said.

"There ain't no trouble in these parts," he said.

Why did he say that? wondered Greg. *Was he being sarcastic? Is he in the know?*

Greg felt sick to his stomach. He was hungry, injured and still very tired.

The clerk collected everything into two bags, and Greg paid with wrinkly cash, damp from the day before, when he was submersed in the pond.

The clerk gave it a funny look. For a moment, it almost looked like he was going to give the currency a sniff.

Susan stood sideways against the counter to watch the other individuals inside the mart. When Greg and Susan first entered, it was empty of customers. Now the mini-mart had at least half a dozen silent, emotionless visitors. She didn't want her back turned on any of them.

Greg received his change. He and Susan each took a bag. They departed from the store in a steady, deliberately casual stride.

Once outside, Susan said, "We can't be in public places like that. We just don't know...."

"As we walk back to the motel, keep an eye out. Make sure no one's watching or following us."

"Jesus Christ, I don't even have my self-defense out of the plastic wrap."

Greg and Susan descended the grassy hill, staying away from the main road and sidewalk. Greg finally said, "I don't think we're being followed. Nobody came out of the store that I could see."

The Finch Motel sign returned to view.

They entered the cluttered room to find Zeke still at the wall, adding copy to the large sheet of paper headlined: *Violence.*

The police radio murmured with a busy tangle of voices. Something was up.

"Now what?" Greg said, closing the door behind them.

Zeke placed the cap on his black Sharpie marker.

He had written down the names Doreen and Clay Mueller.

"Remember the Mueller family?" He pointed to the sheet titled

Disappearances. "Runaway teenager, distraught single mother, very little news on it. To most people, I'm sure it seemed like a typical domestic issue…except the mother claimed to have seen the boy's ghost. She wrote about it on a paranormal forum I follow."

Greg nodded. He knew this wasn't going to end well from the look on Zeke's face.

Zeke gestured to the police radio, still humming with conversation. He said, "They just discovered the mother dead in her kitchen. Chopped up with a butcher knife. The son did it. They have footage from a security camera doorbell. Clips of the son arriving…then leaving, his clothes covered in blood. He's on the loose."

"It's gotta be…" said Greg.

"Fits the pattern." Zeke stepped back. He faced the series of sheets on the wall. "Disappearance. Ghosts. Reappearance. Violence."

Susan slowly moved toward the sheet of names listed under *Disappearances.*

She focused on one entry in particular: Terry Jenkins. The elderly father of Jeff Jenkins. Jeff believed his dad had wandered off in a state of dementia, but that was almost certainly not the case, given the fate of the other missing persons in Engles.

"We have to warn them," Susan said.

Zeke looked at her. "Warn who?"

"Jeff and Marcie Jenkins," Susan said. "Greg and I were in their home and tried to tell them something strange was going on. They could be in danger."

"Oh God, you're right," Greg said. He realized Jeff and Marcie could become a target for violence, especially if they became actively suspicious about their father's fate.

Greg recalled Eryn's chilling cry: "Disruptor!"

He took out his new mobile phone. He pulled Jeff's phone number out of the cloud and quickly dialed him.

Then he listened to a series of unanswered rings.

*   *   *

182 . BRIAN PINKERTON

Terry Jenkins whimpered like a lost dog, floating along the ceiling of his small home, unable to control his movements in any meaningful way, trapped to look down at the carnage below, possibly for eternity.

The corpses of his son and daughter-in-law lay sprawled on the floor, rotting. He had witnessed himself doing it – rather, whatever had stolen his physical existence.

The endless silence and unchanging view felt like he was absorbed into some kind of horrible snapshot.

Then, after countless hours, the stillness was shattered by an unexpected sound. It was the cell phone in his son's pocket.

It rang and rang.

And rang.

But the dead young man on the floor could not answer it. He remained as motionless as ever with his limp wife nearby.

Terry Jenkins cried, not liquid tears, just empty air and nothingness, like his own existence.

CHAPTER TWENTY-SEVEN

Greg hung up after his phone call to Jeff Jenkins fell into voice mail.

"No answer." He stood for a moment in the motel room, staring at the notes on the wall. The sheets were dramatically denser than when they were started just a day ago.

"That's it," Greg said. "We need to go see the sheriff. Right now. I don't care if he's been useless so far. This is getting so much bigger, and we're the only ones who have a full picture of, of..." He gestured to the mural of Zeke's frantic handwriting. "...whatever the hell all this means."

"I'm good with that," Susan said.

Zeke hesitated. "But my exclusive. I don't want to just hand all this over...."

"Forget it, Kolchak," said Greg. "We can't do this alone. You'll still have your story."

Susan agreed. "We can't hide in this motel room forever. Sooner or later, they'll track us down."

"But help is on the way," Zeke said. "The agency will be here soon."

"I'm not waiting around for that," Greg said. "It could be weeks. By the time they get here, we could all be...." He searched for the best word choice. 'Dead' wasn't quite right. He finally landed on, "Seriously fucked up. Like what happened to my family."

Zeke frowned and looked down at the floor.

Greg grabbed one of the mini-mart bags and pulled out fresh bandages, a bottle of antiseptic and rolled gauze. He headed to the bathroom to redress his wound. He said, "I'm getting cleaned up. Then we're leaving."

Zeke slowly nodded. Susan handed him his bag of junk food. "Here's your breakfast," she said.

He brightened as he took it and looked inside. "Yes. Thank you."

Susan sat on the bed and used the sharp blade on her new knife to slice open the packaging for her other self-defense items: pepper spray, tear gas and the noise alarm keychain.

Zeke sat in the big chair. He opened a bag of Cheez-Its, unscrewed the cap on his Mountain Dew, and alternated munching with chugging. He watched Susan stuff her purse with protection.

"I'm not going to be a victim. I'm going to fight back," she said. "Even if it's my brother."

Zeke said nothing. The police radio continued to crackle and drone with bursts of voices filling the silence.

★   ★   ★

Zeke drove the Jeep across town with Greg in the front and Susan in the back. Both passengers sat surrounded by a mess of clutter that ranged from dirty clothes to jam-packed three-ring binders of notes and research to crumpled fast food bags. Neither commented on the smell but they exchanged cringing glances to acknowledge it between themselves.

The roadways appeared weirdly ordinary: cars, trucks and farm vehicles coming and going with regular townsfolk who were carrying on with their mundane lives. Most of them had no idea there was anything strange happening in their sleepy little community, apart from some chatter about missing persons that was largely dismissed as 'family matters'.

Greg was ready with a passionate speech to deliver to Sheriff Casey with maximum urgency. He wasn't going to leave the sheriff's office until Casey recognized the full scope of what was happening and how people were being affected. Just because missing people were returning with casual demeanors didn't mean everything was resolved, case closed. He would rip off his bandage to show the sheriff his stab wound to make his point.

The morning sun was bright in a pristine blue sky, leaving the grotesque terror of the previous night in the dark like a strange dream. Greg wasn't going to let his guard down in this illusion of tranquility. He knew more dangers awaited.

Zeke said, "Before we tell the sheriff everything we know, maybe we can get him to sign something to acknowledge I have exclusive book rights to this story. You know, just so he doesn't—"

"Zeke, shut up," said Susan.

In silence, they arrived at the Engles sheriff's office. They turned off the main road to enter a mostly empty parking lot. Greg noticed a vehicle idling in front of the brick and stone building, stopped between the two flagpoles.

He immediately jumped in his seat at the sight.

It was the white van with the dented door.

"Stop. *Stop!*" Greg exclaimed.

"What?" Zeke said.

"Don't go any closer. Park here in the back."

"Why?"

"Just do as I say!"

"All right, but—"

Susan quickly understood. "The white van – is that the one?"

"I think so."

Zeke backed into a parking space, front windshield aimed for a perfect view of the van as it sat in place. He placed the Jeep in park and kept the engine running. Then it dawned on him....

"On the police radio this morning," Zeke said, dazed by his own words. "They said the Hodges family was seen leaving the hospital in a white van."

"I've been looking for it everywhere," Greg said. "This could be the one."

Then Susan said, "Someone's coming out." The glass front doors swiveled open, catching a moment of glare from the sunlight.

Sheriff Casey and Deputy Billings stepped outside. They moved with a slow, steady deliberation, normal to the casual observer but slightly odd to the three witnesses in the Jeep.

"Oh God," said Greg, under his breath. "They don't look right."

"This is the missing link," Zeke said. "This is the part where they disappear...before they come back."

Sheriff Casey and Deputy Billings climbed into the back of the white van with identical pacing and movements, as if automated. The van door rolled shut with a hard *slam*.

"You still want to go talk with them?" Zeke asked.

Greg shot him a glance. "Get ready. Wherever that van goes, you follow."

"I'm on it," Zeke said. He brimmed with enthusiasm. "This is going to be great. Another scoop." He picked up his cell phone, aimed it at the windshield and started snapping pictures of the white van.

Greg quickly moved to lower Zeke's arm. "Don't let them see you."

"Okay, okay," Zeke said. He placed the cell phone in his lap and fumbled with it some more. "Let me just send a note to my contact." He recited as he poked out the message: "Please hurry. Urgent development. You must respond. Stop ghosting me." He chuckled at the minor in-joke and pressed *send*.

At that moment, the white van pulled away from the curb.

Zeke put his hands on the wheel.

Greg said, "Wait a minute, sixty seconds, then follow. Create a space. Not too close."

"You got it."

The white van maneuvered around the parking lot and then turned right onto the main road.

Greg made a succession of nods, as if counting beats, and then said, "*Now.*"

Zeke pulled forward.

"Wherever they're going, it's part of the brainwashing," Susan said. "Someone has planned this all out."

"That's what I'm thinking," Greg said. "There's a mastermind."

"This is really exciting," Zeke said. "As long as we don't get killed."

He turned right and the Jeep entered the main road. The white van was a hundred feet ahead, merging into traffic. Zeke accelerated.

"Don't get too close," Susan said.

"They're not going very fast," Zeke said.

"I'm sure they don't want to raise any suspicions," Greg said. "I wish we could see who's driving."

"You want me to pull up alongside?" Zeke asked. "You can get a picture."

"No. Definitely not," Greg said. "Stay a safe distance behind."

"The book is going to need photos."

"Don't even," Susan said.

The white van continued on the main road for several miles, passing a deluxe shopping center, before turning right on a smaller road heading into the countryside.

A picturesque residential neighborhood and a high school soon gave way to continuous, rolling farmland.

Greg's eyes remained locked ahead. Zeke glanced in the rearview mirror.

"Jesus, there's some asshole tailgating me."

Greg felt a jolt in his chest. He quickly turned around. He saw a red, four-door sedan with smoked window glass obscuring its occupants.

Susan turned around, too. "Oh no...you don't think?"

"I don't know," Greg said.

"Wait, you think they're part of—" Zeke said.

"Just drive normal. Let them pass if they want to."

"I don't think they want to pass."

The three vehicles continued in a straight line together as the smattering of other cars on the road gradually dissipated, leaving them in isolation.

The white van headed deeper into the green countryside, followed by the Jeep, followed by the red sedan.

Susan was turned around in her seat, staring out the back window. "I can't see their faces. But they are definitely tailing us."

The white van began slowing down, occasionally flashing its brakes.

"Shit," Zeke said, reducing his speed. The Jeep was trapped in the middle of the procession. "Now what?"

The road advanced through a continuous forest of dense trees and overgrown brush. "There's nothing out this way," Greg said. "I know this area, it's just woods, no people."

"Where could they be going?" Susan said.

The white van continued to drop its speed. Zeke kept the Jeep a safe distance behind.

Suddenly the red sedan revved its engine behind them. It began to move into the other lane.

"They're going around us," Susan said.

"Thank the baby Jesus," Zeke said. "They weren't tailing us. We were just going too slow."

Zeke gestured with his left arm through the open window, waving. "That's it. Go around, go around!"

The red sedan sped up until it was parallel to the Jeep.

"That's it," Zeke said, still waving. "Go around. No problem."

In a sudden, swift jolt, the red sedan swerved into the Jeep's lane. Zeke barely had enough time to pull in his arm before the red car slammed into the side of the Jeep, breaking the mirror and delivering a powerful *crunch* of metal against metal.

Susan screamed. Greg fumbled for his gun. Zeke tried desperately to maintain control of his car.

The white van immediately regained speed, leaving the red sedan behind to continue its assault on the Jeep.

Zeke instinctively pounded his foot on the accelerator to escape. Before he could gain momentum, the red sedan struck again, this time more forcefully, and the Jeep was pushed into a new trajectory, heading off the road. Zeke hit the brakes. The imagery through the windshield became a wild blur.

The Jeep leapt off the pavement and tumbled down an embankment, bouncing violently before tipping over. It rolled several times before slamming to a hard stop against a thick tree. The impact burst glass and left the vehicle upside down, wheels spinning helplessly in the air, with the doors, hood and bumpers split at the seams, looking like a torn tin can.

Greg fought off the black spots in his vision to stay conscious. He was trapped in the tangle of his seatbelt and the inflation of his airbag. He grasped blindly for the gun, but it was lost in the wreckage. He could see Zeke stirring with a bloody forehead. He called out to the backseat. "Susan! Susan, are you okay?"

"I don't know," she said, sounding groggy. "I can't move."

"So this is how it ends," Zeke said gravely. "Anybody see my phone so I can record a farewell message?"

Greg pushed back on the airbag and the other debris, including dirty clothes, in his lap. He tried to clear some visibility to see through the window.

He saw a pair of legs outside the car. Blue slim-fit jeans, leather boots. Then another pair of legs entered the scene. Tan khakis, loafers.

Greg tried to stretch for a view of more than just legs, and he got one – two unfamiliar men in nice clothes with rifles.

Then he heard a gruff voice from the other side of the car, a third man, stating: "Get them out of there."

In the following minutes, Greg, Susan and Zeke were pulled from the wreckage. The latter required all three men to extract his large frame from the Jeep.

The presence of three rifles guaranteed there was little hope of escape. They had taken away Greg's gun, which had been launched out on the grass. They also retrieved Susan's pocket knife and confiscated her pepper spray and tear gas weapons.

Greg studied their faces but could not identify any of them – they looked like regular townsfolk, ages between thirty and sixty, not particularly menacing, mostly bland looking.

"Who are you? What do you want?" Greg asked.

"How badly are you hurt?" asked one of the men – he wore a simple, blue cotton shirt with a collar and three buttons. His hair was short and tidy.

"Very kind of you to ask," Zeke said. "Speaking for myself, I'm generally feeling all right. I might have a cracked rib, possibly a small concussion. I really should get that looked at, so if we could put in a quick call to 911...."

The man turned to Susan, expressionless. "You?"

"Cut up with broken glass," she said. "My wrist hurts. Why do you care? You did this to us."

Then the question was directed at Greg. "Are you broken?"

"Broken?" Greg said. "I'm lucky. The airbag saved me, the seat belt. I could have been killed. Isn't that what you wanted? To kill us?"

"No," said the man doing most of the talking. The other two stood on either side of him, shoulders aligned, with identical looks of nonchalance.

"No?"

"You have something that is valuable to us."

"Like what?" Susan said.

"Your shells."

And with that, the conversation concluded, although Zeke, Greg and Susan continued to ask questions. "I just want to interview you," Zeke said, which was met with a nonresponse.

The communication became entirely one-sided. "You will follow us into the woods or you will be shot," said one of the men plainly. He wore a white business shirt, wool slacks and dress shoes, and Greg couldn't help wondering if he was one of the missing travelers from the Engles Imperial Inn.

"I choose following you over getting shot," Zeke said. "I want it to go on record that I am being very compliant."

Hoisting their rifles, the three men from the red sedan took Greg, Susan and Zeke deeper into the woods, several hundred yards, until they found a shadowy, thick area of trees that seemed to satisfy them. One of the men also carried a large black leather handbag. When they stopped at their destination, the man reached into the handbag and brought out coils of sturdy rope.

"That's not for us, is it?" Zeke asked.

"It is for you," said the man in the blue shirt with casual simplicity.

"Oh," said Zeke, disappointed.

The three men tied Zeke, Susan and Greg each to a tree. The ropes were tight, restricting their arms, and the knots were out of reach.

"This really hurts, are you sure you couldn't loosen it?" Zeke said.

"We are done here," said one of the men. He wore a relaxed, V-neck sweater and neatly pressed khaki pants. The rifle in his hands looked out of place with his ensemble.

"Where are you going?" Susan said. "What happens to us?"

"We will be back later," said the man with the business shirt.

And with that, the three men from the red sedan abandoned them, retreating back through the woods toward the road.

Once they were out of view, Zeke said, "I don't get it. They could have just shot us when we were pinned in the Jeep. What's this all about? So we can get ravaged by squirrels?"

"The bastards took my knife, otherwise I could cut through this rope," Susan said.

"My phone is somewhere in the Jeep," Zeke said. "My pictures."

"They took my phone," Greg said.

"Mine too," Susan said.

"So now we just sit here in the dirt, tied to trees." Greg looked skyward. "Is that it?"

Zeke pulled at his ropes. "Crikey. We'll probably starve to death out here. Is that what they want?"

"I don't think that's it," Greg said. "It's something else." He continued to look through the treetops into the sky. "Do you see that?"

"See what?" Susan said, also looking up.

"The sky was blue just a few minutes ago. Now it's graying over. There are clouds."

"Clouds, so?" Zeke said.

"Think back to your narrative," Greg said. "Go to the very beginning."

The three of them went silent.

After a moment of contemplation, Susan said, "Oh shit."

And then the rain started. The droplets fell hard with uncommon abruptness, quickly drenching them and their surroundings.

The pellets of rain didn't look right as they plummeted to the earth. They had a strange color and texture. Silvery.

CHAPTER TWENTY-EIGHT

The afternoon arrived and sunny blue skies returned, but the damage had been done.

"We're going to be surrounded by those gross little eggs," Susan said. "It's only a matter of time. And then what?"

Greg thought back to what he had witnessed inside the Hodges' farmhouse. It wasn't pretty. "We'll be covered by a million bugs, inside and out."

Zeke said, "We're advancing through the narrative."

"I don't want to become one of those things," Susan said.

"Which thing?" Zeke said. "Zombie or ghost?"

"Neither!" She pulled against her constraints and tried again to squirm an arm free.

Greg tried to maneuver out of the tightly wound rope that secured him to the base of a big tree. His clothing was torn and his skin was raw and bruised from repeated attempts to extract himself. He couldn't make any progress.

"I have to pee," Zeke said. Then, almost as an afterthought, "I don't want to die."

Greg thought about the ghosts of Janie, Becky and Matthew. He imagined transforming into his own helpless ghost, floating in the treetops of this forest, never to make human contact again.

Susan, sitting in the dirt with her hands tied down at her sides, was able to raise her butt slightly before sinking down again. While a matter of inches, it was the most movement any of them had accomplished since being bound to the trees.

"Are you able to get your arm out?" asked Zeke hopefully.

"No," Susan said. "I'm actually pushing my arm farther down through the ropes."

"What does that accomplish?"

"I can almost…almost reach into my pocket."

"You said they took your knife," Greg said.

"They did. And the tear gas. And the pepper spray. And my cell phone."

"So what's left?"

"That stupid keychain."

"A keychain?" Zeke said. "How's that going to help us?"

"It makes a noise." She grunted as she continued to wiggle up and down, snug against the tree, driving her outstretched fingers closer to her jeans pocket.

"It's one of those keychains with an alarm," Greg said. "You press it and there's a loud noise to cry for help."

"Nobody's going to hear that out here," Zeke said. "We're totally isolated."

"Maybe," Greg said. "But you never know."

Susan's fingers entered her pocket but then slipped out. She grimaced and squirmed, twisting her torso to the best of her ability, even as it made her gasp out in pain.

"Damn it…almost…I just touched it…."

Greg and Zeke watched her and offered coaching. "A little to your left," Zeke said. "Now straight down," Greg said.

Her fingers reentered the pocket and this time advanced deeper.

"I think I got it…I think I can pull it up…."

Greg saw her hand lift out of the pocket, this time with a delicate pinch on the keychain between two fingertips.

"You got it," Zeke said. "Don't drop it."

She extracted the keychain and palmed it into a tighter grip so it wouldn't fall in the dirt.

"You did it!" Greg said.

Susan nodded, sweaty and panting. She remained still for a moment.

"Okay," she said. "Let's give this a try."

Greg studied his proximity to her. Five, maybe six feet. Zeke wasn't much farther.

"I guess I can't cover my ears," Zeke said.

Greg shut his eyes tight, preparing for pain. "Okay, give it a blast."

"Here goes...sorry, guys."

She squeezed the button on the keychain.

An ear-splitting, high-pitched tone shrieked without mercy.

Birds immediately fluttered from the treetops. Squirrels scampered.

Zeke screamed. "*Holy shit, is that loud!*"

Greg squirmed and tried to turn his head away, barely able to partially press one ear against the tree. It felt like an ice pick going through his head.

When the blast came to a cold stop, Susan murmured, "Oh my God. My ears are ringing. They hurt."

"Great, so I'll be deaf and then dead," Zeke muttered.

"Maybe someone heard it, though," Greg said. "Let's add our voices. Let's do it now."

Then Greg shouted at the top of his lungs: "HELP! HELLLLP!"

Susan joined in. "HELP US, SOMEBODY PLEASE! HELP!"

Zeke added, "WE'RE TIED TO SOME TREES AND WE'RE GOING TO BE EATEN BY BUGS!!"

Greg said, "You probably don't need all that information. A simple 'Help' will suffice."

"This is crazy," Susan said, and her voice turned weary and frustrated. "There's nobody around for miles. We need to keep squirming with these ropes. If one of us can get just one arm free...."

"Uh oh," said Greg.

"Great, on top of everything else, now we have an 'uh oh'?" Zeke said.

"Look straight ahead. Those weren't there ten minutes ago."

"What?" Susan said.

"Look."

Roughly fifteen feet in front of them, the brown dirt and green grass added a new color: a smattering of yellow.

"Eggs," Greg said.

Zeke turned his head to view their broader surroundings. "I see more over there, to the right. Oh – and another batch after that."

Susan said, "And to my left...under that tree over there."

"They're starting to show up everywhere," Greg said.

"That's it, we're doomed," Zeke said.

"Maybe if we're really, really quiet and don't move, the bugs won't see us," suggested Susan.

"Do I look like I'm part of this tree?" Zeke asked.

"Well," Susan said. "We can pretend."

"We don't have a lot of options," Greg said. "I mean, we can close our eyes and mouth as tight as we can. But they can still get in our nose and ears...."

"If I could reach some pebbles, maybe I could block my nostrils," Susan said.

"How am I going to stick rocks in my nose? I can't even move!" Zeke said. "Let's just accept our fate with dignity and see where it takes us."

Greg sighed. He studied the scene before him. The eggs continued to multiply like yellow spots before his eyes.

★   ★   ★

Greg had no way of knowing the time. It could have been one hour later or three or four, but the next step in their destiny arrived inevitably with a tiny sound and image:

A black speck fluttering above the grass, emitting a simple, steady, almost subliminal hum.

"Is that...one of them?" whispered Greg.

Zeke considered it. "Could be an ordinary fly."

"It's just going in circles," said Susan softly.

"Shit. There's another one."

"Another two."

"They're hatching."

"Stop talking. Be still."

Greg froze, which wasn't difficult, because he was bound very tightly to a tree. He kept his eyes open to watch the developments unfold.

The tiny black specks continued to grow in numbers, rising from the grasses in every direction. For several minutes they hovered without destination, aimless newborns.

It didn't last.

Greg watched the insects gradually gravitate toward one another, creating larger and denser formations, as if drawn together by a magnetic force.

No one said anything.

A few more minutes passed, and the mass of insects steadily amplified in both sight and sound. They organized as a single entity, blotting out a portion of the forest, buzzing in tandem like an angry chainsaw. With a sudden swoop, they flowed in one direction toward a common target: Greg, Susan and Zeke, trapped at the base of three trees, offered like food to the monstrous swarm.

Susan screamed.

Zeke joined in, then Greg. It was the only thing left to do, the last act of desperation from hopeless victims.

They screamed in fear, pleaded for mercy and cried for help.

"SOMEBODY! ANYBODY! HELP US!" screamed Susan as the black cloud buzzed closer, filling her vision.

Susan still grasped the keychain alarm, and in a final gesture, she pressed it one more time to send an alert to anyone, anywhere, that might be close enough to hear it.

The shrill tone blasted so loud that it overwhelmed even the roar of the buzzing insects. She continued to press it, prolonging the painful shriek, feeling tears run down her face as she confronted her impending doom.

The black swarm stopped advancing, momentarily frozen just a few feet from her face.

Encouraged, Susan continued to sound the high-pitched alarm, even as her own eardrums throbbed.

Then she witnessed the black cloud break apart, as if punctured. The insects scattered in a million directions and retreated into the woods. She kept pressing on the keychain alarm until there were no more bugs in sight. They had disappeared, driven away.

Susan finally stopped the unbearable noise.

The forest fell into abrupt, stone silence.

She looked over at Zeke and Greg. Both had shut their eyes tight and clamped their mouths shut, hoping to keep the bugs away from their orifices.

Slowly, Zeke opened one eye. Then the other.

Greg opened his eyes.

"Where...did they go?"

"It was the keychain," Susan said, breathless.

"How?" Greg said, slowly regaining some hearing.

"It must be the frequencies, the kilohertz range," Zeke said. "It repelled them."

"How is that even possible?" Greg said.

"Zeke's right," said Susan. A realization dawned on her, and she excitedly relayed a memory. "I – I knew a farmer who used ultrasound frequencies because he didn't want to use pesticides. He said it worked on certain insects to save his crops. Something about overwhelming their senses. A lot of bugs have receptors outside their bodies, like antennae, that are super sensitive. Some pitches are more than they can handle."

"So we scared them off?"

"For now."

"I'm half deaf, thanks to your gizmo, but I guess it was worth it. I don't have bugs down my throat," Zeke said. "So now what happens? We still can't go anywhere."

"We wait," Greg said. "Because if I'm not mistaken, they're going to come back for us in a white van. Like they did for Eryn, the Hodges family, the sheriff, and everyone else."

Zeke said, "So, we're still screwed? Out of the frying pan and into the fire, and all that?"

"No," Greg said. "Not exactly. I have an idea. When they get here, let's act like we've been neutralized by the bugs. It's what they're expecting."

"Yes – yes, we'll fake it," Susan said. "Think back to when they picked up the sheriff and the deputy. They looked normal, they just didn't say anything and moved like robots. We can do that."

Zeke took this in and said, "Indeed. We're at the part of the narrative where the consciousness separates from the physical being. We know the drill. We'll just go along with it."

"And see where it goes," Susan said.

"Fantastic," Zeke said. "We're just one van ride away from getting all of our answers."

CHAPTER TWENTY-NINE

The lush forest colors drained into murky black and white as evening took over with a firm grip. The probing moonlight and a loose scattering of stars provided just enough illumination for Greg to see his two partners outlined as shadows stuck to tree trunks. They murmured to one another to stay awake, awaiting their next fate with open eyes.

Zeke mumbled, "I'm so hungry right now, I would eat tree bark. I really would. Grass. Moss. A frog...."

Susan adjusted her uncomfortable position the best she could – a few centimeters here and there – and voiced her own concerns. "Any wolves or coyotes out here? It would be kind of sad to make it this far and then...."

"Hold it," Greg said in a sharp whisper. "I see something. Everybody quiet."

The three captives stopped talking.

In the distance, in front of them, small spots of white light bobbed like fireflies.

"Flashlights," said Zeke softly.

"They're coming for us," Susan said.

"Remember what we said – nobody talk," Greg said. "Act quiet and submissive...like the sheriff and his deputy. We're just leftover bodies. Be like a robot."

Zeke said, "That would be kind of fun under any other circumstances."

"Ssssh," Susan said. The three of them went silent.

Greg went limp, like a puppet with severed strings. He leaned back against the tree and locked his eyes in a blank stare, looking forward.

Footsteps crunched in the grass, coming closer.

Flashlight beams struck their faces. Greg tried not to flinch.

He could see the shadowy forms of two tall men carrying rifles. One of them spoke in a monotone to the other.

"Untie them."

A nondescript-looking man in his forties – probably a previously captured body himself – stepped behind the trees.

One by one, he undid the knots that Greg, Susan and Zeke had been unable to reach.

Greg felt the ropes loosen around him. He remained very still.

The second man rejoined the first, standing before the trio of slumped, wordless beings.

The first man spoke, again in a flat voice devoid of human emotion, as if reciting programmed lines.

"The three of you will come with us. You will follow our lead. We will take you to base operations."

Greg, Susan and Zeke remained immobile and uncertain. Greg tried not to shift his eyes to look at what his partners were doing.

"Pull away from the tree and stand up!" came the impatient command.

Greg slowly leaned forward, no longer bound tightly by the rope, which slackened and slipped toward the ground. He rose to his feet – stiffly, painfully, fighting off the numbness that painted parts of his body.

Susan followed his lead and then so did Zeke, who made a small, uncontrollable grunt.

The two men with guns said nothing, apparently satisfied.

"Come," the first one demanded, waving the flashlight beam forward. "You will follow our direction."

The mysterious duo led the way. They advanced through the forest, heading back toward the main road. Greg, Susan and Zeke walked in even steps behind them, trading a few secret glances, but remaining devoid of any personality or resistance.

During the walk, they circled past Zeke's badly damaged Jeep. It remained upside down in a ditch below the roadway, dormant like a dead beast.

Head down, Greg continued to march in compliance behind the tall men with rifles, ascending the rugged terrain to the concrete pavement above. The white van awaited, blinkers activated and creating a minor strobe effect in the dark.

There were no other vehicles in sight.

Greg and Susan stopped at the edge of the road. One of the men unlocked the rear door of the white van and slid it open with a hard pull. He turned to face his three new passengers – and discovered only two.

"Where is the big one?"

The other man immediately took the rifle off his shoulder. He stared into the darkness of the forest.

Greg tried not to spin too quickly to see what was happening, keeping his emotions in check. He turned slowly and casually. His heart thumped wildly, betraying his outer calm.

Greg thought, *That idiot! Where did he go? Did he make a run for it? He'll blow it for all of us.*

He looked over at Susan for her reaction. She remained very still, frozen in a standing position, looking back toward the forest.

A single tear of sweat rolled down one side of her face.

The two tall men were prepared to go hunting for Zeke, taking initial steps back down the embankment, when the fat man emerged from behind the wreckage of the Jeep.

He now wore his beloved 'green alien' baseball cap on his head.

He climbed up the hill to rejoin his captors.

He stopped to get his hat? thought Greg incredulously.

The two men with rifles studied Zeke as he struggled up the hill.

One of them rationalized, "He needed to complete his ensemble."

The other said, "Instinct. Force of habit. Stupid creatures."

With Zeke now standing alongside Greg and Susan, the armed men ordered all three into the back of the van.

They obeyed wordlessly.

The back door slid shut with a loud *wham*, followed by the click of a lock.

Greg sat in the middle, with Zeke and Susan on either side of him. Zeke's large form pushed into Greg's space. Greg was careful not to look the others in the eyes, offering no attempt at communication that would question their status as empty vessels.

The two tall men climbed into the front. The one in the passenger seat held the guns. The white van returned to the road and accelerated forward.

The man in the passenger seat turned around to look at the backseat occupants. He stared into their eyes for a long moment and received equally deadened expressions. Then he turned back around.

As the white van sped solo into the dark of night, Zeke very slowly and secretly reached into his pants. His hand slid under his belt, into his underwear.

Greg glimpsed this and tried to follow without making any suspicious movements of his head or eyes.

Zeke extracted his cell phone.

Clever son of a bitch! thought Greg. Zeke had not stopped at the wreckage for his hat. His real motivation was retrieving his phone, which had fallen loose in the crash.

Greg subtly watched what Zeke was doing. Zeke kept his hands held low, out of sight of the two men in the front seat.

Zeke was composing a text message with minimal movements. Greg could just barely make out the letters.

Zeke entered: SOS.

*   *   *

Seated squashed in the middle of the backseat, stiff and staring forward like a stupid mannequin, Greg had a perfect view through the front windshield.

He watched the white van advance many miles deeper into the Engles countryside, a stretch of dark that was occupied by acres and acres of sprawling farm fields with very few residents.

The two tall men in the front did not offer casual conversation. They only spoke when necessary.

Zeke had returned the cell phone to deep inside his underpants, under his fat rolls. Greg reminded himself to never borrow it to make a call and hold it to his face.

After twenty very silent minutes, the white van reached the end of the road, and from glimpses of signage, Greg realized where they were.

Strickland Farms.

Dennis Strickland was a rugged, longtime Engles resident – probably in his sixties or seventies – and owned the biggest farm in the area. He mostly kept to himself and his immediate family members, not a social person but well respected for the size of his successful farming operation.

The location was perfect.

If someone wanted a big, isolated hideout, unseen and undisturbed, this was a wise choice.

The white van entered a long gravel driveway leading to an impressive compound of several buildings – barns, sheds, silos, a stable and an attractive, two-story home. The van made a turn and headed toward the largest structure of the estate – a giant red barn with huge doors, secured shut.

In the dark of night, the barn emitted lights from high windows. Dozens of cars were parked off to one side at odd angles in a large, flat field.

Greg did his best not to react to the dramatic sight.

The white van rolled to a stop in front of the barn.

The driver parked the vehicle. He climbed out, along with his equally deadpan companion, and they circled over to the side door. They rolled it open and issued a simple instruction:

"Get out."

Zeke gracelessly emerged from the van, spilling out with a tumble until he found his footing. Greg and Susan followed, with less of a scene. The trio then stood alert and awaited further orders.

The two tall men slung their rifles over their shoulders. They studied the faces of their captives.

Greg didn't even blink.

"I will announce your arrival," said the taller of the two men, by maybe half an inch. "Wait here."

He left, and his companion remained standing in front of Greg, Susan and Zeke, one hand on the rifle.

The taller man walked over to a small side entrance in the barn. He slid inside, keeping the door from opening fully.

Greg could hear voices coming from the barn. Activity.

After a few minutes, the tall man emerged with a svelte older man with a healthy stock of gray hair, wearing a plaid flannel shirt and cowboy boots.

Dennis Strickland.

Strickland walked toward them in a steady, even pace. His face was weathered and unchanging, without emotion. He had been converted. He was now *one of them*.

Strickland stood before Greg, Susan and Zeke. He studied the trio for a long, silent moment.

"Good," he said impassively. "Three more. I will prepare for their occupation."

Occupation? Greg thought. He tried not to express his elevated fear.

Strickland hesitated, cocking his head like a bird. He took a step closer to Zeke.

He looked into Zeke's face, almost nose to nose, then stepped back.

"Son, remove that hat," he said. "It's disrespectful."

Zeke hesitated, registering the request. He brought a hand up to his head in a mechanical movement.

He gripped the bill of his novelty baseball cap, which displayed a cartoon stereotype of a green alien face with big black eyes.

He removed the cap from his head and dropped it to the dirt.

Strickland nodded his approval.

Then he said, "Bring them inside."

CHAPTER THIRTY

Greg, Susan and Zeke entered the big, red barn.

The transition from middle-of-the-night country darkness to a powerfully lit, indoor space immediately hurt their eyes. There was a lot to take in. The barn was populated with dozens of people, some of them familiar, many of them not, herded like cattle and making small talk. Across the room, Greg glimpsed the Hodges family, Jesse Walton, Carl Peters and Eryn Swanson. He assumed he was also in the presence of Terry Jenkins, Clay Mueller, the Imperial Inn guests, the Riverwoods Campgrounds campers and anyone else who had temporarily gone missing. This was home base.

Dennis Strickland led his three newcomers to the center of the barn, which was dominated by a massive bulk of the strangest machinery they had ever seen. It was silvery and covered with hundreds of tiny slits. One section was dominated by a network of elaborate tubing that looked like a nest of snakes. The entire apparatus glistened and vibrated unevenly, as if pulsing with a living, breathing organism.

It looked like nothing from this world.

"This is the transmission station," said Strickland. "You will remain here and wait your turn. There are two others ahead of you. *Stay.*"

Then he walked away, leaving them standing there. Greg maintained the blank look he knew they expected. For the moment, they were unguarded, assumed to be dormant in bland compliance, stripped of their personalities.

"This is really fucked up," Zeke said between gritted teeth.

"Ssh!" Susan said.

"I really need to take video of this for my blog. That thing looks like a Giger painting."

"If you even try, we are dead," said Greg firmly under his breath. "Don't say another word. I mean it."

The three of them fell silent. Greg wouldn't even look at Susan or Zeke, afraid they might exchange a nonverbal communication that would raise suspicion.

Then:

"Hello, Greg," said a familiar female voice.

Greg did not turn around but waited for the individual to enter his vision. It was Janie.

She held Matthew in her arms. She was accompanied by Becky, who stared wordlessly.

Oh shit, thought Greg, overwhelmed by confusion over what to do. Their previous encounters had turned violent.

But this time Janie regarded him differently, no longer threatened or threatening.

"Welcome to your future," she said.

Greg simply looked at her.

"I know you're unable to speak," she said. "Your current form is raw instinct, physically capable but absent of independent thought. Soon you will receive your new life, like me and the children, and it will be a superior installation that renders your previous tenant obsolete."

She turned toward Dennis Strickland, who was leading Sheriff Casey and Deputy Billings to the large, pulsing bulk of silver machinery. Casey and Billings obeyed Strickland with empty expressions.

"You're next," Janie said. "This is a special occasion. You've met our commander? Your previous identity would have known his previous identity. Dennis Strickland of Strickland Farms. He is 001. The first of a new breed of humanity that will replace the legacy population. The test phase has been a major success. Next, we scale it for the world. A vast migration is coming. You are among the early adopters, a pioneer. Soon your shell will be replenished with a being from a distant star."

Zeke was close enough to eavesdrop and involuntarily released a small gasp. Hearing the impromptu sound tightened the knots in Greg's stomach.

Fortunately, Janie appeared not to notice. She kept talking.

"We either had to kill you or possess you," she said. "We had no choice. You knew too much. This is the better option, don't you think? We can be together again. You, me, Becky, Matthew. We'll go home. We'll resume our lives together as a family unit. That's all we ever wanted, right?"

Greg said nothing, holding everything back, including anger and sorrow. This was no longer his wife and children.

"*Attention!*" shouted Strickland from the center of the room. He stood before the grandiose, pulsating mound of silver machinery. "The time has come!"

His collected audience turned to watch. They looked as though they were attending a play or a church service: ordinary looking people in regular clothes, politely assembled.

Strickland addressed them in a loud, commanding voice. "We are gathered here tonight to welcome our newest brethren. You will bear witness to the activation of 054 through 058 of our initial test series. Remember them. Support them. Know that they are one of us when you see them on the outside. We will add to our numbers every day, infiltrating a failing race and bringing new hope."

The crowd clapped respectfully.

"Now we shall proceed with the rebirth of 054 and 055, known to the locals as Sheriff Earl Casey and Deputy Tom Billings."

More applause.

Janie, carrying the baby and holding Becky's hand, stepped over to get a closer look at the ceremony.

Greg remained stiff and emotionless, watching the process unfold. Strickland placed Sheriff Casey and Deputy Billings in a standing position inside a human-shaped indentation in the machine. As if responding to their presence, the machine shuddered and produced a hissing suction. Various tubes, like tentacles, unraveled and attached to their faces, throats, chests, arms and legs.

One of the thin slits on the other side of the machine began to glow red, selected to partake in the processing. Greg speculated the slit represented a stagnant life-form waiting to be injected into a new host.

"Hello, sis."

Greg's eyes looked over to his right to find the source of the voice.

It was Susan's brother, Steve.

He stood nearby. He had noticed Susan.

Susan refrained from responding, and Greg was grateful for that.

Her brother did not expect her to respond. He simply said, "Watch and learn. You will soon follow." His voice was calm. Then he repeated what Janie had told Greg.

"Welcome to your future."

And he walked away.

The silver machinery began to hum – not exactly a machine-like rattle, more like the unification of thousands of otherworldly voices. The noise filled the barn. Everyone stood perfectly still, observing the proceedings in rapt attention. Strickland stood back, arms dropped at his sides, watching the tubes change color from a milky white to a luminous yellow-green. The machine's entire structure vibrated more aggressively, and the blend of extraterrestrial voices increased in pitch, as if calling out to the stars.

Sheriff Casey and Deputy Billings began to flop around in the tangle of tubing, showing new signs of life, eyelids flickering, jaws moving, limbs shaking with a rubbery looseness.

The audience watched with total concentration, mesmerized. With all eyes on the proceedings, Greg finally felt brave enough to glance over at Zeke and Susan.

Zeke was secretly recording the event on his cell phone.

"God damn it," Greg said. "What the hell, Zeke."

"Listen," Susan said, inching closer to Greg in a sideways shift. "Nobody's watching us right now. They think we can't run away. So…let's run away."

Everyone in the barn, including Strickland, continued to stare at the transformation of the two human beings receiving an injection of alien life-forms.

"I'm up for that," Greg said, trying to speak with minimal lip movement. "Just go slow. Real slow."

"I got what I need," Zeke said, casually slipping the phone back into his pocket.

In small movements, the three began inching toward the side door.

The silver machine continued chugging, streaming a surround-sound chorus of shrill, wordless voices that sounded like ecstasy, pain or both.

Greg took one last look at his wife, daughter and baby son, who faced the proceedings with heavenly rapture. He reminded himself once again that they were not his real family.

He joined Zeke and Susan in slipping out of the barn, undetected.

Once outside in the darkness, they ditched the limp robot movements and picked up their pace, heading for the road.

"*Whoa, stop,*" said Greg in a tight voice, coming to a sudden halt on the gravel. The others did the same, seeing a looming obstacle up ahead.

The two tall, deadpan men who brought them to Strickland Farms were walking back to the parked white van. They were probably heading for another pick-up. They blocked the immediate getaway path, looking the other way.

"Hide," whispered Susan. "Go in there."

A few yards away, there was a large wooden shed with the door already open, revealing a dark interior. The structure was smaller than the barn, but still wide and deep.

Greg, Susan and Zeke hurried inside, careful not to kick up gravel or make any other noise.

Once inside, Zeke pulled out his cell phone and turned on the flashlight app. He pointed it into the dark reaches of the shed, revealing conventional contents: a large and medium tractor, assorted attachments for harvesting, and a broad selection of farming tools and equipment. A crowded workbench dominated the back wall.

"Maybe there are some keys to these tractors," Susan said.

"What, and we ride it out of here? Like nobody's going to follow?" Zeke stepped closer to the big tractor, shining the beam up into its cabin.

"It beats running on foot," Greg said. He walked over to the first tractor and climbed up to peer inside at the driver's seat. After a moment, he scooted down. "I don't see any keys."

He tried the smaller tractor. Also no keys.

"Maybe they're on the workbench." Susan walked over, and Greg soon joined her, with Zeke holding the light steady so they could see.

For a moment, the light beam landed on a pack of Marlboro cigarettes and a book of matches.

"I don't see any keys..." Susan said.

"Those matches give me an idea," Greg said. "Zeke, aim the flashlight over to the left – is that what I think it is?"

The beam floated and landed on a collection of gasoline cans lined up on the floor.

Greg studied the cans for a long moment. Then he said, "Let's burn that son of a bitch to the ground."

Susan looked at him. "Burn what?"

"That machine, spaceship, filing cabinet of alien souls, whatever the hell it is. That ugly thing that's injecting people with other life-forms. Destroy it."

"I don't think they'll like that very much," Zeke said.

Greg was already grabbing a pair of gas cans. "Each of you – take a couple."

Susan said, "But what about all those people inside? What about my brother? Your family?"

"Trust me," Greg said. "That is no longer your brother. My wife, my children – it's no longer them. We can't be fooled. That's how they survive and keep multiplying. They look just like us – but they aren't. That barn is coming down."

But the lingering thought of burning the occupants alive troubled him. He said, "Listen, we'll leave the doors untouched so people can get out, but that – that insane machine will not possess another human being."

Zeke considered the action plan. "It will make for good video."

Susan took ahold of two cans. "I'm in," she said.

Zeke picked up the remaining red containers. "Let's make this happen."

For a moment, they simply looked at one another, well aware that the outcome of their actions could end well – or not.

"Okay," Greg said. "Let's go save the world."

CHAPTER THIRTY-ONE

Dennis Strickland, aka 001, aka chief commander of a prototype race of alien-human fusion, stood before the two newest members of the Great Migration and welcomed them to resurrection.

Sheriff Casey and Deputy Billings now hosted beings from a distant star beneath their skin. The suction tubes fell away from the two men as they separated from the transmission station and took their first, shaky steps forward, reborn.

The gathered crowd welcomed them with cordial applause – a traditional gesture of appreciation inherited from their human instincts.

"We will now proceed to our next three subjects," announced Strickland. "Hosting shells 056, 057 and 058, please step forward so that we may begin the transfer of life."

When his instructions were not met with a prompt response, Strickland stiffened in a moment of confusion.

His eyes searched the barn. Not only did the subjects not advance toward him, they were nowhere to be seen.

"This is not protocol," Strickland said. He turned a complete circle, examining the interior of the barn.

A woman's voice shouted out from the crowd. It was Janie Garrett. Her words created a ripple of panic across the collected masses.

"*They're gone!*"

★　　★　　★

Working quickly in the dark of night, Greg, Susan and Zeke tossed bales of hay against the sides of the barn and soaked them with gasoline.

As the final gas can was emptied, an eruption of raised voices could be heard coming from inside the barn.

"Sounds like our absence has been discovered," Zeke said.

"Stand back," Greg said. The strong stench of gas filled his nostrils. He struck a single match and used it to ignite the rest of the matchbook.

"Oh shit, here they come," Susan said. The first few emerged from the side door, eyes wide and mouths gaping, the surfacing of a furious mob.

Greg tossed the burning set of matches into the hay. With a roaring *whoomph*, flames raced along the trail of gasoline, attaching to the sides of the barn.

"Run!" shouted Greg as a roaring fire lit up the night.

The only clean getaway route led into an adjacent cornfield. Greg, Zeke and Susan dashed for cover. They ducked into the tall, dark cornstalks, hands outstretched to push their way forward, feeling a rising heat wave behind them.

A shrill chorus of voices shrieked in a collective rage. Greg could hear the thrashing and crunching of the horde entering the cornfield in feverish pursuit. He heard Eryn Swanson yelling angrily into the night, "*Disruptor!*"

Greg struggled to sprint between the rows of corn, blinded by darkness, smacked across the face and chest, stumbling on uneven ground but not falling. The rush of followers grew louder and closer, coming not only from behind but also approaching from the sides, choking off avenues of escape.

Greg lost track of Susan and Zeke in the dark, and then his own sense of direction collapsed into disorientation. Everyone in the cornfield became an anonymous, frantic shadow, fighting a path forward in a stampede of trampling, snapping and cracking. He maintained a distance from everyone else, pushing through openings where he could see them.

Then he heard Susan scream – perhaps twenty or thirty feet away – and instinctively ran toward her. He bounced off another body crossing in his direction and tumbled hard. He hurried back to his feet and then felt a strong grip on his shirt collar.

"I caught one!"

Greg fought hard, but a small crowd engulfed him, grabbing at his limbs and hair. He felt himself being lifted off the ground – then tossed into someone else, fat and soft. It took him a few seconds to realize he was on top of Zeke, who lay sprawled on his back. Then he saw Susan on the other side of Zeke, sitting up with nowhere to go. He moved off Zeke, and they slowly sat up together.

A large crowd surrounded Greg, Zeke and Susan. They stood around them, shoulder to shoulder, forming a wall. The cornfield quickly fell into silence.

Greg could hear the distant crackling of fire consuming the barn. He smelled the acidic smoke.

"Your noisemaker," whispered Zeke, looking at Susan.

She stared at him for a moment, eyes wide and scared, and then realized what he meant. She casually reached into her pocket and slid out the keychain with the sonic alarm.

Greg covered his ears.

She abruptly held it up and squeezed the trigger.

The device shrieked, shattering the silence and sending the wall of people stumbling backward, grimacing in pain.

Susan extended the sharp tone without pause, slowly standing up. Greg and Zeke also rose from the ground, hands clamped over their ears, cringing from the audio attack.

The circle of possessed human bodies continued to back off, and for a moment, Greg felt hope even as his eardrums were ready to explode.

Then a man stepped forward, raising a shovel. He swung it hard, striking Susan in the back of the head. She collapsed to the ground, dropping the keychain, bringing the high-pitched shriek to a sudden halt.

The man with the shovel advanced closer, and Greg recognized him as Steve, Susan's brother.

"That was bad," he said to his sister.

She struggled to a seated position, blood trickling down one side of her head.

Steve brought the blade of the shovel down to the ground, scooping up the keychain. He lifted it up and then gave it a toss deep into the cornfield, out of reach and lost in the darkness.

Susan stared up at her brother. She faced a stranger.

"Why?" she said.

He did not answer.

Dennis Strickland entered the circle. He stared down at Susan, Zeke and Greg. No one spoke for a long moment. Smoke continued to fill the air.

"They have destroyed our means of transition," Strickland said in a plain voice. "But it has not stopped our mission. It has only caused a delay."

He looked at Steve. "Use your shovel to kill them. Use the blade to cut off their heads. Then use the shovel to bury them, here, in this cornfield. They are the enemy. Execute them."

Steve looked down at the three prisoners with a flat expression, unmoved by his duty. He simply said, "Yes."

Susan looked up at him, tears trickling down her cheeks.

He stared back, impassive.

He lifted the shovel, prepared to deliver a fatal blow.

Then he froze.

A sudden snap of bright lights shocked the space around them, piercing the cornfield from multiple directions. The lights, combined with the smoke, took on an eerie, hazy glow.

An approaching rush of movement rustled through the cornstalks, spread wide in a semi-circle and drawing closer.

Strickland turned and faced the sudden commotion, staring into the cornfield with blazing eyes.

"*Who goes there?*" he shouted.

The oncoming wave rippled through the corn, revealing hulking shadows with circular white lights that expanded larger and brighter until they nearly blinded their targets.

A brigade of soldiers in combat fatigues burst into view, aiming powerful flashlights mounted on automatic rifles.

"Stand where you are with your arms raised above your heads!" ordered a voice through a megaphone.

Greg stood up alongside Zeke and Susan, obeying the instructions with everybody else.

Steve dropped the shovel and raised his hands.

Strickland was one of the last to submit, surrendering only when a soldier brought the barrel of a gun to his head.

The show of force was resolute. There appeared to be one armed soldier for every person apprehended.

Greg, Susan and Zeke said nothing as they joined the others in a single-file march out of the maze of bent and broken cornstalks and into a clearing on one side of the farmhouse, away from the burning barn.

The lawn was crowded with military vehicles and teams of soldiers in green and gray uniforms. The Strickland farm had been taken over.

"Hold on!" cried out a voice from the darkness. "Not them! Those three – bring them here!"

Greg quickly discovered these orders pertained to him. A soldier directed Greg, Zeke and Susan out of the larger group of captives to join a gathering of officials in dark jackets, standing apart from the military forces.

"Zeke," said one of the officials, stepping forward from the shadows. He wore a dark blue windbreaker. He had short blond hair, rimless glasses and a broad smile.

Zeke recognized him instantly. "Darren!"

"I told you it would only be a matter of time," Darren said. "We received all your messages. We used your cell phone to triangulate your location. That fire certainly helped. You can see it for miles."

Zeke eagerly introduced Greg and Susan to Darren Callahan. "This is my contact at the agency, the guy I've been telling you about." He turned back to face Darren. "So now do you believe me?"

"I never stopped believing," Darren said. "We've been receiving intelligence from a variety of sources, not just you, and more of it every day. This is big, my friend. This one is for real."

Dazed, Greg turned and watched the soldiers frisk and handcuff about fifty prisoners. He couldn't see his family but knew they were somewhere in the crowd. Then he looked back at the burning barn, a raging monster of orange flames reaching high into a night sky of stars.

He knew that going forward, those stars would have a new meaning.

CHAPTER THIRTY-TWO

Greg sat in a large orange chair in the lobby of the Engles Imperial Inn in the middle of the night, dirty and exhausted, with Susan and Zeke seated nearby. His past and present crashed in a dizzying throb of déjà vu. He used to manage this hotel and spend a lot of time here, talking with staff, overseeing the operations, and observing the parade of strangers that floated in and out of the building in a small chapter of their ongoing lives.

U.S. Special Forces had taken over the hotel as a command center, which made some sense, given that it was a big empty building and had a lot of rooms. The fifty-five 'inflicted' citizens rounded up from the Strickland farm had been placed in fifty-five individual hotel rooms on floors three through five and subjected to interrogation, medical inspection and full-time watch by armed guards. In an ironic twist, many of the prisoners previously occupied these hotel rooms as travelers, prior to the invasion of extraterrestrial insects that purged their true personas. In the middle of the night, a white van made multiple trips to relocate their physical beings.

The individuals captured at Strickland Farms each received an initial analysis that found them physically sound but mentally remote, clinging to inherited memories and instinctive routines but possessed with stubborn, new personalities.

Greg, Zeke and Susan had been subjected to their own lengthy interviews upon arrival, sharing every shred of information they knew with agency officials, including their own narrow escape from becoming 'one of them'.

Now they had been placed in the hotel lobby to await further instruction. Susan's head injury was bandaged, and she was told she had a mild concussion from the whack of the shovel wielded by her brother, who was now one of the prisoners being held in an 'interrogation space' with a queen bed, television and private bathroom. Zeke was busy scribbling notes on a pad of paper he found behind the front desk, trying to capture every moment of his adventure for future posterity. Greg stared at the carpet and its ugly brown and orange patterns, representative of the Imperial Inn corporate branding. He thought about Jesse and Carl Peters undergoing questioning on the floors above him. He felt sorry for Jesse. He didn't care about the fate of Carl Peters.

A round wooden table in front of them had been filled with a variety of snacks and sodas taken from the hotel's small mini-mart selection. Most everything had been consumed, leaving wrappers and empty plastic bottles.

It was a little after three a.m. when Darren Callahan entered the lobby to check on them, breaking their tired silence with an energized, "How's it going?"

"Worn out," Greg said. "What are you learning?"

Darren stood before them and sighed. "Not much. Like you all said, they're possessed. They aren't the same people. And they're not anxious to tell us a whole lot."

"Your best bet is Strickland," Zeke said. "Apparently he was the first one and then directed everything that followed."

"He's been difficult as well," Darren said. "He just looks at us... and scowls."

"So what's next?" Susan said. "I need to lie down. In a real bed."

"That's why I'm here," Darren said. "We have rooms prepared for each of you. On the second floor, away from the interviews. You can sleep, shower. We'll make sure your rooms are guarded – and that you receive fresh clothes."

Greg, Susan and Zeke exchanged weary glances. Susan finally said, "Okay."

"I only ask that you refrain from contacting anybody about this right now," Darren said. "It'll interfere with our investigation. We're trying to keep it classified for at least a couple more days, but we know that word could get out. Once it does, we expect a crush of media like no one has ever seen before."

"Don't forget," said Zeke, holding a handful of notes, "I'm the authorized chronicler of this story. You and I have a relationship that goes way back. Remember all those great collectibles you got from me? Well, consider this. I'm willing to part with my grandest prize. My Kenner 1978 Darth Vader action figure in the original packaging, unopened. There isn't another mint one available in the world."

Darren broke out into a grin. "I'm sure we can work something out."

Susan stood from an orange chair, impatient. "All right. Lead me to one of these rooms. I'm done."

Greg and Zeke also stood. Zeke brushed away a lap full of crumbs from a meal of cookies and potato chips.

Darren said, "I'll provide you with my cell phone number. Call me from the room phone if you need anything. I mean it, anything at all."

⋆   ⋆   ⋆

Greg was assigned to room 206, which looked just like all of the other rooms in the hotel, presented in an all-too-familiar layout and colors.

Greg locked the door – bolt and chain – and checked through the peephole to make sure the promised armed guard remained at his station. He did.

Greg stripped down to his underwear, closed the heavy shades and turned off all the lights. He slipped between the cool, crisp sheets and lowered his head on a fluffy pillow.

For a moment, he simply lay motionless and felt the beating of his heart – still accelerated, locked into panic mode. He attempted breathing exercises to slow it down. He desperately needed rest.

His mind swirled. It was deeply strange to be back at an Imperial Inn, staying in one of the rooms, a routine he had endured over and over for his job. It gave him a strange, floating feeling, moving through the crosscurrents of time and space, somehow equally present and absent.

He remembered how often he'd lain awake in one of these beds in locations across the Midwest, riddled with guilt. Another evening away from his family. Abandoning them as his wife struggled with two small children. Even though staying at the hotels was related to work, it could feel like a vacation. An escape. He regretted that feeling, but it always persisted.

Greg had almost drifted off when a vision appeared above, skimming the ceiling with a grainy luminescence.

His heart began beating faster again.

He focused his eyes.

Ghosts.

A man and a woman. Unfamiliar faces but recognizable as ordinary travelers in life, middle-aged, losing youth to wrinkles and added weight, staring down at him with expressions that begged for empathy.

The gentleman had sideburns and a receding hairline. The woman had bags under her eyes, thin lips, no makeup.

Greg stared at them and knew their circumstance.

When the hotel had been attacked by the storm of bugs, this couple occupied this room. The insects invaded their bodies and purged their consciousness. A white van took their physical presence away to Strickland Farms to accept a new life-form under the skin. Their consciousness stayed behind.

My God, thought Greg. *This same couple probably exists elsewhere in this hotel, undergoing examination by the investigators. Along with Janie, Becky and the baby.*

Greg shut his eyes but he could still sense the apparitions hovering directly above him. Watching him. Sad travelers distanced from their lives....

He finally pulled himself out of the bed and turned on the lights, erasing their images.

He yanked on his filthy, torn clothes and grabbed for the room phone.

He called Darren, who answered on the third ring.

"What's up?" Darren asked.

"I want to go home."

★   ★   ★

A crew-cut soldier named Roberto drove Greg back to his house.

The front porch remained damaged from where Zeke's Jeep slammed into it during the escape from Greg's faux family members and other maniacs. The getaway in Zeke's Jeep felt like weeks ago. In reality, it was one night earlier.

Roberto dropped off Greg but did not drive away.

"I've been instructed to stay here, stand watch and guard the house," said Roberto in a stiff monotone that could almost be mistaken for the speaking patterns of one of the alien-infested people. "We don't know for sure that we've rounded up all the crazies. There could be a few others out there, and they could try to hurt you."

"Thanks, I appreciate it," said Greg, before closing the car door.

Greg entered his house, flicking on a single light and waving back at Roberto before closing the front door.

Standing for an awkward moment in his home, Greg looked around at the weirdly ordinary surroundings. He called out, "Honey, I'm home."

He went into the kitchen for a drink of water.

Then he headed for the bedroom, turning off all the lights behind him.

He fell back on the bed, too tired to remove his clothes or peel back the sheets.

It would be dawn soon, but for now he remained covered in the dark of night. The bedroom disappeared into blackness, window shades drawn, every house light extinguished.

He stared up at the ceiling, waiting.

After a few minutes, his true family reappeared.

Janie, Becky and Matthew existed as soft wisps of light and muted colors, moving with the delicate slow motion of clouds.

He looked into their faces, and the more he focused, the more depth and clarity came into view – a melding of his memories, his imagination and the vague spirits that persisted.

Lying on his back, he reached up with his arm, extending his fingers, as if to touch the intangible.

"I know you still exist," he said.

Then he was certain he saw Janie smile.

He felt awash with comfort, a feeling he hadn't felt in a very long time, extending well before this entire alien episode even began.

He waved his hands at the visions in his darkened room, as if conducting them in some kind of personal symphony, and they circled gently, faint dashes of light, hanging on, staying with him.

CHAPTER THIRTY-THREE

The next morning, Greg returned to the Imperial Inn, driving his own car, with Roberto dutifully following him. Earlier, Roberto helped Greg repair his engine from the damage inflicted by Jesse and Carl – essentially, reconnecting the battery cables and spark plug wires.

Greg felt rested for the first time in a long time but was still burdened with layers of anxiety. Roberto's close watch on him was a steady reminder that his life could still be in jeopardy.

Back in the orange hotel lobby, he joined Susan and Zeke, who were eating breakfast. Someone had revived the hotel kitchen and created a minor buffet for the federal agency staff and various witnesses participating in the investigation of extraterrestrial 'infections'.

Greg filled a plate with scrambled eggs, bacon and a bagel. He sat next to his two comrades, and asked, "How'd you sleep?"

"I had ghosts in my room," said Zeke enthusiastically. "I studied them in the dark. It was phenomenal."

"I had one, too," Susan said, sipping from a Styrofoam cup of coffee. "It was creeping me out, so I slept with the lights on."

Greg explained he had gone home to see his family.

Susan frowned. "I went upstairs to see my brother," she said. "They have him in one of those rooms, with three people watching him and questioning him. A doctor probing him, taking all sorts of readings." She made a deep sigh and continued. "He showed no remorse for hitting me with the shovel. He was chained at the ankles and wrists. He wouldn't say much. It's him on the outside but someone else on the inside. His expression never changed. Basically, it's like before. He has my brother's memories to fall back on, to make it sound like he's the same person, but it's obvious he's not. It's an alien, wearing him like a costume."

After a long silence, Zeke asked, "What about you, Greg? Are you going to go upstairs to see your family?"

"No," Greg said. "I already saw them. The real them, back at the house. Those things upstairs...it's somebody else. Like Susan said, it's just a costume. I want to know what's next. Can they put these people back together like they were meant to be? How do you evict what's inside of them?"

Zeke shrugged. "It's a whole new area of science. If you can call it science."

"Science from another planet," Greg said.

Zeke removed an empty paper plate from his lap and placed it on a nearby table. He picked up his laptop bag from the floor. "They collected my things from the motel and brought them here. I've been working on my notes. They expect a lot of media when all this gets out. The three of us will be bombarded. Listen, while I have you here, do we have an understanding that I have an exclusive on your stories? I mean, hell, we should stick together on this, don't you think? We're like the Three Musketeers meets *The X-Files*. What do you say?"

Susan shrugged, staring tiredly into the room. "Whatever."

"Sure," Greg said. "You can put me in your book. But who will play me in the movie?"

Zeke chuckled gleefully. "I hadn't thought of it. But of course! I wonder who they will get to play me? Someone dashing and handsome, I hope." He ran a quick hand through his hair to smooth it out and then brushed the breakfast crumbs from his shirt.

★   ★   ★

An hour later, Darren stepped into the lobby, shirt untucked and rumpled, face long and exhausted, no doubt from being up all night sorting through the biggest case in the history of his agency – and possibly the only one that turned out to be legit and not a hoax or illusion.

He stood before Zeke.

"He won't speak to us," Darren said. "He wants to talk with you."

Zeke looked up from his orange chair. "Who wants to talk with me?"

"The leader of the pack. Strickland. I mean…the thing inside Strickland."

"He…he asked for *me*?"

"Don't worry, you'll be protected. He's restrained. He can't touch you."

"But why me?"

Darren shrugged. "Let's go and find out."

Zeke stood up, clutching his laptop.

"Leave your things here," Darren said. "If we need them, we'll come back for them. For now – just you."

Zeke looked back at Susan and Greg, who offered no commentary, just blank looks. He placed his laptop on the chair. "Okay then," Zeke said. He gave his arms and legs a small, nervous shake before stepping forward. "Let's do this."

★   ★   ★

The physical presence of Dennis Strickland sat in a hard wooden chair in the center of a secured King Room on the top floor of the hotel. The window shades were drawn, the lights were low, and four agency staff members stood in different spots around the room, wearing sour, frustrated faces.

Darren brought Zeke forward and shut the door behind him. Another man promptly applied the deadbolt and chain.

Zeke slowly approached Strickland, who stared emotionlessly at the floor. His wrists and ankles were in chains.

After an awkwardly long stretch of silence, Strickland raised his head. He stared directly at Zeke with dark eyes ringed with wrinkles.

He said, "Hello."

The agency members in the room exchanged quick glances, as if this was the first word uttered by Strickland in a long time.

Zeke licked his lips nervously, cleared his throat and responded. "Hello."

"Someone get him a chair," instructed Strickland, as if he still led all the actions around him.

Darren quickly obeyed, dragging another wooden chair to the center of the room, positioning it to face Strickland.

Zeke sat in the chair. It creaked under his weight. He said, "Thank you."

Strickland studied Zeke for a long moment. The room around them remained very still.

Then Strickland spoke.

"So, 058, I understand your name in your native tongue is Zeke Abernathy Gorcey."

"Yes...."

"An interesting discovery."

"It is?"

"Indeed. I had no idea. You see, I'm familiar with your work."

"You are?"

"I've read your writings."

"Oh...."

"It's quite alluring," he said. "Your passion. Your perseverance. Your open mind. Your belief in life beyond your own planet."

"Thank you," Zeke said. He guessed this was a compliment, although the flat tone offered no clues.

"You have been writing about extraterrestrial life for many years, am I correct?"

Zeke nodded. "Yes. I mean – it's been speculative. But hopeful. I knew there had to be something else out there. It's been a lifelong obsession, the potential for life on another planet. Ever since I was very young."

"Your lack of arrogance and bias is commendable," Strickland said. "Most of your human counterparts believe only in themselves. They can't fathom the existence of intelligent life somewhere else in the universe. I'm sure my presence is quite unsettling to them. I'm a threat to their sense of supremacy."

"Well," Zeke said, searching for a diplomatic response, "we didn't know...what we didn't know."

"But now you do."

"Yes."

"And I need someone to document it."

"Document...what?"

"Our heritage."

"Your...?"

"Our heritage, Zeke Gorcey. I have chosen you to be our historian. The recorder of a new society on planet Earth. I call it 'Earth' because that is your nomenclature, but I assure you, there will be a rebranding."

Zeke froze. He attempted a string of words and then simply stated, "... What?"

"Someone needs to transcribe our origins, our evolution, the story of how we came to be, the launch of a new generation of intelligent life on this planet. You have the right perspective for this testimonial. You are a keen observer, a researcher, a seeker of truth, an enemy of xenophobia, an eloquent wordsmith, a witness to this interplanetary transition, fully immersed in the changeover from what used to be to *what will*."

Zeke took it all in, awed.

"So what do you say, Mr. Gorcey?"

"I...I would be proud to write your story," Zeke said. "I am humbled."

"I will tell you everything you need to know. Why we came here. How we took over this distant star and made it our own. How we released the lesser beast from inside your shells and replaced it with a significant upgrade, something more worthy of this glorious habitat that you have squandered."

Zeke recognized the insult, even as it was delivered in a casual tone. He wasn't sure of his response and allowed for a moment of silence. You could hear a pin drop in the room. No one moved. Everyone was listening.

"There will be one critical difference in your approach to this story compared with the others you have constructed in your repertoire," spoke Strickland. "You will not be referring to us as the alien. When we populate your entire planet and only a chosen few of your current race remain, *you* will be regarded as the alien."

Zeke mustered the courage to express what was on his mind at that moment. He chose his words carefully to protect his elevated relationship with a visitor from the stars.

"Um, with all due respect, sir," Zeke said, offering a polite smile, "I don't understand the part about...populating the planet. It appears we – they – have stopped that from happening. I – I was in the presence of someone, a – a person, persons, no names, who burned down your barn and destroyed your...people-changing machine. What you were doing...it appears to be canceled. You've been captured. You're here in chains. Your mission…it's over, isn't it?"

Strickland's expression did not change. "No. Not at all. You are wrong about that, Mr. Gorcey. Very wrong."

"So…how…. What do you mean?"

"I came to this region to oversee a simple test. I'm nothing more than a district manager. I report up through a much larger, much more powerful chain of command. We chose a small, isolated country town, not very sophisticated, rather insulated, to conduct a proof of concept. We took over a large barn and set up one of our exchange systems containing an initial batch of preserved life-forms from our home, removed from their physical entrapments in order to adapt to something more appropriate to your atmosphere, namely your own human biology. We executed a series of captures from single residences, farms, a campsite, this hotel. We accomplished our objective to effectively inhabit your shells. You may have brought the test pilot to a premature finish, but it has no serious consequences to the larger mission. We have achieved our goal to confirm the viability of our strategy for a full-scale reinvention and relocation of our species. My superiors are well aware of everything that is happening at this moment, and they are moving forward at a rapid pace with a global infestation. What you experienced in your simple and naïve small town will soon be replicated in every town, every city, every community, every *continent* in your world. If you don't believe me, just take a look. Walk over to that window, which you have concealed to deny your outside environment, and open the shades to reveal the fate that awaits you."

Zeke remained seated, looking at the other faces around the room. No one moved. Finally, Darren broke the hypnotic stillness. He stepped over to a large window. He took ahold of the cord and opened the shades with a long pull.

Dark skies stretched for as far as the eye could see, heavy with ominous, black clouds.

Strickland continued, "The experiment has been a resounding success. Now the full plan can go into effect. We will complete what we started, bringing it to your entire population. We have taken control of your atmospheric conditions to commence the cleansing. Much like you yourselves have manipulated your environment with harmful climate change, we will make our mark to reverse course. You endangered one of the most magnificent planets in the galaxy. We are here to save it. This is not a massacre of life on Earth, it is a rejuvenation, a cause for celebration."

"That's a really big storm…" said Zeke softly, staring out the window.

"Yes," Strickland said. "First comes a purifying rain that sends our front-line troops, small to you but mighty to us, to expel your defective core so that we may replace it with a superior being with a higher purpose."

One of the agency officials in a plain business shirt and slacks finally spoke, voicing his skepticism. "Rain clouds. You expect us to be threatened by a few clouds? We'll stop you everywhere you go."

"No," Strickland said. "I'm afraid that's not possible. But don't take my word for it. This room has a television. Turn it on. Any channel. Every channel."

The agent hesitated, then cautiously stepped over to where the TV remote sat idle on one side of a table. He aimed it at the flat-screen monitor hung over the dresser and clicked.

The first image to appear was a newscast about an 'international weather event'. Out of nowhere, black clouds were covering the entire globe. The sunlight had been snuffed for every citizen on Earth.

The agent began advancing through the channels – and the story remained the same even as the voices, news desks and graphics varied. Programming was interrupted on every network to report on an unprecedented atmospheric activity with desperate, stammering speculation over the root cause – global warming, upper stratosphere pollution, ozone contamination, biological warfare experiments gone awry….

No one could ever imagine the truth, thought Zeke, terrified and fascinated at the same time.

"You failed your habitat," Strickland said. "You were sending it on a crash course with irreversible destruction, so we stepped in, better citizens for a better world. You are the problem. We are the solution. There is nothing to be gained by prolonging the human race. Your souls are as poisoned as what you did to this planet. You see, we've been watching for a long time. Your wars, your riots, your injustices, your greed, your cruelty. It is time to turn over this landscape to new ownership. You have failed as a civilization. You've had more than enough time to get it right. Now we are here to take your place. We will replace each and every one of you, with very few exceptions for study and special projects. We will settle in gradually. We will keep things operating as status quo in the beginning to get our footing, but not for very long. We will undertake a full evaluation of what you started, your societies, your behaviors, your structures – and we will make significant improvements in every way possible. We do this out of love. We have long admired the majesty of your planet. And we have reached the conclusion you no longer deserve it."

The agent continued to flip through the channels, amplifying the scope of impending doom. Reports of a massive cloud cover poured in from every country in a medley of voices, flicking by like an atlas. Germany... Great Britain...China...Russia...Australia...Africa... Brazil...India.

Finally, at wit's end, Darren rushed over to the television monitor and snapped it off. He was sweating. He turned around. His face was ghastly pale. "That's enough," he said.

Strickland focused his eyes on Zeke. "So what will it be, Mr. Gorcey? I am offering you protection. You can stay on as a unique specimen, evidence of this planet's primitive past, a forthright chronicler of the last days of your people and the birth of a new day. You will be saved from termination to serve a noble calling and share this extraordinary account of evolution for future generations, an everlasting readership. You can be the esteemed author of the bible for how we came to be, the truth teller about a savior from the stars. I need your answer, Mr. Gorcey, and I need it *now*."

Zeke took a deep breath. He did not look at Darren or anyone else in the room, keeping his eyes steady on Strickland.

"When do I start?" he asked.

CHAPTER THIRTY-FOUR

"Oh no!" Susan leapt from her chair in the lobby of the Imperial Inn and ran over to one of the large, floor-to-ceiling windows. She pointed to the skies. "It was sunny just minutes ago. I don't think those are normal clouds."

Greg joined her at her side. "Shit, I think you're right."

"We have to get out of here," Susan said.

"Let's call Zeke."

Greg hurried over to the phone at the front desk and dialed Darren. Darren picked up after four rings.

"Is Zeke with you?" Greg asked.

"Yes."

"Put him on."

After a moment of muffled voices and fumbling, Zeke's voice said, "Yes?"

"It's Greg. I'm with Susan. Have you looked outside?"

"I know."

"We have to get out of here. Out from under these clouds. We're a target. You know what's going to follow...."

"Yeah, I'm aware." His voice failed to express the alarm that Greg expected.

"Then – we're leaving. We're going somewhere safe. Are you coming?"

There was a long silence on the other end. Then Zeke said, "You go ahead. I'm staying."

"Seriously?"

"Yes."

"The silver rain, the bugs – we can get out of range, *now*."

"I'm sorry," Zeke said. "I'm going to stay here. Listen, I can't explain it, but it's for the best. I promise. Go without me."

"Really?"

"Goodbye, Greg." Zeke hung up.

Greg turned and looked at Susan, dumbstruck. "He said for us to leave without him."

"Why?"

"I don't know."

"Well, maybe he feels safe here but I know I don't. This building is too big. There are probably a million ways that bugs could get in, all the vents and doors and windows. The clock is ticking. Let's just pick a direction and keep driving until we're out from under this cloud."

"All right," Greg said, shaken by the turn of events and Zeke's indifferent attitude. "Get your things."

Within minutes, they were exiting the Imperial Inn and headed to Greg's car. The dark, charcoal cloud cover extended for as far as they could see.

"Shit," muttered Greg. "Where does it end?"

They climbed into the car. Greg started the engine.

The first plop of rainfall splattered on the windshield.

Susan studied the residue.

"It's not normal," she said. Her voice began to rise. "It's not clear, it's shiny, it's silvery."

Greg powered the car forward with a squeal of tires.

He rapidly entered the main road and accelerated. More raindrops struck the windshield – not yet a downpour, but just enough to cause them to jump with every pop and smack.

Greg turned on the windshield wipers, smearing the ivory drops into a series of blotches.

He passed cars obediently going the speed limit and glanced at the faces of drivers coming from the other direction. No one appeared to be in a panic, it was just another average day as far as they were concerned. A simple rain.

Greg turned on the radio.

A disc jockey was stammering his way through breaking news, unsure of what to make of it.

"...so it appears those clouds you see overhead, they're everywhere. And I don't just mean Marion County, or the state of Indiana. There are reports of rain clouds in every geographical region of the world. There's never been anything like this, as far as I know, and meteorologists are scrambling for an explanation. Even areas that rarely get rain.... Very, very strange. The wire reports.... No one seems to know what's going on, exactly. It wasn't in our weather forecast, blame the weather man, ha ha."

His chuckle was strained, the tone of a man desperate to dismiss the notion that anything bad or dangerous could be happening. It was a voice more familiar with AM radio comedy hijinks and promoting pop singles than confronting disturbing world headlines.

Greg quickly switched over to another radio station. He found the same information, an equally bewildered radio personality, but more somber. He hopped several more times across the dial, and there was a common denominator in the reports: this cloud cover canvassed *everywhere*.

"So where do we go?" said Susan in a quiet, stunned voice.

Greg said nothing, but he had his answer.

At the next stoplight, he turned off the main road. He continued on a succession of smaller streets, entering a residential area.

Susan remained silent, listening to the increasingly distressed radio reports about an atmospheric abnormality as the windshield wipers continued their hypnotic sway, tackling a gentle drizzle.

Within ten minutes, Greg brought the car to a stop. In his driveway.

Susan sat up, alarmed. "Why are we at your house? We don't have time to get your things!"

"We're not getting my things," Greg said. "I'm staying here." He parked and turned off the engine. He handed her the car keys as she stared at him, open-mouthed.

"Here," Greg said. "Take my car. Drive it wherever you want to go. You don't have a car, take this one."

"But—"

"Don't worry about me. I'll be fine."

Greg stepped out of the car and entered the rain.

"Greg!"

It was difficult, but he kept his back to her. He advanced along the walkway to his front door. He climbed the damaged steps to his front porch. His lawn was wet, receiving steady rainfall.

"*Greg!*" she cried out a second time.

He unlocked his front door and entered. He shut it closed behind him without looking back.

Susan sat for a moment in the passenger seat, stunned. The discolored raindrops grew heavier, filling the windshield without swipes to clear it away.

"God damn it!" she finally blurted.

She jumped out of the car, circled it in the rain and climbed behind the wheel.

Susan took one last look at Greg Garrett's home and then started the engine and backed out of the driveway.

She resumed the windshield wipers.

As she sped down the street, she made a mental map of her escape route – getting to the highway as quickly as possible and heading east.

She could have chosen north, south, east or west with equal ambivalence. East was random with no time to overthink it. She knew the route, she could speed, and it would take her away on a straight path.

As she entered the highway, she continued to examine the skies – front, back and sides of the car – for any break in the heavy, gloomy cloud cover to reveal a safe destination.

But the darkness appeared to spread forever.

★   ★   ★

As the rain continued to fall, Greg moved throughout his house opening all the windows – glass and screens.

He opened the front door so wide that the inner door handle touched the wall.

He watched the raindrops, milky and unnatural, soaking the earth.

He knew what was next, but it no longer bothered him. He felt overwhelmed by feelings of calm. In the end, the decision was simple, not hard. He drew strength from the firmness of his resolve.

I am not leaving my family.

CHAPTER THIRTY-FIVE

Susan sped furiously on the highway, desperate to reach a break in the stormy cloud cover, finding none.

Greg's car had three-quarters of a tank of gas, and it got her out of Indiana and into Ohio with no difference in weather across state lines. The downpour continued to pummel the car, pavement and surrounding fields. The windshield wipers worked frantically, in vain, to slap it all away.

The rain pelted the roof inches above her head with a steady, torturous rhythm. It became the soundtrack of her drive. She had turned off the voices on the radio because their confusion was becoming panic, and she already knew more about what was happening than anyone she would hear over a broadcast.

Susan feared it was futile to seek out a sanctuary but still grasped at thin strands of hope that something could be gained from fleeing as fast and far as possible. While the pounding rain had slowed down most traffic, it galvanized her to achieve speeds she had never reached before behind the wheel of a car. She kept her eyes off the dashboard but knew she was close to triple digits.

She had been driving for nearly two hours when all of a sudden, without warning, the downpour stopped. There was no transition, no gradual reduction in the level of rain. It was as if someone had shut off a faucet.

For a moment, her heart jumped with joy – she had broken free of the silvery storm and discovered an outer parameter.

But reality quickly settled in. The roads remained wet, the surrounding acreage soaked. The territory she approached had not been spared, it had simply finished receiving a heavy deluge.

The end of the rain became more frightening than the start of the rain because it brought the next phase of a horrifying sequence of events she knew all too well.

Yellow eggs would begin appearing everywhere. Those eggs would release a monstrous mass of vicious winged insects. The insects were capable of blackening car windows and sending her off the road. Again.

Susan screamed in frustration and pounded on the steering wheel.

She figured she had only a matter of hours to prepare herself before the eggs developed, matured and hatched. She couldn't flee, but she could hide.

Susan pulled off the highway at the next exit ramp. She entered a small, nondescript town in Ohio she had never heard of before. She needed to find a small and confined space and seal every possible entry point for the tiny insects. As she sped through the sleepy, rain-soaked community, her mind raced through options: Rent a storage unit and hide inside? Gamble on a hotel room, shut the air vents and squeeze wet washrags under the door? Park in a random parking lot, secure the inside of the car and wait it out? For how long?

She drove past a strip mall with a predictable assortment of big box retail stores and hearty restaurants. She advanced into a residential area of old Midwestern houses set back from the road on generous lots. After a couple of miles, something caught her eye that offered a quick, possible solution:

A modest split-level home with a long driveway and large, detached garage. A sign out front, hanging from a white post, announced: ROOM FOR RENT.

She was moving too fast to make the turn, so she had to pull a sharp U-turn. She returned to the driveway, soared over its potholes and parked close to the house. She removed the awkward bandage from her head wound and tossed it in the backseat, primping her hair so it concealed the injury. She hurried up the front steps to ring the bell.

She forced herself to calm down and act casual. The last thing she wanted was to be sent away for looking wild eyed and crazy.

An old man in his seventies answered the door in a slow shuffle, wearing a gray sweater over a collared shirt. His wife appeared behind him, in a plain blue dress and pearls, offering a natural smile. They looked comfortable, pleasant, unrushed.

Perhaps they had not turned on the news, and they assumed this recent spell of rain was the most ordinary thing in the world.

"Hello," Susan said with a smile, speaking slower than her mind was racing. "I saw your sign out front. I wanted to ask about the room. Is it available...now?"

"Well, yes," said the man. "Please come in."

The next fifteen minutes served as an informal interview. She made up a story about being new to town, accepting a teaching job at the high school, looking for a place to stay for a couple of months before finding a house or apartment.

The old couple, Don and Ruth Keillor, were very nice and explained they had a small room and bath over the garage. The previous homeowner was an artist and used the space as a studio. More recently, the Keillors used it as a guest room for visiting family, but those visits were becoming more infrequent and they already had enough space in the house to accommodate guests.

"I get a decent pension," said Mr. Keillor, leaning back in his chair, relaxed and chatty with nothing else to do but engage with a stranger. "I was an engineer with the Frietag Group, next town over. Good people. Fine people. Retired seven years ago. Thought I was set. We've been doing well, knock on wood, but we're not getting any younger. Honestly, with the cost of medical, we could use the extra income, and the room just sits empty most of the time anyway. It's very nice. It's furnished, clean. There's working plumbing, a toilet and a shower. Water pressure isn't bad. Would you like to see it?"

Susan jumped at the chance to end his rambling and seal the deal. "No. I'm sure it's wonderful. Can I write you a check? First two months, whatever you want. I need to move in now."

"Now?" said Mrs. Keillor. "As in today?"

"Yes, ma'am. As in immediately. I really...love it here. I don't want to look any further."

The Keillors exchanged glances, then settled on a smile.

"Sure," said Mr. Keillor. "We can take you today. You're sure you don't want to see it first? To be sure?"

"No," said Susan firmly, forcing her own smile. "It's been a long morning. I'd love to settle in."

★   ★   ★

The room above the garage was perfectly adequate. A wooden staircase attached to the back of the garage led to an isolated unit. It was very simple: one door, four windows, a bed, a dresser, a small bathroom, some throw rugs. It was dusty but not dirty. Mrs. Keillor brought a fresh set of towels and linens. The décor was decades old, floral and faded, with a lot of brown wood. Everything looked sturdy, without noticeable drafts from the outside. A space heater sat on the floor, plugged into the wall. "For air, we just open the windows," Mr. Keillor said.

"Uh huh," Susan said. She was never opening these windows.

Susan handed over a check and minimized her end of the conversation to accelerate its conclusion. The old couple finally got the hint that she wanted to be alone and began a slow transition to departure.

"You sure you don't need help with your things?" said Mr. Keillor one last time, assuming her car was filled with suitcases.

"No, I'm fine, honestly."

"Well, you need anything, just holler. Maybe we could have you over for dinner in the next day or two? Ruth cooks a mean meatloaf with mushroom gravy."

"Sure. In a couple days."

She thanked them. They left. She watched from a window as they returned inside the house, disappearing from view.

Then she scrambled for the car. With a place to stay secured, she quickly needed to stock up on necessities for the long haul.

Susan returned to the strip mall she had passed earlier. She went on a speedy spending spree, rolling carts quickly through the aisles of Walmart, Target and a Family Fare grocery store.

She bought weeks' worth of food and bottled water.

She bought a small microwave oven.

She bought some extra clothing and basic toiletries.

She bought multiple rolls of thick duct tape.

She bought every ultrasonic keychain noise alarm she could find in every color and variety.

The pimply, teenage Walmart clerk scanned her items with an agonizingly slow pace, making small talk.

"Whoa, a lot of keychains," he said.

"Party favors," she mumbled.

"What do you make of all this rain? They say it's raining all over the world. Was supposed to be sunny today. Stupid weatherman."

"The weatherman has no idea..." she said.

Driving back to her apartment rental with a car filled with purchases, she spotted something on both sides of the roadway that caused her to gasp.

Small yellow dots.

In front of one home, two little girls in matching dresses stood in the grass, poking curiously at the eggs with a stick.

Susan wanted to burst into tears, but she held it in.

She parked in her designated space, a dirt-covered slot that veered off the main driveway. She made several quick trips to carry everything up the stairs and into her rental unit before the old man could come out and offer to 'help' by slowing her down.

After she finished bringing everything in, she shut the door to the outside and locked it. She grabbed the duct tape and began covering every crack and crevice she could find that was exposed to the outdoors. The apartment filled with the constant screech of tearing off new sections of tape, which she bit apart with her teeth. She clawed at the rolls for the start of new pieces until her fingernails broke. She secured the window frames and the door.

Finally, out of breath, she dropped an empty roll of tape to the floor and stood back, surveying her work.

The interior of the apartment was sealed in silver tape. She could not find a single small opening where a bug could sneak in.

Susan went into the bathroom to wash her hands. She splashed her sweaty face with water. She wiped it on a musty towel. Then she stared at her haggard expression in the mirror.

It looked like she had aged ten years in the past three weeks.

Get used to that face, she told herself. *It's the only one you're going to see for a long time.*

She was prepared to stay locked up alone in the apartment for as long as necessary.

As she stared at herself, she noticed something stuck in her tangled, messy red hair. She squinted and brought her face closer to the mirror.

It was a small, yellow egg.

Susan screamed. She staggered backward, away from the mirror. Then she jumped forward for a closer inspection.

It was definitely one of the eggs, ripe but not hatched. She thought back to when she had climbed out of the car in Greg's driveway to circle to the driver's seat, rain falling on her....

"*Get out!*" she shrieked. She pulled the egg out of her hair, and it slipped through her fingers and landed in the sink. She pulled off her shoe and slammed it hard into the sink bowl, repeatedly, flattening the egg and squishing its contents with so much angry force that she nearly pulled the sink out of the wall. *Die, die, die!*

She blasted the sink faucet, hot and cold, to send the residue far down the drain. She wiped the bottom of her shoe with toilet paper and flushed it down the toilet – six flushes to make sure it traveled far, far away.

Then she inspected her hair with maniacal detail for any more eggs.

She found none, but the paranoia remained.

She moved to the center of the apartment. She stripped down to her underwear and pulled a new piece of clothing out of a bag: a sporty jumpsuit with a zipper. She tore off the tags, climbed in and sealed herself tight. She put on heavy wool socks, then thick boots.

She opened another bag and brought out more items. A respiratory face mask to cover her nose and mouth. A pair of protective goggles for her eyes. And then wireless headphones to snugly cover her ears. There was no music to be played through them – just silence.

Wearing gloves, she arranged a semi-circle of sonic keychain alarms in front of her for quick access, if needed.

Susan sat on the floor, hung her head, and waited.

After ninety minutes, she heard a pop.

She looked around the room.

The pop came from the window.

She slowly stood. She walked over. She took a sideways peek through the drawn vinyl shade.

Flying black insects were striking the glass.

The invasion had begun.

They can't get in, she told herself. *They can't get in. Don't let them see you.*

She returned to the center of the floor, seated with her legs crossed Indian style.

Even though she wasn't religious, she prayed.

It wasn't long before she heard screaming. It penetrated her headphones. It was coming from the house on the other side of the driveway.

It was the Keillors.

Susan tried not to fill her goggles with tears.

The screams lasted for about five minutes, painful shrieks from the old man and old woman, and then the sounds halted into a dead silence.

Susan couldn't avoid thinking about this exact same scenario being played out in massive numbers around the globe. The insects had risen to start the chain of events that would lead to world domination by an alien race. The end was beginning.

Susan remained very still on the floor, listening to the occasional smack of bugs hitting the windows and door.

She thought about everyone she had ever known, and what was happening to them at this very minute. She felt very, very alone.

*   *   *

In a small town in Indiana not noted on many maps, Greg Garrett stood in the open doorway of his one-story brick home in a small residential community surrounded by lush countryside.

The sun was emerging from dissipating cloud cover, returning brightness to the neighborhood.

Black clouds of insects began rising from the ground in dense pockets, buzzing in unison like industrial noise, visible over his lawn, across the street, down the block and everywhere.

He no longer feared them.

He raised his arms, stretching them out in a grand gesture. He let out a powerful bellow, summoning his fate.

"*Come and get me, you little bastards!*"

The harsh buzzing elevated, incited. A spread of insects pulled together from around the area, summoned by a single instinct, forming one giant blob of pulsing darkness.

Then they attacked.

Pouring like liquid in a horizontal stream through the air, the onslaught of winged insects rushed the entrance to the Garrett house.

Greg did not try to escape as they splattered against his body, hitting him with a united physical force. He staggered backward into the living room, and they entered with him.

The bugs covered Greg, his walls, his floors, his ceilings. They took over the inside of the house and turned it into a massive, writhing nest.

Greg felt the tiny, clutching insects cover every inch of his skin. They crawled inside his clothes. It felt like a layer of hot, stinging lava. The pain grew so intense that it entered a stratosphere of agony he never knew existed.

Then everything started slipping away.

He lost his sense of sight, hearing, smell and taste.

His outer surface became numb.

Stolen.

He felt his consciousness disappearing down a long, narrowing tube of diminishing light. Darkness took over. It consumed him.

His body fell to the floor with a thud of finality, like a large slab of meat, inert.

Greg Garrett had been expelled.

CHAPTER THIRTY-SIX

One month passed before Susan felt brave enough to venture outdoors.

She had remained contained inside the small room and bath on top of the Keillors' garage, not seeing them or any other human beings since the massive insect attack. The scenery outside her windows was deceptively calm and pleasant, nature gently shifting from summer to autumn, evidenced by the leaves starting to change color before they fell to the ground.

Two days earlier, there had been a scare when a new rainstorm rolled into the neighborhood. She had watched anxiously from the side of a window shade, fearing a fresh round of terror. But the rain appeared natural – clear, not silvery. No yellow eggs appeared.

And there had been a rainbow.

The sight of the rainbow made her cry. She had lost track of how many times she had cried over the past several weeks. Her entire body felt weighed down by terminal sadness.

In the mirror, she looked gaunt and pale. She ate small meals from her stash of groceries, but not much. Her appetite just wasn't there. She had lost a lot of weight from an already skinny frame.

The air in the rental unit was stale and disgusting. The lighting was dim. She maintained minimal exposure to the outside. She knew she needed to acquire fresh lightbulbs, more food and water, and some additional clothes.

She felt certain she wasn't the only survivor. Surely across the globe there had been others who somehow survived the insect infestation, although very few people would have been aware of the lethal dangers of such a tiny enemy. No doubt, the element of surprise had been deadly on a massive scale.

Still, there had to be others, like herself...somewhere. Maybe in the

Canadian Rockies…remote parts of Africa, Europe and Asia…inner city high-rises in New York, Tokyo or Melbourne….

"I'm not alone," she said to herself in a small, cracking voice.

She put on a jacket. She filled her pockets with noise-producing keychains. She went outdoors.

She walked slowly to Greg's SUV, which remained parked where she had left it the day she moved in.

She didn't want to go near the Keillors' house. She didn't want to think about their horrific screams. She felt guilty – she could have warned them, sealed them in a space with food and water.

But her warnings about bugs and aliens would have sounded like the ravings of a lunatic. They might have had second thoughts about allowing her to rent a room. That's how she finally justified it in her mind to relieve some of the shame.

Despite being idle for a month, Greg's car started fine, only a moment of engine coughing.

She made a three-point turn and cautiously retreated out of the driveway. She entered the roadway, eyes wide to take in her environment.

There were birds, squirrels and other common signs of everyday nature. She did not see any bugs. They had performed their duty and become absorbed into their victims.

And what had happened to their victims?

As she drove the speed limit, another vehicle passed her, coming from the opposite direction, a blue pickup truck.

The driver wore a beard and a cap. He looked perfectly ordinary.

Susan thought back to her brother's transformation. *Now multiply that by billions*, she thought to herself.

On the way to the shopping mall, she encountered more traffic, more blank faces. None of them glanced at her or regarded her in any way.

Just another day in this small Ohio town.

The mall parking lot was half-filled. She parked alongside other cars. She saw a few people coming out of stores and walking toward stores.

Aside from their lack of expressions and identical, unrushed rhythms, they appeared perfectly normal.

Susan was very careful to fit in.

She went shopping with a steady, almost robotic rhythm. She remained stoic. No one gave her a second look.

Inside Walmart, there were very few conversations – words were exchanged only when necessary. She heard:

"Where are the grapes?"

"Can you help me reach that can on the top shelf?"

"Paper or plastic?"

Susan knew the signs. The town's population was possessed, returning to their routines with faint remnants of memory and instinct, maintaining structure and order. Every movement was evenly paced, every interaction was emotionless.

It was the same but different.

Occasionally the zombie-like behavior caused fumbling – a dropped orange, a shopping cart bumping into things. The aliens were settling into their human bodies, taking care of their physical needs, continuing the necessary activities to maintain their predecessors' biological requirements.

She felt a growing confidence that she could blend in with this new civilization. All she had to do was remove her personality and avoid any unusual physical motion. She could conform to this society.

As she rolled her cart into a new aisle, she nearly struck an elderly couple and then almost gasped when she realized who they were.

She quickly regained her composure.

They froze and stared at her for a moment.

It was Don and Ruth Keillor. The new versions.

"Hello," said Mr. Keillor in a plain voice, as if their encounter was the most ordinary thing in the world.

"It's nice to see you, dear," Mrs. Keillor said, with frozen features and eyes that did not blink.

"Hello," responded Susan in a monotone. She didn't know what to follow up with and finally offered the most mundane cliché she could think of. "Have a nice day."

"Yes," Mr. Keillor said. "You, too."

He made a stiff wave. Then the elderly couple returned their attention to their grocery shopping.

And Susan continued with hers.

When she was finished filling her cart, she waited in a small line in a checkout lane. As she reached the clerk at the cash register, she recognized him as the same pimply teenager from her last visit, one month ago.

Back then, he had been chatty.

Now he imparted minimal words, probably the same string of dialogue he offered every customer, stiff one-liners like, "Do you have any coupons?"

She placed her items on the conveyor belt in a steady, even pace, one at a time, emptying the cart.

As she waited for the cashier to finish ringing up her purchases, she glanced at the supermarket tabloids. They filled a rack beneath the candy and chewing gum.

She scanned the headlines. It was an old habit, something to fill her attention for a few minutes.

The tabloids were all a month old – the new society hadn't gotten around to reviving them.

There were headlines about celebrities and miracle cures and cooking and fitness.

Then she noticed one of those one-off specialty magazines that no one ever took seriously. It was devoted to the paranormal, featuring a dramatic illustration of a flying saucer.

The headlines screamed with cheesy hysteria.

I WAS ABDUCTED BY ALIENS!

13 GHOSTS IN HAUNTED HOUSE!

UFO COVER UP: EXCLUSIVE DETAILS!

Susan stared at the headlines, and her head began swimming with emotions. Absurdity crashed with reality, and then she lost it.

All of the tension built up inside of her for so long was finally released in a loud fit of laughter. Once started, she couldn't stop. Tears rolled down her cheeks. She roared with hysterics, shattering the mundane mood of the superstore, breaking from the pack, letting loose with her true colors.

Susan shrieked with laughter even as the people in the store stopped what they were doing, turned and stared. All eyes were on her.

Their deadened, unamused looks only caused her to laugh louder, an audience of phonies, hopeless stiffs with dopey faces, pretending to be real.

Slowly, in measured steps – because that was the pace of everybody and everything – the circle of people tightened around her.

They didn't rush the outcast, they simply surrounded her and moved in until there was nowhere for her to go.

Susan let go of all fear. All that was left was hard laughter.

She continued to laugh until they silenced her.

CHAPTER THIRTY-SEVEN

Greg Garrett drifted weightlessly, swimming in air, reunited with his family for eternity in a home within their home – the attic. He moved slowly above floorboards filled with forgotten possessions and beneath exposed rafters of a slanted roof, gliding past Janie, Becky and baby Matthew, sharing smiles, unable to touch but fully capable of love. He felt a soothing comfort in this new form of existence, sharing it with those he cared for the most. The separation of consciousness and physical form was healed by rejoining his wife and children. With them, he felt whole again.

They floated across and around in a continuous circling, like goldfish in a bowl, wide eyed and silent, an effortless life without complications. No stress, no work, no distractions, just being.

Occasionally they had fun – producing the only noises they could, murmurs and moans, to alarm the family that had moved in below. The new occupants were naïve and boring replicas of themselves, learning and settling into the expectations of a prescribed society. They filled their days with imposed routines and activity.

Although confined to the attic without physical functionality, Greg felt freer than he had ever been. His mind was pure. His affection for those closest to him was absolute. Not a whole lot else mattered.

The real joy of living was here, not there, in the simple spaces.

EPILOGUE

And then one day there was a mighty storm to wash away the debris of a failed civilization. From those cleansing rains, a new life-form emerged. The undesirable first draft of the human race was evicted from its biological host so that better tenants could move in.

The new society that took control institutionalized peace. It was a harmonious people, working together without conflict or exaggerated emotions. They demonstrated devotion for their planet with the respect of an outsider who did not take the wonders of their habitat for granted.

Around the globe, citizens reported occasional sightings of ghosts representing expired life-forms from a lost era. The ghosts were harmless, hanging on to a marginal existence, incapable of inflicting any more trauma on the physical world.

More troubling was the truth that the new breed of humanity still carried biological remnants of its predecessor, potentially toxic residue that could reintroduce the faults and failures of the prior form of *Homo sapiens*. This book, by detailing the dangers of the past, aims to protect the future.

A small scattering of survivors from the old civilization continue to exist, mostly in hiding, with the exception of a chosen few, like yours truly, kept on for precious insights and study purposes, but not allowed to procreate.

When I am gone, only my words will remain to serve as a bridge between two chapters of human existence to be studied and understood.

From what I have seen, I am encouraged for the future. There are no wars. The air is cleaner. People are unified to protect the planet and serve one another. Everyone exists within the template of an ideal society with a contained temperament and mutual demeanor. No one is out of line.

However.

As I write this initial draft, I also wonder if civilization will regress. The conditions are ripe for a growthless primitive state, reflecting the absence of individualism coupled with the intellectual loss of creative disruption. I think about it every day. But I recognize with a heavy heart that my obligation is to delete those words from the final manuscript before others witness them. My stream of consciousness is not a wise path to self-preservation, and my best course of action is to praise the beginning of a better world.

Perhaps I will create an alternate, hidden narrative and unleash dueling sources of truth. In one, Earth's intruders came from a distant star. In the other, we were already here.

Zeke Abernathy Gorcey, *Revealed! The Untold Story of the Human Race* [A work in progress]